THE TREES HAVE BUDS

FRANÇOIS HOULE

Dawn Rainbow Books

OTTAWA, ONTARIO

For permission requests, email: francois@francoisghoule.com

www.francoisghoule.com

The Trees Have Buds/François Houle. -- 1st ed.

ISBN: 978-1-989734-02-5

Published by Dawn Rainbow Books

Cover Design: KD Design

Cover Art Image: Sergii Mostovyi©123RF.com

Editor: Geffen Semach

For my brothers

Gaétan, Robert, Martin, Benoit

ONE

S arah woke up to a dreary autumn morning with the odd sense that the perfect harmony that had unexpectedly found her less than three years ago would someday soon be impossible to hold onto—thin and misty like the fog that wisped by her bedroom window.

Jack was in the shower, getting ready for work. Sarah had gotten up with the intent to join him, but the fear she'd been harbouring lately, like she was a fraud and soon Jack would figure it out and cast her aside like the nobody she used to be, paralyzed her.

Giving up her former life had been easier than she'd ever dreamed of, but it was never far away, almost like an imperceptible mosquito buzzing around her head and keeping her awake at night.

Sarah hated it when Jack went to work and left her alone. She'd always loathed being alone, mostly because she had spent the majority of her life alone with her mom, moving from place to place. Always the new kid at school, on the perimeter of other kids' lives, watching friendships from the boundary of the play-ground or the lunchroom. Never venturing closer, never becoming one of them.

She watched others live while she waited to be invited to join in. By the time others kids had warmed up to her, she would be long gone, her mom already hooking up with another *boyfriend* in a new place. That is, until they'd outstayed their welcome and Mr. Boyfriend dumped her mom's sorry ass, leaving them with no-where to live once again.

Sarah put her fingers to her lips, but the cigarette that had been a fixture in her hand since she was twelve was absent—a phantom of her old life. She had been all too happy to give that up when Jack had suggested that it might be best for her health.

And his.

He didn't smoke and she had figured it was as good a time as any to give up the habit anyway. Besides, at almost twenty dollars a pack, it made little economic sense.

But still, while her mind agreed with the common sense of quitting smoking, at times her fingers seemed to have a mind of their own. There was still the odd time she had a craving, espe-cially on mornings like this when she was feeling completely out of her element, and could feel her anxiety coming at her from everywhere, desperately trying to suffocate the happiness she felt she so deserved.

The shower stopped, and Sarah knew Jack would be on auto-pilot now getting ready for work. She'd only get in the way and she really didn't want to pick a fight this morning just because she was feeling insecure.

Again.

Thanks to her mother.

And her mother's *boyfriends*.

So many men.

So many towns.

So many disappointments.

Sarah closed her eyes and took several deep breaths. Remembering to breathe had helped her get through some really bad moments, but today it wasn't really helping. Maybe because this morning wasn't really a bad moment. She was married to the most amazing man she had ever met and had never been this happy.

Well, things could be better with Hailey, but she was a teenager going through adolescent stuff and clearly had no intention of sharing any of that with Sarah. If anyone could understand the troubles of teenhood it would be Sarah, but Sarah had not yet managed to earn her stepdaughter's trust or respect.

She really had no clue how to be a mother, and she hadn't had much experience with friendship, either. So, when she was left alone with Hailey, both just kept to themselves while they waited until Jack came home.

Being a firefighter, he'd be gone for the next twenty-four hours.

No wonder Sarah was feeling anxious.

☙ ❧

Sarah was still standing in front of the window that looked out across an expansive farmer's field when Jack crashed out of the bathroom—Jack never seemed to do anything with delicate finesse, always seeming to destroy as he moved about. Sarah had remarked this early on in their relationship and he'd simply laughed it off, telling her that when your life was spent rushing into burning buildings to save lives, delicate finesse wasn't going to get the job done.

"No," she'd said. "I guess it wouldn't."

Still, it wasn't like their house was burning, so he really didn't need to act like he had to rush in and out of rooms as if it were.

Stop it, she told herself. *You're doing it again, finding faults where there are none to be found. Are you trying to ruin this beautiful life that basically fell into your lap?*

Sarah felt Jack wrap his arms around her, his naked body against her bare skin.

"Good thing we don't have neighbours," he whispered into her ear.

"It's such a great view from up here." Dawn had just begun to push the night away. "Except right now, even if we did have nosy neighbours, that fog blocks everything. It makes me feel like we're cut off from the world."

Jack kissed her neck and she felt him against her lower back—he was a big man, nearly a foot taller than she was, and she wasn't short—and reflexively, she reached behind her and grabbed him.

"You don't have time," she said sadly.

Jack spun her around and kissed her like it was their first time, deep and long and eagerly. No one had ever kissed her like that before she had met him and she wondered why that was—why hadn't anyone before Jack ever made her feel like she was that desirable?

She felt a tear sneak out of her right eye.

"Hey, what's wrong?" he said after their kiss ended.

"Nothing," she said. "I'm just so happy."

He looked at her with a frown.

"Are you and Hailey getting along?" he asked. "Do I need to talk to her again?"

Sarah shook her head. "We're good."

He looked at her a little longer, and she could feel his gaze trying to reach her lie, but then she started to run her hand up and down and next thing she knew he'd led her onto the bed and loved her until they were both spent and he was running super late.

"I'll grab something at Tim's," he said as he rushed out the front door. "Love you, babe."

"I love you more," she said.

Sarah stood just outside the open front door and watched Jack back his car out of the garage and into the little two-car parking area off to the side of the driveway designated for guest parking. He gave her that big smile she loved so much and then blew her an air-kiss before heading towards the main road. Their driveway was so long that Jack owned a tractor-snowblower because there was no way anyone could shovel that much snow in the winter without getting a heart attack. She saw the tail lights turn bright red, and then Jack aimed the car toward town and out of Sarah's sight.

She then closed the door and began to shake.

03 80

Sarah let herself slide down against the wall until she was sitting on the floor. She pulled her knees up against her chest and wrapped her arms around them, making herself as small as she could.

Small things went unnoticed.

She hated when this happened. The shaking, the sweating followed by chills, that invisible hand around her throat cutting off her airwaves, as if she had no control over anything. It would be easy for her to blame her mother, or at least her upbringing for these panic attacks, but she'd basically been taking care of herself since she was barely ten and had never made excuses for anything.

Her mom wouldn't have cared anyway, so complaining about things wouldn't have mattered. Nothing would have changed. She had learned to live by being unseen and unheard.

The panic attack would pass. It always did. She just didn't understand why she was still getting them, especially now. She had never been more loved, cared for, or safe.

Which was probably the problem.

She was afraid of losing it all.

Her eyes stung.

The day her mother died when Sarah was seventeen didn't even bring a tear to her eye. She'd been too busy trying to figure out how to survive.

Sarah had no idea who her father might be, and she had no brothers or sisters.

At seventeen, she'd been all alone.

Grieving for a mother who had dragged her around like she was a used piece of luggage had been a luxury she couldn't afford; her new reality was that she'd become an orphan, was homeless, and no one in the world cared about what happened to her.

She never returned to school.

What was the point? She had still been just in grade ten because of all the moving around, and she had been tired of being made fun of by the other kids when they found out she was old enough to be in grade twelve. Being called stupid and worse had long ago made her despise school anyway.

And it wasn't like she could have afforded to go to college after graduating. Besides, there was only one thing she'd been meant to do, and although the thought hadn't ever crossed her mind until that day, she'd known that following in her mother's footsteps had been the only option she'd really ever had.

Jack had saved her from that life. She couldn't imagine life without him and every time he went off to work, she felt like that seventeen-year-old who'd suddenly found herself all alone.

Something rough and yet wet touched her bare feet repeatedly, and through the cascade of grief pouring out of her eyes, she saw the one, true thing that really belonged to her.

"Hey, Peanut," Sarah said as she scooped her little Maltese into her arms and buried her face into its fur. Jack had brought her home last July. One of the guys he worked with had a dog who'd had a litter, and Jack had surprised Sarah by bringing a little puppy home. Not that she'd ever expressed any desire to have a dog, but Peanut was so cute and friendly and lovable that Sarah had simply fallen in love with her. "Mommy is all right. I'm just being my silly old self."

Peanut acknowledged her mommy's silliness by licking Sarah's tears from her face.

"You'll never leave me, will you?" Sarah said and was greeted by more kisses. "Of course, you won't. You love your mommy, yes you do."

Sarah held Peanut up against her chest, feeling the Maltese's warmth and comfort. Slowly, her shaking stopped, the chills vanished, and she was able to breathe again as the pressure around her throat eased and disappeared.

Sarah put Peanut down and pulled herself up. She took a deep breath and straightened her nightgown. "I bet you're starving."

She let the dog out to do her business in the back yard and took Peanut's bowls to the sink to give them a quick wash before filling one with water and the other with dry lamb and rice kibble. Peanut came in and dashed toward her food while Sarah went to make a cup of coffee and put a couple pieces of bread into the toaster. She smothered peanut butter on her toast but after a couple of bites she found that she didn't have much of an appetite. She sat at the kitchen island with her cup of coffee in her hands, watching Peanut eat, wondering how she was going to fill the next twenty-four hours until Jack came home.

She heard the old pipes rattle as the upstairs shower came to life. Her heart began to beat a little faster.

Her stepdaughter was up.

TWO

Hailey turned on the hot water tap in the shower and peed while she waited for the room to fill with steam. It normally took a couple of minutes for the cold water to be pushed out of the pipes as it moved from the cold, dank basement tank all the way to the second floor. The house had been her grandparents' home, and before that had belonged to her great-grandparents. It was old and cold in the winter and, really, she wished her dad would just sell it and buy a new one.

She really didn't care for old things. Bulldoze the damn thing if he really wanted to stay here and build a nice modern house. Maybe one of those sprawling bungalows that went on forever. She wouldn't mind having a wing to herself. The farther away from *her* the better.

Hailey had no idea why her dad had married Sarah. She seemed rather useless. She didn't work, didn't cook, didn't do much of anything. Hailey guessed Sarah must be good in bed because Hailey couldn't see any other reason for her father to keep Sarah around.

Hailey flushed without thinking and when she stepped into the shower, the scalding water made her shriek and she stepped back quickly. Another thing she hated about this place—her dad had promised to install one of those anti-scalding thingys but never seemed to get around to it. He was too busy renovating the spare bedroom into a workout room for *Princess* Sarah to care that his own daughter constantly burned herself in the shower whenever someone flushed a toilet in the house.

While she waited for the water in the shower to return to a more moderate temperature, she grabbed her phone and put on one of her podcasts. Her friend Madelaine had turned her on to podcasts a couple months ago, and Hailey had become quickly addicted. It seemed that no subject was taboo.

Hailey used her hand this time to test the water and, feeling it was fine, stepped in the shower again and spent the next twenty minutes washing up as the podcast blared over the noise the old pipes made. She then spent another ten minutes examining her blemishes in the steamed-up mirror that she kept having to wipe with her towel—another thing her dad hadn't done yet was to replace the useless old fan that seemed to suck the humid air out of the bathroom about as good as a straw full of holes.

Then she examined her body. Her shoulders were broad, her arms muscular. And her thighs were strong and powerful, which may have made her one of the fastest skaters on the ice but she definitely wasn't delicate like Madelaine or some of the other girls at school.

A big angry sigh escaped from between her lips, which were her best feature: naturally full and inviting; at least, that's how she liked to think of them. Unfortunately, no boys were kissing her these days, and definitely not the one she wanted anyway. Her hair was long and twilight-dark like her mom's (from what she had seen from the few pictures she had in her baby album), and she had her dad's lawn-green eyes. Her nose was a problem. She felt it was too big, especially compared to Sarah's perfect Emma Stone celestial nose. In fact, Sarah could almost pass as Emma's twin.

Another angry sigh.

"You look too intimidating," she said to the image in the mirror. "Maybe that's why Connor hasn't asked you out."

And she was smart. Her overall average was ninety-three. Things just came naturally to her. She knew she could get her average up above ninety-five, but she purposely kept it below that. She never studied and still she often had to purposely sabotage her tests to bring her grades down, which were still better than all her friends'. She already got called brainy as it was and she just couldn't imagine how her friends would treat her if she started getting A pluses.

Smart and intimidating. She heard the rumours of what the non-athletic girls called her: a dyke on steroids. So, she was grateful for her small circle of friends.

She couldn't wait to be done high school. High school was the ultimate institution populated by teenage fraudsters. Everyone was trying to fit in, look *cool* as her dad would say—such a prehistoric term—and for what?

So they could survive the four worst years of their lives.

Hailey hated it when her dad tried to tell her that these were the best years, that she should enjoy them. Was he nuts? Had he completely forgotten his own teenage years?

She looked at herself one more time and then wrapped a towel around her body and walked back to her room. She closed the door, threw herself on the bed, and grabbed her phone to open Snapchat and see what was going on with her friends. Madelaine was going on about the math test today and how she wasn't prepared; Sylvie was complaining about her weight again—the girl was as thin as a rail, so Hailey really had no sympathy for her; Jessie was bitching about her younger sister who kept coming into her room and taking her stuff; and Connor, who Hailey had a secret crush on, was just being his goofy self and making fun of everything and everyone.

Hailey was about to start her morning rant about Sarah but decided that was too predictable. She searched for something else and couldn't think of a thing to say.

Then Andréa piped in about the show *You* on Netflix she'd been binging on—hockey practice three times a week squeezed in between two games didn't leave Hailey and Andréa much time to stay current with the latest shows, so they were always trying to catch up. Still, the conversation got heated and Hailey's imagination easily began to place Sarah as Joe and her dad as poor, trapped Guinevere.

And then something dawned on Hailey. Sarah was only twelve years older than Hailey and twelve years younger than her dad. Strange coincidence.

She quickly shared it with her group.

That is weird, Andréa texted.

Really weird, Sylvie added.

High-five for your dad, Connor texted and added smiley faces.

You're such a guy, Hailey texted back.

Hey, don't blame the player, he texted.

Yeah, yeah, hate the game, Hailey texted back.

So, how's the wicked stepmom? Jessie asked.

Hailey glanced back at her bedroom door, as if to make sure Sarah wasn't eavesdropping. Not like she could know what they were texting about.

Haven't seen her yet, she texted, including the hands raised emoji. Gotta get dressed and grab something to eat. See you all at school!

Hailey rummaged through her closet and settled on a pair of blue jeans and a loose-fitting, midnight-coloured sweater. She brushed her hair and tied it in a ponytail, didn't bother with makeup—she rarely wore any, something she'd noticed Sarah rarely wore either, which really annoyed her because Sarah still looked gorgeous.

Everything the woman did annoyed Hailey.

The fact that her mom had left when Hailey wasn't quite five didn't have any bearing on her quest to dislike her stepmom. It was just that she'd had her dad to herself all those years before Sarah showed up. Ten wonderful years where her dad gave her his full attention. In the summer, he'd take her camping almost every weekend that he didn't have to work; in the winter, they went skiing at Camp Fortune. He never missed her hockey games or lacrosse games. Before she'd gotten her G2 licence a few months back, he'd driven her and her friends to the Kanata or Barrhaven cinemas.

Now he was always too busy with *Sa-rah*.

Arrrggg!

Sure, at seventeen she didn't spend as much time with her dad as she used to, but it irked her to share him. He was her dad. Sarah was just a third wheel. No one needed a third wheel. She had ruined the family dynamic. If Hailey could blame Sarah for the hole in the ozone layer, she'd do it.

As much as she loved her dad, she despised his wife. And the last thing she was going to do while she still had to live at home was be nice to Sarah.

Not a chance.

ᘓ ᘔ

Lately, Hailey wished she could go stay with her mom. Her mother lived in the Glebe in a beautifully renovated, century-old home. Hailey had only been there once, last summer when she and her friends decided to go to a Redblacks afternoon game. Not that she liked or knew anything about football, but Connor was a fan. Afterward, she'd convinced them to take a walk by her mom's place.

She hadn't exactly gone inside. In fact, she hadn't even gone up to the front door and rung the bell. She hadn't seen her mom since the day her dad had picked her up at daycare when she was four—they'd had to call him when Hailey's mom had been a no show. When they'd gotten home, the house had been void of all her mother's things. On the kitchen counter there was a short note that even Hailey, in her limited reading ability, had been able to read.

I'm sorry. Mom

"Why is mommy sorry?" she'd said and had showed her dad the note.

Her dad had then gone searching through the house and come back down to the great room. "She even took her Caroline Larsen painting."

Hailey had looked at the empty spot above the fireplace where her mom's favourite painting had been. Then her dad had sat her down and explained to four-year-old Hailey that her mom had decided to leave.

"For how long?"

"I think, for good."

"Why?"

"I don't know."

Hailey had looked again at the place where the painting had been. "She liked her painting more than us."

"I guess so."

Just like that, her mom had packed what was precious to her and left.

Leaving Hailey behind.

It wasn't until years later that she truly understood that she hadn't been one of her mom's precious possessions. By then she'd learned to hate her.

Not that it didn't hurt.

It did.

While she'd cried that first night her mom hadn't been there to tuck her in, she'd quickly figured out how to live without a mother. Her dad became enough. And when he was off working, Hailey's grandparents looked after her.

But when she was seven, the questions started. Hailey wanted to know why, kept pestering her dad for weeks why her mom had left. Had it been her fault? Had she been a bad child? Had she been the reason Mom had left?

Her dad had reassured her that it wasn't anything that she had done. It wasn't anything that he had done. Mom had just needed a change.

A *change*?

At seven, Hailey had known her dad was lying to protect her, but she hadn't wanted his protection—she'd wanted to know why. Because her mother leaving had made her feel insignificant. And what if her dad left her too?

That's about the time when she really started to excel at school, at sports, at home. She figured her dad couldn't leave her if she was the perfect child. And it worked. Hailey and her dad spent all his free time together. He told her all the time how proud he was, how much he loved her, how incredibly lucky he was to have such a wonderful and beautiful daughter.

But then he'd married Sarah.

Cʒ ʁC

Hailey heard the old floor outside her room protest as Sarah walked by, followed by the tiny click-click-click of nails against hardwood. Her mood instantly turned, like the sun breaking through thick clouds. As much as she disliked her stepmom, she loved Peanut.

Such a good dog.

Too bad it wasn't hers. If Sarah was around, Peanut stuck to her like a second skin. Which was almost all the time since Sarah rarely went out. Other than her dad, her stepmom seemed to have no one else. Hailey knew Sarah had no family, that her mom had died when Sarah was about the same age as Hailey was now, but she must have had friends before her dad lassoed her and brought her home?

Another notch against her, in Hailey's eyes. Who doesn't have friends?

And their wedding had happened so quickly. Her dad was mister let-me-think-about-it until he found a reason not to do it. Had he been so desperate to show her mom that he was fine without her, that he'd found someone better?

Maybe he'd been lonely for someone other than his daughter? She knew that when she wasn't around Connor, she missed him a lot and could only think of him, and maybe once her dad had met Sarah, that's how he'd felt?

She recalled their conversation the night before the wedding.

"When you told me you were getting married three months ago, I didn't think it would be this soon," she said. "What if mom—"

"Your mom and I are never getting back together," he'd said. "I really love Sarah."

"But why can't you just date her for a while?" she'd said. "You barely know her."

"We've been dating six months, and she makes me happy and I make her happy."

"She's so young."

"She's a bit younger than me, but once you're an adult, age pretty much ceases to matter."

"It's just . . . weird to see you—" She'd been about to say *with someone other than Mom* but truthfully, she'd had no memory of her parents together.

"Give Sarah a chance," he'd said. "She's actually really nice." *Really nice.*

What exactly did that mean? Some serial killers appeared to be really nice, too. Didn't mean you had to marry one.

Hailey knew she was being ridiculous now, that Sarah wasn't a serial killer. And yes, she was nice. That's really what irked Hailey. Sarah tried too hard to be her friend. It showed. Besides, Hailey had plenty of friends.

She didn't need her dad's wife to be her friend.

She didn't need her dad's wife to take him away from her.

She didn't need her dad's wife for anything.

They'd been fine without her. Hailey and her dad had been a family of two for a very long time, and she had accepted that her mom was gone and not coming back. He'd actually looked happier after her mom had left, and he was more fun; at least, that's what she seemed to remember. It's like her mom leaving had liberated him.

She'd often wanted to bring that up, but had never quite found the right words or the right moment. She hadn't wanted to spoil whatever good time they were having by pestering him with questions as to why he'd been so solemn and strict when her mom had been around.

Sarah had made him even more laid back and, in a way, Hailey was thankful, but her time with her dad had almost all but disappeared. So, being thankful was hard, impossible really.

Oh, why should it even matter? None of her friends spent any time with either of their parents. Why should it be different for her?

Because she and her dad had survived the abandonment of her mother. That's why it mattered to Hailey. And that's why it hurt that her dad seemed to have forgotten the bond they'd built during all that time.

And that's why Hailey couldn't be nice to Sarah.

THREE

S arah closed her bedroom door and went to take a shower. It was so nice to have this new spacious ensuite now that Jack had finished renovating it. He'd taken a third of the adjacent spare bedroom to make the ensuite bigger, and was going to turn the rest of the spare room into a small workout space. There was a workout room in the basement that Hailey used, but Sarah didn't care much for the basement; it was dark and damp and uninviting with too few windows and a low ceiling that made her feel claustrophobic.

Jack had just gotten her one of those new Peloton Bikes and she loved doing yoga. He was so good to her. She felt guilty for not working, but he'd told her she didn't need to rush into it, to think about what she really wanted to do. Problem was that she had no idea.

She'd only ever had the one *job*, and she'd promised herself on her wedding night that she'd never go back, that she was finally shedding her old life for good, every aspect of it.

Gone.

All of it.

At the age of twenty-seven she had married the most wonderful man, but she had been petrified the morning of their wedding—worried that he wasn't going to show up that day, that he'd get cold feet and stand her up.

But Jack had been waiting at the altar for her, a grin so wide and bright it had pulled her toward him, like a beacon guiding her to the life she'd always dreamed of but could never find.

If only Hailey could accept her, not as a mother—good God, she had no idea how to do that and a seventeen-year-old girl didn't need Sarah in that role anyway—but as a friend. Maybe Sarah had been naïve to think that was possible. She'd hoped that since they weren't so far apart in age that it might come naturally, but she had quickly realized that Hailey would never see her as a friend.

Sarah was the competition.

Hailey's enemy.

Sarah knew that Hailey couldn't accept her because doing so would mean that she was giving her assent to sharing Jack, and Sarah could tell that Hailey didn't want to share her dad.

She'd lost her mom.

She wasn't losing her dad.

Not to some woman who was barely older than her—that's how Hailey had put it. The first time Sarah had tried to talk to Hailey about it, to reassure her that she wasn't stealing her dad away from her, Sarah hardly got two words in before Hailey walked away. Then Sarah had made the mistake of trying to assert her status as Jack's wife and Hailey had just laughed in Sarah's face and then spent the rest of the day in her room until Jack came home.

And before Sarah could talk to Jack, fill him in on what had happened, hoping he could give her some pointers when it came to Hailey, her stepdaughter had flat out told him that Sarah wasn't her mother, that she didn't need a stepmom, and there was no way in hell she was ever going to listen to a girl that was barely older than her.

Then Hailey had stormed off to her room again and Jack had stood in the hallway by the front door, his jacket half off one arm, staring at Sarah like he'd just been shot and was seconds from collapsing to the floor.

And for a split second, Sarah had seen hesitation in Jack's eyes as he tried to figure out whom to side with. Later as he slept beside her, and she lay awake staring at the darkness of their room, her heart beating too hard and her fears choking her, she'd cried silent tears.

Because in that moment earlier, she had seen all the disappointment and hurt of her old life, the failing of the one person, her mother, who should have been her protector. In that second of hesitation, Sarah had seen her mother standing by the front door instead of Jack, yelling at her, demanding what the hell had she done this time to piss off yet another man who was kind and good enough to let them stay with him; that if they found themselves homeless again, Sarah would only have herself to blame.

She was so afraid of disappointing Jack.

He'd quickly taken his jacket off and had wrapped Sarah into his arms and reassured her that Hailey was just a typical teenager and that she shouldn't worry too much. That someday Hailey would come out of her teen angst and the two of them would become as close as mother and daughter could.

She'd wanted to make him promise but had caught herself, knowing that he couldn't do such a thing, that the best he could do was to tell her what she needed to hear.

Two years later, Sarah still felt like she was a stranger in the house and that she would never quite fit in. It killed her to be cast out again. All her life, she'd always been on the outside and she had so wanted to believe that finally, with Jack, she was on the inside.

She had a family.

Maybe she was making more of it than it was. Maybe Jack was right and someday Hailey would stop seeing her as the enemy and embrace their relationship. And maybe her life had always been wonderfully perfect and she had imagined ever being abused.

Sarah stepped into the walk-in shower and let the hot water soothe the tension she'd been holding in her neck and shoulders. She thought of how tenderly Jack had made love to her earlier, and for a moment all her qualms about Hailey were washed away along with her feelings of inadequacy. Someday Hailey would be an adult and would move out.

Until then, Sarah would do what she'd always done.

Hide the scars of her past and survive.

ര ഇ

Hailey heard the shower going and headed down to the kitchen to make breakfast. Her dad had drilled into her the importance of eating in the morning, to fuel the body and most importantly, the brain. How could she expect to be at her best if she was starving her decision maker, her reasoning partner, her commander in chief.

Yeah, her dad could get a little melodramatic about breakfast but she didn't care. But that was back when he'd made her these wonderful meals—western omelets, scrambles eggs with a sprinkle of Gruyere or Morbier, a stack of blueberry pancakes, or her favourite, homemade waffles.

These days, she made smoothies. Hailey put a banana into the blender and added some frozen blue berries and raspberries, poured some milk, and sprinkled a scoop of protein powder on top.

Mixed the concoction for about a minute and drank it right from the blender. No need to dirty a glass. Something quick and easy.

She didn't want to linger in the kitchen too long and have Sarah come in and try to make conversation. It just didn't happen between them. It was as natural as a pair of fake boobs.

Sarah's, not Hailey's.

She didn't know for sure, but they sure didn't look real to Hailey. Way too perky. And too big. Sure, Sarah was a tall woman, but she wasn't big boned. In fact, she had a killer body which made Hailey hate her more.

And the sexiest voice. Not too high pitched, not too low pitched. Kind of like Cobie Smulders.

Hailey noticed Sarah's wallet on the counter and started to look through it. She wasn't sure what she was looking for, anything that she could use against her stepmom. But of course, there was nothing. What sort of incriminating evidence could she find in a woman's wallet? She did find a twenty-dollar bill and was tempted to take it. It would be fun to lie to Sarah that she hadn't taken her money, but she knew her dad would be disappointed with her. Because Sarah would definitely tell him.

She left it and put the wallet back.

Then she changed her mind and took the twenty anyway. She walked into her dad's den and put the twenty on his desk, held down by the corner of his laptop. Technically, she hadn't stolen the money.

Just displaced it.

Hailey headed back to the kitchen while studying her phone for what was going on in the world. The world being her circle of friends. She got bored and checked out how the Sens did last night. It was another tough year. The team had been stripped of all of its stars a couple of years ago and were still rebuilding. She missed Karlsson and Stone, but that Brady Tkachuk was hot. She and her dad used to go to a lot of hockey games. They hadn't been to one yet this year. Sure, the season was just a month in, but in previous years they would have already been to three or four games by now.

Sarah didn't know anything about hockey. Her idea of entertainment was watching *The Bachelor* or some *Housewives of Stupidtown* reality show.

And Hailey would shake her head when she saw her dad wasting his time watching those shows with Sarah instead of watching their favourite team with his daughter.

At least she had Connor, and they'd Snapchat all through the games which she'd watch up in her room on her laptop. She knew he liked her. Both Andréa and Madelaine had told her. She'd thought she'd dropped enough hints that she liked him too but maybe she should get her friends to make it known that she was looking for more than just snapchatting through a hockey game.

Connor could be a bit dense.

He made her laugh, though. He didn't take anything seriously—she realized that maybe that was the problem, that he didn't see them as a couple. He never missed a chance to make fun of someone or something. He was such a contrast to her dark moods. Although, when she was around him, she did lighten up and forget about her problems at home.

Hailey was still hungry. She searched the fridge for something else to eat and spotted a raspberry yogurt on the middle shelf, behind a jar of pickles.

That's not where the yogurt went.

She took one of the little containers and then moved the rest to the bottom shelf, beside the bags of milk. Dairy all went together.

Sarah should know that by now. The fridge had become complete chaos with her around. It didn't seem to matter how often Hailey told her where things went, and she'd almost stopped bothering because it was just easier to move things to where they should go. Like, it wasn't really hard to notice where things went.

Not hard at all.

Hailey peeled the cover off her yogurt container and emptied it in four spoonfuls. She rinsed the plastic cup and placed it in the recycling bin under the sink. She felt pretty full now and couldn't be bothered to make a lunch. She'd grab something in the school cafeteria.

A reminder on her phone beeped three times. Time to go brush her teeth and head out to catch the bus. She lived about three kilometers from the school which was way too far to walk, especially in the winter; she'd hoped her dad would let her drive the older Outback now that she had her G2, but he'd told her he didn't want Sarah to be left stranded.

Of course not. Wouldn't want little Sarah who didn't work, who didn't need to go anywhere, to be left homebound without a car.

Not precious little Sarah.

Instead, Hailey had to sit in a bus full of immature freshmen who still behaved like they were in elementary school. So humiliating.

Hailey dashed up the stairs and saw Peanut staring at her when she reached the top.

"Hey girl," Hailey said and tickled the dog's chin. Peanut wagged her tail so wildly that her tiny bum wiggled along. "I've got to go to school now."

Peanut followed her into the bathroom where Hailey brushed her teeth and then looked herself over to make sure she was good.

"You look great," Sarah said.

"Jesus!" Hailey jumped back. "You scared the crap out of me."

"Sorry."

Hailey wanted to step out of the bathroom but Sarah was just standing there in the doorway, staring at her, blocking her, a weird smile on her lips.

"I gotta go," Hailey said and motioned for Sarah to move. "Don't want to miss my bus or you'll have to drive me."

"I don't mind," Sarah said and moved back.

"I'd rather drive myself," Hailey said, curtly. "Not like you really use the car."

"I have to get a few things at the grocery store."

Hailey brushed passed Sarah, grabbed her laptop and stuffed it into her backpack, searched for her lip balm and found it under her desk, and left her room but double tracked to get her phone which she'd left on the desk. She stuffed the phone in her back pocket and raced down the stairs, slipped into her fall jacket, and was about to leave when Peanut came and sat in front of the front door staring up at her.

Hailey bent down.

"I've got to go to school," she said in her tiny voice. "But I'll miss you."

Peanut barked and wagged her tail. Hailey kissed her nose and stood. For the second time in the last few minutes, Sarah was just standing there staring at her.

"Do you need to do that?"

Sarah just stood there, fiddling with her wedding ring, saying nothing.

"Jesus," Hailey said. "You're really weird."

"I'm doing the best I can," Sarah said in a voice full of despair. "I didn't exactly have a role model growing up."

"Yeah, yeah, yeah," Hailey said while rolling her eyes. "Your mom was awful. You keep saying that, but you don't really say how she was horrible. Did she just sneak up on you and stare at you like you do to me? It's kind of creepy but not traumatizing. But feel free to stop doing that."

"I'm sorry," she said and looked at the floor.

Peanut barked. Hailey saw that she was stuck in the middle, torn on whom to go to. Normally the dog would side with Sarah but right now the pup was undecided. It was like she was trying to pull them together by getting them both to come toward her.

"Clever," Hailey said.

"Pardon?"

"Peanut," Hailey said and nodded at the dog. "She's trying to draw us together."

"Would it be such a bad thing?"

Hailey glared at her stepmom. Just thinking of her in those terms sat in the pit of her stomach like food poisoning.

"Why do you hate me?"

"I don't have time for this," Hailey said and turned toward the door. Peanut moved quickly to stand in front of the door. "Sorry P, but I have to go."

Peanut just barked and wagged her tail, looked toward Sarah, then back to Hailey. She barked again.

"I'm not trying to replace your mom," Sarah said.

Hailey shifted her glare toward Sarah. "I don't need her re-placed. I don't even remember her being here. All I remember, and maybe it's because Dad told me so many times, was that she spent all of her time in her *art studio* and the few times I went in there, all I saw were pathetic paintings that looked like a three-year-old had dipped her fingers in paint and smudged them all over the canvas. When she wasn't in that room, she was in bed, too depressed to get up and *be* a mother. So I definitely don't need you to be my mother. I've been doing fine without one my whole life."

Sarah looked like she'd been punched in the gut.

"And I don't need you to be my friend," Hailey said. "Unlike you, I have friends. My dad and I were just fine without you."

Hailey saw Sarah's eyes well up, and a tiny smirk pulled at the corners of her mouth. For some sadistic reason, she felt a small pleasure in upsetting Sarah. Good God, the woman had the worst waterworks of anyone Hailey knew.

"Your father is the best thing that's ever happened to me," Sarah said with a voice that did its best to stay composed. "I'm a good person—"

"Funny," Hailey said, the smirk on her face growing, "how people who really aren't good always try to convince others that they are. Why is that?"

Sarah's facial features suddenly turned hard. "Maybe you're the one who's not a good person. You treat me like crap and I haven't done anything but fall in love with your dad. In fact, I did all I could to push him away."

"Guess you didn't try hard enough," Hailey said.

"And maybe he saw that I really am a good person."

Hailey just eyed Sarah. Neither broke the glare. A duel for the attention of the man in their lives. Hailey had never really shared her dad, not even with her mom. He'd always been there for her—when she fell off her bike when she was just four and had scraped her hands and knees, when she was sick in the middle of the night and puked everywhere—he was the one to clean up her mess, change her bed, tell her that everything would be all right.

When her first heartbreak happened when she was fourteen. And he was always the loudest one cheering at her hockey games.

Her dad.

She couldn't share him. She didn't want to believe that he could love someone else just as much, or worse, more than he did her. She couldn't accept that.

Sarah was so beautiful, how could he not love her more? It hurt Hailey to think that. Despising the woman was the only thing that made sense, that brought her world within her grasp.

Hailey swallowed the words she wanted to fire at her stepmom. She was mad at her dad, at the guys at work for setting him up with Sarah, at Sarah for stealing him from her. Why couldn't he have waited a few more years, until she was older and didn't need him as much?

Would that really have made a difference?

She didn't know. Maybe. But right now, it did matter and venom filled her veins.

СЗ ВО

Sarah watched Hailey and could see that her stepdaughter was fighting internally. She could relate. Not once had Sarah ever liked any of her mom's boyfriends, but then again, they'd all been seedy men.

Especially that creep Axel.

Which was why Sarah was trying so hard to be nice, to be someone Hailey could like and trust. When she'd met Jack, it was his eyes that had convinced her that she could trust him. Those beautiful, honest, dark green eyes that seemed to reach deep inside of her and bring serenity to her life, a calmness she had never known.

Passing that up had been impossible.

It would have been foolish on her part. At first, she had tried to turn away, refuting his request for dates a dozen times, and then she'd finally accepted, figuring he'd see that she wasn't who he thought she was, that she wasn't for him after all.

Best date she'd ever had.

He took her skating on the Rideau Canal and they'd sampled the various foods available from the vendors along the skateway, and of course there had been BeaverTails—no one went skating on the canal without getting a BeaverTail. It being Winterlude, they'd also spent the evening admiring all the ice sculptures and taking in the multitudes of activities.

Such a simple date.

It had been perfect.

A sweet kiss as he dropped her off and a phone call—an actual phone call, not a text—the next day had told her that she'd be a fool to let this man get away.

She had been waiting—hoping—for someone like that her whole life. A girl like her didn't get that sort of fairy tale love. And when he'd told her he had a fourteen-year-old daughter, it had scared her at first, but then she'd embraced the chance to be part of a family, a loving family. She could tell how much Jack adored his daughter by the way he talked about her.

"When your dad asked me to marry him, all I could think about was you and how wonderful it was going to be to have you in my life, too. He was bringing me into his family. Do you have any idea how special that felt to me? I couldn't wait to get to know you."

"Guess that didn't turn out how you expected?"

"No," she said softly. "But it doesn't have to be that way. I truly love him as my husband. He's your father. He can love us both the way we are meant to be loved by him. This isn't a competition for his love."

Hailey turned her head. "He's all I have."

"And he's all I have, too," Sarah said. "You're young and someday soon you'll fall in love with someone and you'll have a life with that someone. And your dad will continue to love you. My being in his life will never change that."

"You just don't understand."

"Yes, I do," Sarah said. "Probably better than you. I never knew my dad and my mom . . . she went through men like Pez." A distressed frown crossed her face. "Mostly they ignored me, tolerated that I was there as long as I was quiet and stayed out of the way."

A memory flashed by and she closed her eyes. Her mouth turned into a tight line, as if she was supressing a cry. Her hands went up to protect herself against an invisible blow, and she closed her eyes. She started to shake.

"Please don't hurt me."

CS BO

Hailey heard Sarah's plea, but she didn't think her stepmom was talking to her. She actually began to take a step backward but realized she was already pressed against the front door. Something wasn't right with the woman.

"What?"

Just then her phone began to vibrate in her back pocket. She looked at it and at first, the name on the display didn't register. Then a smile spread across her face. Must be her dad calling her from the fire station's landline.

"Hey, Daddy."

She didn't recognize the voice. She didn't understand the words. Something about a fire and an accident. He was really sorry to tell her this. Jack was such a great man, the best fire-fighter he'd ever served with.

Hailey felt the air around her vanish. As much as she tried, she couldn't draw a breath.

"I don't understand," she said, her throat closing fast. Her chest felt too small. She couldn't have heard him right. "I don't understand."

"Hailey, what is it?"

"It's nothing," she said and tried to walk away, but Sarah grabbed her arm. "Let go!" She yanked her arm free.

"Maybe I can help if you tell me what's wrong."

But Hailey wasn't paying attention to her stepmom. She was listening to the man at the other end of the phone. And she was beginning to understand and she didn't like what he was telling her.

Not one damn bit.

"Is my dad all right?"

She saw Sarah turn into a statue. Only her eyes moved as they filled with fear.

"Did something happen to Jack?" she said, her voice sounding nothing like Cobie Smulders now. "Hailey, is your dad okay?"

"I don't know," Hailey said in a spat of anger. "I'm trying to listen to what the fire chief is saying."

Sarah reached for Hailey's phone. "Let me talk to him."

"NO!" she said and headed for the stairs. "He's my dad."

"He's my husband," Sarah said, following Hailey up the stairs and into Hailey's room. "Why didn't they call me?"

"I don't know," Hailey said. "Just shut up."

Sarah stared at Hailey.

"Can you not," Hailey said.

"You better tell me everything."

Hailey turned her back to her stepmom to shut her out. The fire chief was telling her what had happened. Her mind was racing. Her dad was the best. He never took chances. He knew how to stay safe.

Hailey fell to her knees by the foot of her bed, her face streaked by silver lines. Her breaths were quick and shallow and she swallowed back bile. Everything around her was closing in. Her entire room was crushing her.

Crushing the life out of her.

Her phone went silent and she stayed there on her knees on her bedroom floor, her upper lip covered in snot, her eyes so blurry she couldn't make out Sarah or understand what she was saying.

In one swift moment, Hailey Cormier's life had changed forever.

CB EO

Sarah watched her stepdaughter fall apart in front of her and instantly knew that something bad, really bad, had happened to

Jack. This was no time for subtleties, to be nice, to walk on thin ice. As his wife, she had the right to know.

"What happened?" she nearly screamed. "Is your dad all right?"

Hailey wouldn't answer her. Her stepdaughter just looked up at her from where she had crumpled to the floor and shook her head.

"He's just hurt?" Sarah said, her words hanging to hope. "What hospital is he at?"

Hailey kept shaking her head, her chin quivering, words unable to come.

Sarah knelt in front of Hailey and took her hands. Overwhelming grief crushed her words as she waited another devastating moment. "Please don't . . . he can't be . . . I just talked to him not two hours ago. We made—"

"Daddy is dead!" Hailey shouted. "My daddy is dead."

Sarah shook her head. "No, no, no."

This couldn't be happening. Not know. Not when her life was finally, *finally*, perfect. Their second wedding anniversary was five days away, and then Christmas. He was going to make sure he got it off this year. They'd even talked of taking Hailey south for a vacation. Something different. His parents had moved to Vancouver just last year to be closer to Jack's younger brother who had met his wife at university there. They'd just had twin girls and his parents had felt they could lend a hand.

Christmas in the Bahamas or the Virgin Islands had sounded like a great idea to both of them. There had been no planning of him dying today, not tomorrow, not anytime soon. Jack was too young to die. He was just forty-one. Great shape. He ran 5K almost every day. Lifted weights. He was adamant about staying fit. Being a firefighter, his job demanded it.

She could smell him.

Sarah closed her eyes and she could see the grin on his face, the one he always got after they made love, like this was the best damn thing in the world. She loved that grin. Made him look like a little boy who'd found that one hockey card missing from his collection.

Jack had to come home. She had to see that grin again. She had to feel his strong arms around her. She had to smell him again.

It had to be a mistake. Maybe the chief was wrong and it wasn't Jack, but someone else. Yes, it was someone else. Not Jack.

Couldn't be Jack.

She wouldn't allow that.

Jack couldn't die today.

No.

Jack had promised to finish the spare bedroom. He'd also talked about redoing the great room, of knocking a wall down and make it into a grand room. Put crown molding along the ceiling and create an accent wall where the fireplace was. He had too many things left to do in the house.

She couldn't do all those things.

She couldn't do any of those things.

She needed him to come walking through that front door right now, *right* now, and bring balance back into their lives.

Sarah needed Jack's balance. He was the only thing that made any sense in her life. What would happen if he was no longer there to provide that equilibrium?

Sarah looked at Hailey.

What would happen to them both if Jack wasn't here to bind them as a family?

FOUR

Hailey pulled her hands from Sarah's and wiped the snot from her upper lip with the back of her hand. Her phone chirped and she glanced at the text. It was Madelaine asking her where she was. The bus was waiting at the end of her driveway but the bus driver was getting impatient and would leave any second now.

Tell him to go, she texted.

What's going on? Madelaine texted back.

I'll tell you later.

You okay?

We'll talk later.

Hailey wasn't ready to tell anyone what had just happened. She wasn't sure it was real anyway. It definitely didn't feel real. Any second now, she'd wake up from this nightmare.

It just had to be one.

Or some cruel joke.

No, that would be too cruel and Hailey didn't think the fire chief would do such a thing. He'd said her dad had just gotten to work when they got their first call, an old building downtown that was burning, a restaurant at the bottom and a couple floors of apartments. As always, her dad was first in and radioed that the restaurant area was too far gone. He'd come back out and headed up the separate stairwell up to the second floor. One of the guys said he then headed to the third floor, but before he could come back safely the fire had engulfed the stairs and cut him off.

Two tenants also died, a man and woman in their fifties.

Sarah stood and walked to the doorway. "Did he say anything else?"

"No," Hailey said. "That's all the chief told me."

Sarah gnawed at her lower lip. "Always worried about others."

"He should have been thinking of us," Hailey said.

"Knowing him," Sarah said. "I'm sure he was. But he also had to try. He believes he can save everyone."

"I don't care about everyone," Hailey said. "He should have been thinking of me."

"I'm sure he was, Wiggles."

Hailey turned sharply, and if her glare could kill Sarah would have been struck down instantly. "Don't ever call me that. That was for my dad. Only him."

"I just thought—"

"Not even my mom ever called me that. Just Dad. Only he was allowed to call me that."

"Sorry," Sarah said and chewed at her lip harder.

"You can leave now," Hailey said and turned her back to Sarah. "I want to be alone."

Sarah didn't move. "Did the chief tell you what we should do?"

"I don't know. Maybe." Hailey stared at her phone, as if willing it to give her some good news. At the very least, take back the news it had delivered. But it stayed silent. "I can't remember."

"Maybe I should call him."

"Do what you want," Hailey said. "I don't care. Just leave me alone."

"Maybe we shouldn't be alone—"

"*Fucking* leave!"

೮೩ ೮೦

Sarah stood there like she'd been slapped so hard her bearings had been knocked right out of her head. She stared at Hailey's back while anger rose in her throat.

"I lost the man I love, too."

"I don't care what you lost," Hailey said, not looking at Sarah. "I don't care about you."

Sarah struggled with what she'd just heard. The immature child in her wanted to lash out, too, hurt Hailey with sharper words, but reason prevailed.

She left the room quietly, Peanut at her heel. Out in the hallway, she stopped in the spare bedroom doorway and looked at the mess Jack had left behind.

Sarah wasn't just thinking of the room.

And then it hit hard. Shock had kept her from falling apart, but standing alone in the mouth of the spare room, her body started to shake and shiver while her throat became so small that she couldn't swallow. Her breaths felt like brad nails shredding her lungs.

Jack was gone.

Her Jack.

Gone.

Sarah walked aimlessly around the room, touching the drywall that Jack had started to pull apart where the closet was because it wasn't needed anymore and he'd told her it would make the room bigger if he removed it. Especially since he'd stolen a third of the room already for their ensuite, removing the closet made sense.

She took his hammer in her hands and cuddled it like a prized possession. She saw his dust mask sitting on top of the bucket of drywall compound. On the window sill, his protective glasses rested along with his utility knife, the glasses never to be worn by him again. His eyes no longer needed to be protected. There were clean rags hanging on the ladder that leaned against the wall and dirty rags on the floor.

"Jack," she whispered. In her head, she heard Hailey's words, *he should have been thinking of us,* and there was a lot of truth in that. For once, she wished he'd been selfish and thought of his well-being, his family's well-being, before attempting to be the hero again. "Oh, Jack."

She remained there for a good five minutes, cuddling the hammer, grief pouring down her pale face. She rarely wore makeup unless she went out—even then, Jack had told her she didn't need it, that she was naturally beautiful.

Who was going to tell her that now?

And mean it.

Men had been telling her how beautiful she was all her life, but no one had truly meant it until she had met Jack.

Jack.

He was so good at what he did, but he also pushed the limits. She knew it was in his nature and it's what made him great at everything. But she reminded him every day when he went off to work of what he had at home, to never forget that. He always reassured her that he never forgot the ones he loved, that she and Hailey were always first and foremost on his mind at all times.

Especially when he was called out to fight a fire.

But this morning, he'd been running late and she couldn't remember now if she had reminded him. In fact, she was pretty sure she hadn't.

This was her fault.

Her fault.

Jack was gone because she hadn't reminded him to be careful. Of course, it was nonsense, Jack had been doing this job long before he'd met her. He'd never needed to be reminded before she'd come into his life.

Maybe his ex-wife had.

Sarah wiped her runny nose with the back of her hand. Jack had been a professional firefighter for nearly twenty years. She knew he hadn't needed her reminders. She knew this wasn't her fault.

She knew bad things happened to good people and no one was to blame.

But blaming someone or something was easier than accepting that life had just randomly killed the man she loved. If that fire hadn't happened, Jack would be alive this very minute. Something had caused that fire: faulty wiring, a burner left on, a fired employee with a grudge. It had to be something because she couldn't accept that it was just fate.

Fate couldn't be faulted.

And she needed to blame something or someone. In the worst way. She'd been alone for so long and she couldn't go back to that life. She hated that life. But without Jack, she had no family.

Hailey hated her.

Hailey didn't want anything to do with her.

Hailey already had a mother.

A mother who'd left her. Jack's parents were on the other side of the country. There was no one in Ottawa who could take care of Hailey. She'd be eighteen next August, but until then she was a minor.

Who really couldn't take care of herself.

Hailey wasn't her family. Jack was Hailey's family. Sarah was just the stepmom, the stepmom Hailey probably wished had died instead of her dad.

Without Jack, Sarah and Hailey were two strangers living in the same house. A house that had belonged to the Cormier family for generations. She didn't even know if Jack had a will. People their age never talked about such things. Dying wasn't a concept that came to mind.

They had so much time.

Considering what Jack did, Sarah realized that she should have thought about the possibility of him dying. So many things she wasn't aware of. She was so naïve.

No wonder Hailey didn't like her, didn't trust her. Sarah barely knew more than Hailey. How could she ever be a parent figure when the concept actually eluded her? She'd been Jack's wife. Jack took care of everything.

Jack took care of them.

Of her.

Sarah had been too happy to let him do that. She'd had to take care of her mom all her life and then herself, but she really hadn't. All she'd ever done was survive one more day. The things normal people worried about, planned, had been foreign to her and, she now realized, were still foreign to her. She had been living in Jack's adult world but had yet to grow into an adult herself.

Was she living on borrowed time? Who did the house belong to? Hailey? Or Jack's parents? She wasn't a real Cormier. She was the last stranger into the family.

She was probably homeless now.

Sarah sat hard on the bucket of drywall compound, crushing the dust mask that was resting on top of it. Peanut rubbed herself against Sarah's leg and Sarah put the hammer down and scooped the little dog into her arms. She patted the Maltese with slow, absentminded strokes. She really didn't care about being homeless.

She cared about being a widow.

A *widow.*

It tasted bitter, sounded surreal, made her feel cold and very lonely. Old women were widows, not a twenty-nine-year-old who had finally found love.

And lost it too quickly.

She hated feeling sorry for herself, but dammit, she'd just lost her husband . . . what was she going to do now?

"I don't know," she whispered to Peanut. "Your daddy isn't coming back." Peanut looked up at her, twisting her neck in an unnatural position, and cried. "I know baby. It feels like someone pulled my heart from my chest and left this big empty hole that I can't imagine ever filling."

She looked the room over.

"Jack, you left me like this room," she said through choking sobs. "Broken and unfinished."

Someone spoke and pulled her out of her trance, slowly. At first, she could only see her mother, standing in the doorway, blocking her escape.

But it wasn't her mother. She was dead.

Like Jack.

"It's your fault," Hailey said, ice in her voice. "Everything is your fault."

Sarah stared at her stepdaughter, feeling her anger wrap its cold fingers around her throat. She began to shake her head.

"My fault?"

"That my dad died."

Sarah felt her forehead tighten as her brows pulled downward. "How . . . how is it my fault?"

"All he ever thought about was you," Hailey said, her face red. "He was careless because of you. He was probably thinking about you and made a mistake. Dad never made mistakes until he met you. Look at this room. He would have had that done in a weekend before you."

Sarah shook her head. "I love him. He's a good man. He loves me."

"Don't you know your tenses?" Hailey said. "Dad is no longer in the present tense. Dad is in the past tense now. You're so dumb. GOD! I wish he'd never met you. Why couldn't you be the one that was dead? I hate you. This is all your fault. I hate you, I hate you, I *hate* you!"

Sarah couldn't listen to this anymore. She stood quickly and Peanut jumped out of her arms and looked frantically at the two women. Sarah bolted toward Hailey, pushed her out of the way, knocking the younger girl back against the hallway wall, then swiftly rushed to her bedroom and locked the door before Peanut could follow her in.

Sarah heard scratching on the door and moved away, fear ripping her apart. Could Hailey be right? Was Jack careless because of her?

No. This wasn't her fault.

She hadn't killed Jack.

She loved Jack.

Her mother had always blamed her for everything. Sarah folded herself in the far-left corner of the room, by the window, her knees pulled to her chest, her arms covering her head like a shield. Any minute now, the blows would start. It always ended with her mother beating her for something, anything. It didn't matter. Her mom blamed her for everything that was wrong with her life.

Jack had been the first person who had never physically hurt her, who had loved her for all her simplicity and her faults. She would take a thousand beatings at the hand of her mother if it would bring him back to her.

Someone pounded on her door. Sarah didn't dare look, she just buried her face into her knees. She wanted it all to go away. Her mother and her deadbeat boyfriends who were always trying to feel her up when her mother wasn't looking. She hated them so much. They had taken any self-esteem she'd ever had, and left her bare to the bones, broken, feeling worthless.

Jack had made all of that go away.

"You don't belong here!" Hailey shouted. "This was never your home."

"Please," Sarah whispered. "It wasn't my fault. I love Jack with all my heart. Hailey, please, this wasn't my fault."

The only reply was Peanut's quiet whimpering.

And the slamming of the front door.

FIVE

Hailey walked down the long driveway to the main road, a little shorter than the length of a football field, and turned to look at the house. Her dad had bought the house from her grandparents years ago, when she was one or two, so it was really the only home she could remember. Her mom had left when she was four, and then it had just been her and her dad until Sarah tipped the balance.

And now her dad was gone.

And opposing forces remained.

She had no idea what was going to happen now. All she knew was that she couldn't stay another second in the same house as Sarah and needed to get out. Her dad's presence was all over the house and even from way out here, his ghost filled every inch of the property. She could see him mowing the lawn on his ride-on-mower, building that tree-house where that gigantic hundred-year-old elm tree was on the east side of the house; she could hear his belly laughter from when they used to play in the back-yard pool.

She was angry and confused and tired of crying. She didn't really know what she should do regarding her dad—there had to be people to contact and a funeral to plan, but she was going to leave that up to Sarah. All she wanted right now was to get away from this place and all its haunting memories. Maybe she could stay at Andréa's for a couple days.

Thoughts of her mother crossed her mind.

Would she care that Dad is gone?

Hailey had no idea. A more pressing question was whether her mom would take her in for a while, until she came of age to be on her own. Her future had just taken a sharp wrong turn.

Maybe the house was hers, maybe it was Sarah's. Maybe it would go back to her grandparents. She had no idea if her dad had written a will. It was obvious that he'd forgotten to change his emergency number at work, because then the chief would have called Sarah instead. What else had her dad forgotten to do?

He'd forgotten to be careful.

She was so pissed off with him right now. And she hated that she couldn't tell him. Who would drive her to the out-of-town hockey games? Who would be there in the stands to cheer for her? Who was going to be there to watch her graduate high school next June?

They were supposed to look at colleges and universities before Christmas because her applications would need to be sent in soon.

School seemed so pointless right now.

Everything felt small and insignificant.

Hailey had to go. She didn't want to cry again thinking about how horrible her life had become. She just wanted to get to her friends, lose herself in them, not think about her dad's funeral, or Sarah, or her mom. She just wanted to be blissfully numb.

The wind coming across the wide expanse of the farmer's field that surrounded their home was cold and Hailey shivered. She hesitated just for a moment thinking about going back to the house to get a warmer jacket, but decided to pull up her collar, shove her hands in the pockets of the windbreaker she'd grabbed hastily, and started walking toward town.

Away from the pain that suffocated her and toward the people she trusted and loved.

CB ∙ EO

Sarah was standing in front of the living room window watching Hailey brace herself against the wind as she started to walk away. Jack would be so disappointed that she and his daughter couldn't get along, especially now that they really just had one another.

Sarah totally understood Hailey. She had been that girl not that long ago, which made it worse for Sarah because she wasn't like the men her mother had shacked up with. Sarah wasn't a fly-by-night stranger who didn't care.

She put her hand on the window as if she could will Hailey to come back. Real life didn't have magical forces that could bend minds. Real life was hard and unforgiving at times. Real life had sucker punched them both.

And instead of coming together, they'd been torn apart.

Peanut gave a sad, weak bark and Sarah scooped the Maltese into her arms. She patted her head gently.

"I don't know how to fix it," Sarah told Peanut. "Do you?"

Peanut let out a quiet whimper.

"Yes, it makes me sad too."

Sarah stayed in front of the window for as long as she could see Hailey, and once her stepdaughter was out of sight she let Peanut down and walked back to the kitchen. Jack had completely gutted it last year, knocked down a non-load-bearing wall to make the room bigger, and had turned the old kitchen into a dream: a huge island, marble countertops, a walk-in pantry, and more cupboards than they could ever need.

Sarah stood in the middle of the room, feeling completely lost and defeated. And very alone.

Jack was everywhere. His handiwork over the last couple of years had really transformed the old house into a home that Sarah absolutely loved.

Home.

I wasn't just a house. A house was four walls and a roof, but a home was filled with love and memories. She had really hoped that Hailey would warm up to her in time, and as long as she'd had Jack, she'd figured she had plenty of time.

But now?

It felt like a house, a big empty box void of love and full of painful grief. Anger rose in the back of her throat and hardened her facial features. This wasn't fair. Hadn't she had a difficult enough life? Didn't she deserve some happiness? She'd just gotten a taste of it and now it had been ripped from her grasp, taken back like it had never belonged to her. But she didn't want to let go. She wanted to hold on to everything this house represented, but she wasn't sure how to do that or if she'd even get the chance. The doubts inside of her felt like sledgehammer blows, each one destroying everything she and Jack had built since finding one another.

Hailey's harsh words blasted inside her head. Could her stepdaughter have been right? Had Jack become careless because of her?

Was she the cause of his death?

Sarah didn't want to believe that. He'd even told her just last weekend as they sat under a blanket, watching one of those Hallmark movies—this one was about a man who Jack had been quick to point out had looked an awful lot like him and Sarah had laughed and told him not even close, that he was way better looking and sexier than that actor—that since he'd met her, he felt all his senses had undergone some sort of augmentation because he felt like he could hear, see, feel, and think clearer than he ever had before.

A sad smile forced itself on her face as she remembered that they'd never made it to the end of the movie, and not because they had fallen asleep. Hailey had been at a Halloween party and they'd had the house to themselves.

As quickly as the smile had come, tears followed in an uncontrollable torrent. She could hardly believe she had any left, but just like her love for Jack was endless, so would be her grief. She now understood how someone could die of a broken heart, how someone could throw herself in front of an oncoming train to stop the pain and loneliness.

He should be here, holding her like he often did when she had one of her horrible nightmares. He never asked her what they were about and even after all these years, she still couldn't tell anyone. She felt guilty for not confiding in him, knowing he would never judge, but the memories were too raw and painful.

Shameful.

She didn't want to have anything to do with that Sarah, with that past. Problem was that *it* wasn't done tormenting her. And now that Jack was gone—she still couldn't quite believe it and thought she should call the fire chief to find out what had really happened instead of relying on what Hailey had told her, but she wasn't ready for that yet—she wondered whether her past would catch up to her, pull her back.

An oncoming train would be a better fate.

And she was worried about Hailey. The girl was full of hurt, and she remembered when she'd been her stepdaughter's age that she'd had no idea how to deal with the hurt she'd had and had made all sorts of wrong decisions that had taken her ten years to make right.

And really, if Jack hadn't come around, she'd probably still be living those mistakes.

She didn't want that for Hailey.

But she knew you couldn't help someone who didn't want to be helped. She had no idea how to get herself through this nightmare, let alone help an angry teenager who blamed her for what had happened to her dad. How could a high school dropout with so few life skills help anyone? Jack had encouraged her to go back to school, pursue her passion, and she'd told him that she would—except that she'd been petrified of going back and looking dumb in front of everyone, and she'd had no idea what her passion was anyway.

She loved to read.

"Then become a writer," Jack had said.

Reading had simply been her way of escaping the cruelty of her life. And how could she confess that she could barely spell? Okay, maybe she wasn't that bad, but still . . .

She did like gardening and seemed to know more about flowers than she ever thought possible. Of course, Google was a wonderful friend.

"Then become a horticulturist," he'd said a few weeks back when she'd talked non-stop for an hour about her garden and how she wanted to move things around to create a better synergetic environment that would allow the plants currently being suffocated to thrive. "I love it when you talk dirty."

The memory chased away her melancholy, but just as quickly she yearned to hear his deep, confident voice. All he ever had to say was *"Hey, babe"* and whatever trouble she'd had on her mind would dissipate like thin fog. She knew some women would find it sexist or maybe even a little demeaning, but to her, those two innocuous words wrapped her in the comfort of his love for her.

A sudden chill travelled across her skin and left a trail of tiny goosebumps everywhere.

She wanted a cigarette really bad.

This was the second time today that she'd had the craving. This morning when she'd stared out the bedroom window while Jack had been in the shower, and now. Had it been some sort of omen earlier? A reminder that her past was finally catching up?

Going out with Jack in the first place had felt all wrong. Where she worked, you simply didn't agree to go on a date with a patron, a complete stranger. But his honest face . . . and those green eyes had just seemed to reach deep inside of her and something had convinced her that she'd be a fool to turn this guy down. She'd had no idea why he'd wanted to go out with a girl like her . . . well she'd hoped it wasn't for that same reason that always made her say no when guys asked her. Her rules had told her to turn him down and send him away, and she'd tried, but fortunately Jack had had other ideas.

"Jack," she whispered. "How am I supposed to move on without you? What am I going to do with Hailey's hate?"

The only answer she got was Peanut's tiny whimper.

The house phone shattered the silence around her. Jack insisted on keeping a house phone even though they each had a mobile phone. No one ever answered it, preferring to let it go to voicemail and if it was important, whoever was calling would leave a message and they could call them back.

She noticed it was the school calling.

"Hello?" Her voice sounded strange and thick with grief.

"Mrs. Cormier?"

"Yes, this is Sarah Cormier." She always wanted to make sure that whoever was calling knew that she wasn't Natalie.

"This is Forest Creek High School calling regarding Hailey's absence."

Sarah always found it strange that whenever someone from the school called, they identified themselves as "the school." As if a building could phone. "Oh, yes. Umm. We've had some terrible news this morning. Hailey probably won't be in for a few days."

"I'm sorry to hear that," the woman at the end of the line said. "If possible, could we get a phone call early each morning that Hailey will be absent, otherwise we have to follow up with a call? Schoolboard directive."

"Yes, of course," Sarah said. "I understand."

She hung up and looked down at Peanut who was practically lying on her feet.

"What do you think?" she asked the Maltese. "Should I call Hailey and find out where she is?"

Peanut raised her head at the mention of Hailey, and then she got up and went to the front door. She wagged her tail expectantly. Sarah walked up to the foyer and scooped the dog into her arms.

"Sorry, honey," she said. "Hailey isn't here."

Peanut's face turned sad and she lay her head on Sarah's arm. The dog sighed.

"I'm worried too," Sarah said. "But right now, Hailey is hurting too much to want me." She patted Peanut a few times. "She'll probably never want me."

Peanut reached up and licked her chin.

"I'm glad someone still wants me," she said and kissed Peanut's nose. "Mamma's girl, aren't you?"

Sarah got a faceful of kisses from the little dog. She then put Peanut down on the floor and stood motionless by the front door, unable to make a decision. Making decisions would mean moving on, moving to the next stage of this nightmare, and she didn't want to do that.

Not without Jack.

Nothing nauseated Sarah Cormier more on this dreary cold autumn morning than the thought of facing the rest of her life as the widow of Jacques (Jack) Cormier.

SIX

Forest Creek was still considered a village even though in the last two years it had seen its population grow by almost fifteen hundred new faces thanks to the new housing development on the west-end. Business owners loved the influx of new revenue, but for the long-time residents it just meant more traffic down Franktown Road which divided the village between north and south, and connected the village to its Richmond neighbour on the east side as well as the still undeveloped space on the west side; not to mention more waiting in lines at the local grocery store—which was now busting at the seams on Saturday mornings—and just a whole lot more strangers invading their once peaceful and secluded little piece of tranquility.

Madelaine Dupont was a new kid whose family had moved to town over the summer and Hailey had instantly connected with her. Andréa Laperrière, who had been Hailey's best friend since Junior Kindergarten hadn't been as keen to accept Madelaine and it sometimes created friction between the three.

Hailey reached Franktown Road and a sigh of relief escaped her when she saw her two best friends standing on the other side of the road waiting for her.

She had texted them as she'd walked toward town to let them know what was going on and, although she hadn't asked, she was glad that they'd both ditched classes to come and support her.

Hailey really needed her friends right now.

She waited for the light to change and crossed quickly, falling into their open arms. All three started to cry as they stood there by the side of the road, oblivious to the world around them, overwhelmed by personal grief.

"Thank you," Hailey said once the crying eased off and they'd pulled apart. She watched her friends wipe their own tears and a timid smile appeared unexpectedly. "I love you guys."

"We know," Madelaine and Andréa said at the same time. "We love you too."

They stood in awkward silence, the traffic rushing by them the only sound audible.

"I'm sorry," Andréa said. "Your dad, he's the best. The way he drives us around to all our hockey games, lets us hang out and sleepover whenever we want."

"I don't always like my dad," Madelaine said, "but I can't imagine not having him around. This must be so hard." She touched Hailey's arm. "Are you okay? I mean, I know you're not really, but—"

Hailey put on a brave face.

"I don't think it feels quite real just yet," she said. "I mean, I just talked to his boss on the phone. What if he's not really dead?"

Andréa bit her lip and looked from Hailey to Madelaine and back to Hailey. "He wouldn't have called—"

"I know," Hailey said and any other words she'd meant to say faded in the back of her throat. She bit her lower lip while her eyes shined. "I have no one now."

Madelaine glanced at Andréa.

"What about Sarah? Or your mom?" Andréa said.

Hailey snorted. "My mom left me when I was four. She obviously doesn't want me. And Sarah . . ."

"She's nice," Madelaine said.

Hailey looked away.

"I know you don't like her," Andréa said. "But maybe you can give her a chance."

"She's barely older than me."

"Isn't she like, thirty?"

"Twenty-nine," Hailey said.

"My mom is only thirty-five," Madelaine said.

"Yeah but she's been your mom all your life," Hailey said. "She knows how to take care of you. Sarah just dropped into my life. She's not mother material."

"She doesn't need to be your mother," Andréa said. "Think of her as your big sister."

A frown crossed Hailey's features. "Would you listen to Alexi?"

Andréa shrugged. "She's only four years older, but maybe if I'd lost my parents and she was all I had, I guess I would."

"So, what are you going to do?" Madelaine asked.

"I don't know," Hailey said. "Right now, I'm cold and could really use a Caramel Mocha."

"We could go to Charlie's," Andréa said. "It's a lot closer than walking across town to Tim's."

"Tim's doesn't have real Mochas anyway," Madelaine said.

Charlie's was a small local coffee shop just a few blocks from school, so all the juniors and seniors frequented the place. The owners made their own breads and pastries, but for the best dessert treats in town, everyone knew you had to go to Sarah's Bakery, *Forest Creek's Yummy Treasures*.

Although lately, Hailey had boycotted the shop because she couldn't bring herself to go in a place called Sarah's Bakery. Silly really, because the store had nothing to do with her stepmom, but the name just grated on her a little, which really annoyed her because they did have the best chocolate walnut brownies in the world.

And she could use one of those, too.

The girls made their way to Charlie's in silence, heads down and shoulders braced against the cold wind. No one was really dressed for the sudden turn in temperature. November in Ottawa could hardly be trusted. It could go from plus ten Celsius to below freezing in a matter of hours.

The little bell above the door announced their arrival and Cecilia, who owned the shop with her husband Charlie, greeted them with a warm smile.

"Hey girls," she said. "No classes this morning?"

"Spare," Andréa said. "And Hailey was craving a Caramel Mocha."

"Should I make that three?"

They all nodded. Hailey whispered something and Madelaine left the coffee house.

"Oh!" Cecilia said. "Should I just make two?"

"She'll be right back," Andréa said. "Hailey is also craving a chocolate walnut brownie."

Cecilia nodded. "Nothing better than Sarah's Bakery for one of those."

"You have good treats, too," Hailey said.

"No worries," Cecilia said. "Emily makes the best desserts in town. I go there too to satisfy my chocolate fix."

The girls paid and grabbed a table. The place was quite small with just half a dozen round tables. There was just one table occupied by a woman who was probably about the same age as Hailey's father and a small boy of maybe one, one and a half.

Andréa took a sip of her coffee.

Hailey watched her.

They sat in the comfortable silence of friends who really knew each other. They'd gone through all the grades together, fell in love with hockey when they were five, had had crushes on Justin Bieber when they were twelve. Andréa was the first one Hailey had told that she really liked Connor, but that was last summer before they'd met Madelaine.

"I have no idea what you're going through," Andréa said after putting her cup down. "But I'll do anything I can."

"I know."

"I'm sure my parents won't mind if you stay at our place for a few days, if you need to."

"Thanks."

Hailey watched the little boy. He was in constant motion, climbing down from his chair, walking over to the counter—his mother telling him not to touch anything—coming back to his mom and taking a bite of his snack, dashing across the shop,

coming back again. The woman—Hailey thought she was absolutely beautiful—seemed to take it all in stride. Hailey could
remember her mother getting flustered with her all the time and
telling her dad how exhausted Hailey made her.

"He's cute," Hailey said to the woman.

"Thank you," the woman said. "He's a busy bee."

"What's his name," Andréa asked.

"Callum," the woman said.

"How old?"

"Almost eighteen months," the woman said. "He doesn't realize it yet, but he's going to be a big brother in about four
months."

"He'll be a great big brother," Hailey said, not knowing if that
was true. She didn't know these people, but she wanted to believe
that there was good in the world, that maybe her dad dying had
made room for that woman's unborn child.

Hailey had never set foot in a church in her life—as far as she
could remember—so the thought was like a bucket of cold water
dumped on her head. She knew life didn't work that way, but she
wanted to have some reason, however farfetched it might be, for
her dad dying today. Suddenly, the coffee house seemed too
small, the air too thin, Callum's cries of joy too shattering.

She didn't want her dad to be dead.

The woman stood and Hailey saw her belly semi-full. Four
months wasn't very long. It would be March break in four
months. The last high school March break for Hailey and her
classmates. Four months ago, it had been summer and her dad
had rented a cabin in the Gatineau Hills and Andréa had come
with them for the two weeks. They'd had a blast using the paddle

boards and the canoe they'd rented, and she and Andréa had had awesome tans to go back to school with.

Four hours ago, her dad had still been alive.

The little boy ran up to Hailey and crashed into her legs. He looked up at her and grinned, showing his tiny baby teeth.

"Callum," his mother said in a tone that showed authority. "What do you say?"

"Thorry," he said and dashed away.

"It's okay," Hailey said. She watched them put on their jackets and the woman put a hat on Callum. She wondered why her parents had never had another baby, why they had stopped with just her. Maybe she wouldn't feel so alone if she'd had a sibling.

The little boy turned and waved. "Bye."

Hailey waved back. "Bye."

She watched them leave, Callum holding his mother's hand, his world unshattered.

CB ८০

Madelaine came in as the woman and her son left and put down three delicious chocolate walnut brownies on the table. She pulled up a chair and joined them.

"He was cute," Hailey said.

Madelaine glanced at Andréa, and gave her an *is-she-okay* look.

"The little boy who just left," Andréa said.

"I wasn't really paying attention," Madelaine said.

"Me neither, usually," Hailey said. "Why is that?"

Madelaine and Andréa tore small pieces from their brownie and popped them into their mouth.

"Because teenagers don't pay attention," Hailey said. "We think the world rotates around us. We think nothing bad can happen to us. We don't think our dad could go to work today and get killed."

Madelaine and Andréa were stunned into silence. They didn't even dare reach for their coffees or treats.

"I mean," Hailey said, as if thinking out loud. "My dad is a fireman so I know it's a dangerous job. But I guess I never expected him to ever get hurt. His job was to help other people who got hurt. He wasn't supposed to get hurt. He was supposed to save those people and come home to tell us about it." She battled to keep her composure. "But he's never going to tell us anything more. It's just me and Sarah. She's not my mother. How can it be just me and her? Without my dad, we're just strangers. He was our connection."

She looked at her friends.

"Me and Sarah, we're not family."

"But maybe she is," Madelaine said. "I know I don't know her very well, but whenever I've been to your house, she was always nice to me."

"She is nice," Andréa said. "It's more complicated than that."

Hailey looked off, focusing on a shelf of cups with Charlie's logo on them. They looked more like mugs that could hold a lot of coffee. "What if my parents couldn't get back together because of her? Maybe my mom had wanted to come back but because of Sarah, she couldn't."

"Do you really think so?" Madelaine asked.

Hailey turned to her and shrugged. "Probably not. I'm not sure my dad wanted my mom back. He always seemed angry whenever her name came up."

Hailey thought back to Callum's mother and how she'd looked at her son, with utmost love. Her mom had never looked at her that way. It seemed that her mom's eyes had always been full of regret, like her life had taken a horrible turn. Maybe that was why Hailey had never had any siblings. Her mother had never wanted Hailey in the first place.

Didn't her leaving them confirm that?

It was a truth Hailey had closed her mind to for a long time. It was too painful of a truth. To accept that her mother, the woman who had carried her in her womb for nine months and gone through the grueling process of giving birth, really hadn't wanted her at all. It was the hardest truth to accept. Even now, sitting here with her friends in this quaint little coffee shop, Hailey was contemplating showing up on her mom's doorstep and forcing the woman to be the mother she should have been.

The only other choice was to go back home and learn to live with Sarah. Both options squeezed hope out of her. If only she'd had more time to prepare to be on her own. She glanced at her friends and realized that even though they were trying to share her grief, it wasn't really possible. Their lives hadn't been turned inside out, their perfect worlds were still intact. Bitterness fueled her anger, made her dislike her friends.

This wasn't fair.

She knew she sounded like a five-year-old, but her dad had died this morning and she had no idea why she was sitting in a coffee house with her friends bitching about her stepmom.

Before she could stop herself, she began to fall apart, her shoulders rolling and her wails coming out in uncontrollable waves.

She hated her mom.

She hated Sarah.

She hated Madelaine.

She hated Andréa.

But most of all, she hated her dad for trying to be someone else's hero and getting himself killed.

Who was going to be her hero now?

SEVEN

S arah put her phone in her back pocket and walked up the stairs. Each step felt like her legs were made of lead, the longest climb to the second floor ever. She really didn't know why she was going up to her room. She just needed to move around.

She'd been talking with the fire chief for more than thirty minutes and her mind had tried really, *really* hard to refute what Jack's boss and friend was telling her.

She'd yelled at him, sworn at him, pleaded with him. Why had he allowed Jack to go up to that third floor? Why had Jack even been out there? He couldn't have been in the station more than a few minutes when the call had come in. It had been one of those strange calls that had come while a shift change was happening, but no matter, that hadn't played any part in the outcome. Jack was a veteran, and he would have assessed that it was still safe to go to the top floor and rescue whomever was up there.

The fire chief promised Sarah that he'd take care of everything for her, and apologized profusely for not calling her first. Seemed their emergency contact had never been updated and still listed Hailey as Jack's next of kin.

Sarah reached the landing and stopped in front Hailey's messy room. She took a hesitant step forward and pushed the door wide open. It looked like the closet had vomited all her clothes onto the floor. On her little desk that she used as a makeup table was a clutter of mascara and lip balms and rings and earrings and bracelets, none of which Hailey used or wore often. Sarah had had nothing like that growing up. She'd been lucky if she'd gotten something decent to wear from a second hand store.

She pushed the jealousy back where it belonged. It felt petty. Not how a grown woman who had known hardship should think. She understood that not everyone had the same hard upbringing, and that it was not Hailey's fault that she had been spoiled. Probably Jack had doted over his daughter more so than he would have had Hailey's mother not left. In that way, Hailey has known hardship as well; maybe not to the same degree as Sarah, but she'd lost plenty. More so now that Jack was gone, too. Jealousy had no room here. It didn't belong.

Hailey was all Sarah had left. No matter how much her step-daughter didn't want her, Sarah had made vows to Jack, and those vows included taking care of Hailey.

She'd have to find a way.

Absentmindedly, she started to tidy up but then realized Hailey would see it as an invasion of her privacy and the last thing Sarah wanted right now was to give her stepdaughter more reasons to hate her.

Sarah needed Hailey to trust her.

Sarah needed to find the Sarah Jack had believed in. Maybe that Sarah could reach Hailey.

But what if that Sarah had only existed for Jack?

She didn't like that thought. That Sarah had to be there inside of her.

She had to be.

Sarah backed out of the room and left the door like it had been and walked away. She was scared of what was ahead for them. Her world had become a great big unknown. There was no one out there for her. Jack had been everything.

Flashbacks to her old life invaded her thoughts and she shuddered. Selena was the only one she'd stayed somewhat in contact with, but she wouldn't consider her a true friend. They had worked together.

Nothing more.

Walls started to go up, trying to keep *that* part of Sarah's life out. But she could feel those walls coming down on her, letting her old life back in and reminding her of those homeless nights when she and her mom had held on to each other to stay warm as they slept under a bridge or in a cemetery where they would go unnoticed. Or worse, she could feel Axel choking her, his grip on her throat so tight she knew she'd either pass out or simply die.

Sarah put her hand against the wall. She closed her eyes and waited for the moment to pass. Axel couldn't hurt her anymore. Her mother couldn't hurt her anymore. But knowing something and not feeling that something were two different things. Emotional scars were the hardest to survive. Those memories pressed hard against her chest and every shallow breath felt like she was breathing in fire.

She didn't want to give in to these attacks anymore.

Sarah remembered her first night here as Sarah Cormier instead of Sarah Kincaid. She couldn't have gotten rid of her mother's maiden name more quickly, finally shedding the last of her past. Of course, that night wasn't the first time she and Jack had slept together in this room, but before it had been his room, not theirs. Even the next morning, it had felt strange to look at her left hand and see that beautiful ring on her finger. Knowing that someone like Jack felt that she was worthy of his love brought her to tears as she stood naked in front of the mirror, her hair a tangled mess, her eyes caked with sleep, her breath still tasting of last night's celebration.

And then Jack had come in and wrapped her in his big, muscular arms and all her silly fears had evaporated, all the painful memories of her old life banished, leaving all the new possibilities staring back at her from their reflection in the mirror.

And now it was all gone.

Sarah opened her eyes and barely gave a glance to the unfinished spare room as she hurried passed it—a room she loved to stand in because it was filled with Jack's handiwork and presence. Instead, she reached the walk-in closet in the master bedroom and stood in its dimness, having no idea what she was looking for. The conversation with the fire chief seemed like hours ago and, after hanging up, all she could think about was getting up to her room, but now she couldn't remember why.

And then it hit her. Jack's essence was everywhere, but instead of bringing her comfort it brought on a medley of painful solitude.

She pulled one of Jack's Ottawa Redblacks hoodies over her head and inhaled his sent. From his dresser she grabbed a pair of his pajama bottoms and slipped them over her jeans. She then curled up on their bed and hugged his pillows.

Tears streaked unnoticed down her face.

She couldn't do this. When her mom had died, Sarah had felt liberated, like for the first time in her life she was finally in control. Jack dying imprisoned her in a gluttony of fear and doubt and isolation.

A broken arm would heal.

It seemed unlikely that her shattered life could ever rise from the depths of her despair and regain any semblance of normalcy.

Anger exploded from deep inside of her, obliterating her grief. How dare he make her fall in love with him, show her how wonderful life could actually be, and then leave her. He couldn't do this to her, to them. They loved him. He couldn't leave them. It wasn't right.

"I hate you Jack!" she screamed. "I hate you," she whispered, her face buried in her pillow. "I love you."

After a moment, she sat up and reached for the box of tissues on her night table. She grabbed two tissues and wiped her nose. Peanut, who had been waiting for Sarah, was lying down on the floor, her troubled eyes looking up at her owner.

Sarah's anger began to fade. She knew she was being stupid. It's not like Jack had left her on purpose. He'd been doing his job. He was the quintessential firefighter—tall, strong, handsome, and fearless.

And so damn funny.

After his green eyes, she loved that he never took himself seriously and always made her laugh. It had been such a change from the joyless harshness of her life, and laughing so much had felt like a drug she couldn't get enough of.

If only she could have bottled his goodness so that she could continue to sample him whenever she needed it. She wasn't fooling herself. That bottle would already be empty.

She was so addicted to her husband.

In that way, she understood Hailey. Her stepdaughter hadn't wanted to share her dad with her, with anyone. She and Hailey were both selfish when it came to Jack. And now she realized that they'd been adversaries for his love and attention instead of coming together as a family.

That had been a huge mistake on her part. A mistake that was costly now that she and Hailey needed each other but couldn't even be in the same house together without Jack. She worried about her stepdaughter. Not where she was—Hailey had her friends and was likely with them. What she worried about was the anger she was carrying deep inside of her and that the only release she had was to direct it at Sarah.

She'd been there long ago. And she remembered how draining it had been to always be angry at her mother. When she had married Jack, she had promised herself that she would never make the same mistakes her mom had made, that she would never alienate Hailey.

She hadn't expected Hailey's hostility.

But she'd hoped that in time, with Jack's help, that Hailey would come around. But now, she saw little hope of that happening. Sarah had also found herself alone at seventeen. And all she'd known had been the life her mom had dragged her into. She'd struggled. Lived with the wrong kind of people because it was better than being on the streets. It had taken her years to save up enough to get her own place. And the only furnishing she'd been able to afford was an inexpensive mattress from Ikea.

She didn't want that sort of life for Hailey.

When she'd met Jack, she'd been horrified that he'd want to come up to her apartment one day. The last thing she'd wanted, once she'd realized she'd fallen for him, was for Jack to see how out of her league he really was. And she still felt that way now. She'd been too happy to let him take care of everything. She had yearned for someone to take care of her her whole life and now she was regretting it. She felt very unprepared for what lay ahead, and completely lost when it came to caring for an angry teenage girl who wanted nothing to do with her.

The situation felt utterly hopeless.

Sarah's gaze fell on their wedding picture sitting on top of the dresser and feelings of loneliness grabbed her once again. She suddenly didn't know if she was going to be able to stay in this house. Too much of Jack roamed these walls. Two years of wonderful memories.

Mostly.

At least for her and Jack.

And Peanut.

She'd never had a pet before Jack brought the puppy home last summer, and Sarah had taken to her instantly. She'd seen that Hailey was going to be hard to reach and Peanut could fill that void. Besides, the puppy had been irresistible.

As if the Maltese could read her thoughts, Peanut raised her head and looked expectedly at Sarah. A smile softened Sarah's troubled face and she made a calling noise with her tongue and mouth. Peanut leaped to her feet and jumped up onto Sarah's lap.

"I need to plan a funeral," she said before realizing the fire chief had told her he'd take care of everything. "When Mom died, I just told the hospital to take care of it. I don't even know what they did with her," she told Peanut. "I want to know what happens to Jack. I have to make sure the fire chief tells me. I want to know where Jack is going to be. I don't want him to be dead anymore."

She pulled Peanut against her chest and held on to her as though she feared losing the dog, too. Her shoulders were tense, her neck was too tight, and her thoughts turned dark and bitter.

"Damnit Jack! Come home. Come home right *fucking* now!"

EIGHT

S arah woke up on Christmas Day abruptly, suddenly feeling nauseated. She kicked the blankets back and rushed to the bathroom. She just managed to pull the toilet seat up before retching last night's dinner of chicken noodle soup and crackers.

She hated throwing up. The way her body tensed and forced everything out left her achy and exhausted. Nothing tasted worse than bile coating the back of her throat.

Which made her dry heave a couple of times.

Sarah wiped her mouth with a handful of tissues and flushed. She stood on wobbly legs and looked at the pale reflection of herself in the mirror. There were dark circles under her eyes and her hair was a tangled mess full of knots.

She splashed cold water on her face but it didn't help ease the puffiness under her eyes. She looked like someone battling a horrible flu.

Crawling back into bed sounded so inviting.

Not like she was going to celebrate Christmas. There was no tree in the great room, no decorations, no lights hanging on the eavestrough, no presents.

December twenty-fifth was just another day. It had been six weeks since her husband had died, five weeks since he'd been cremated. His ashes sat in a beautiful urn that she had placed on the mantle above the fireplace.

She had no idea what else to do with it.

Hailey had been against it, telling her it was creepy to keep her dad's ashes where they'd be reminded all the time that he was gone. Not that Hailey spent much time in the great room. She preferred the solitude of her bedroom.

Hailey had come home after staying at Andréa's for a couple days after Jack had died, and if Sarah and her stepdaughter had exchanged more than a dozen sentences since then, that would be pushing it. There was a lot of silence, harsh stares, and derisive snorts.

Sarah had given up.

She couldn't force a relationship with her stepdaughter when it was obvious Hailey didn't want one. The house belonged to Sarah now—Jack's will had been updated shortly after the wedding, naming her as the beneficiary of most of his assets—but this would always be Hailey's home no matter the status of their relationship. At least until Hailey was old enough to live on her own.

Which Sarah figured would be the last time she'd ever see Jack's daughter. It was hard to think of Hailey as her stepdaughter now, given the hostility she directed at Sarah. Part of it was teenage angst, part of it was the loss of Jack, but Sarah knew that all of that was also rooted in Hailey's resentment toward her.

And she was tired of trying.

Sarah brushed her teeth and headed down to the kitchen, passing by Hailey's closed bedroom door and feeling like such a failure. It was difficult not to be so hard on herself. She remembered the first time she'd met Hailey. It was late July, and she'd been dating Jack a few months by then. He had invited her to spend the day here at the house, her first visit here. He'd wanted to enjoy the summer day around the pool. Hailey had been guarded and had tried to exclude Sarah until her friend Andréa showed up. Jack had cooked burgers on the barbecue. A simple day, but she'd enjoyed his company and watching the girls have fun in the water.

Dinner could have gone better, though.

The next day, she'd been tender around the shoulders where she'd gotten a bit of a sunburn. It had also been the first time she'd slept over, and Hailey had given her the cold shoulder when she'd seen her sitting at the kitchen island with a cup of coffee.

Hailey had obviously still been angry about the news Jack had delivered at dinner. Anger Sarah had become all too familiar with by now, but back then she'd completely missed its significance.

Her head had been in the clouds.

She had never been in love like this before, and when she was with Jack the world around her could have burned down and she wouldn't have noticed.

Jack had been her first true love . . . and would be her last.

Sarah reached the kitchen and made a pot of coffee. She glanced out the kitchen window and watched big, fat snowflakes cascade down in a lazy back and forth motion, nearly hypnotising her. Peanut's tiny bark pulled her out of her reverie and she let the dog out for a pee. While she waited for the coffee to brew, she refilled Peanut's bowls, one with fresh water and the other with her kibble.

The little Maltese attacked her food with dedicated fervour.

Sarah watched her little bundle of joy for a moment and then walked back toward the stove. She wasn't really sure if she was hungry, and the coffee didn't seem to call to her this morning either. In fact, the smell was too strong.

Instead, she poured a glass of milk—something she rarely did—and put a heaping spoonful of Nesquik in it. She mixed it well and then drank the whole glass in one big gulp. Nothing else appealed to her, except for a yogurt.

Well, if she ate like this all the time, she'd easily lose those five pounds she'd put on since Jack's accident. It seemed that all she'd done in the last six weeks was watch TV and eat. She'd had little motivation and tears came unexpectedly, draining her. Thankfully those moments usually happened when Hailey was at school. She had stayed home for a couple of weeks but had then decided that being with her friends would be better than moping around the house, and Sarah had been grateful when Hailey had climbed onto the bus that following Monday morning.

Except it had left her alone with her grief.

And anger.

Without a mechanism of releasing it. She'd never been the sort of person that would scream and hit and break things. She had learned to cry in silence, to be angry in silence, to hope in silence. Her mother had not tolerated anything else.

Sarah rubbed her forehead. She could feel another headache coming, something that had become a daily occurrence. She should take a walk to clear her head, but the past week had been quite cold and just the thought of having to put on several layers of clothing dampened the idea of going outside.

Peanut barked and looked at the front door.

"Oh, sweetie," Sarah said. "Mommy isn't up for it. I'm sorry."

Peanut barked louder and rushed to the front door. She turned and looked at Sarah. Barked twice more. Wagged her tiny tail. Spun around.

Sarah felt horrible for disappointing Peanut. Again. Each day the little dog tried to coax her into going for a walk and Sarah kept telling her no, that she wasn't up to it. How long could she hide inside these walls? She was becoming a hermit. Alienating herself from the world. If only she had a friend, but there was no one. A couple of time she'd thought of contacting Selena, but the idea had died almost instantly. Their lives were so different now. The conversation would be strained and fake. And there was nothing of her old life that she wanted to reminisce about.

That hit her hard.

It was really sad that, before Jack, there was nothing worth remembering. Just nameless towns her mom had dragged her from and deadbeat men who were mean and violent. And then nearly ten years of surviving doing the only thing she was good at.

Sarah punched the wall and barely left a dent in the drywall. Her hand ached so badly she hoped she hadn't broken anything. But she'd punched the wall and it actually felt damn good. Jack would probably have laughed at her for leaving such an insignificant dent. He'd have probably made her punch the wall harder, just so he'd have an excuse to fix it. Or tear it down. He was all about open concept, and if a wall wasn't load-bearing—he'd had to explain to her what that meant—then it had no purpose.

Thinking of Jack ignited a warmth inside of her. If he were here, he'd be telling her to get her ass dressed in as many layers as she needed and to get outside. Just because Jack Cormier was no longer here to enjoy a beautiful snowy day didn't mean that his wife shouldn't enjoy it without him. He wouldn't stand for the way she'd been falling into herself and hiding. Jack had believed that every day was a precious gift that shouldn't be wasted.

"Give me a minute," Sarah said to Peanut and headed upstairs. She returned shortly after, dressed for winter. "Let's go see what's going on outside."

Peanut dashed out as soon as Sarah opened the door and she lost site of the Maltese as it blended with the falling snow. Sarah took a few steps and then realized that it had snowed quite a bit overnight, and that she was going to have to figure out how to operate Jack's ride-on snow blowing tractor.

CB EO

Sarah grabbed her phone and googled how to use a John Deere snow blowing tractor; twenty minutes later she was sitting on the little, green machine blowing snow off the driveway. She made sure that Peanut was standing far away—the dog seemed to be a bit afraid of the noise anyway, so she was standing on the highest snowbank watching Sarah and barking like crazy. There must have been about six inches of snow on the ground and considering the driveway to the main road was probably three hundred feet—Sarah had never realized how long it was—it took a good hour for her to clear it.

She pulled the tractor into the garage and killed the engine and brushed off the snow. Satisfied, she headed back outside and smiled.

She'd actually done it. Her. The girl who'd always stayed clear of trying things she thought were completely out of her reach. It was all because of Jack. He was always telling her not to be afraid, that the worst that could happen was that she'd fail. And then all she had to do was try again and again until she no longer failed.

She'd nailed the snow blowing on the first try.

Peanut barked, as if congratulating her.

"I did it," Sarah said, her hands in the air. "Mommy actually figured out how to use the John Deere and clear the driveway."

Peanut barked and twirled, joining the celebration. She then ran down from her mountain top and rushed toward Sarah who scooped her into her arms. Peanut licked her face.

"I did it," she said again while putting Peanut down.

She looked at the front steps and saw that some of the snow had blown and covered the walkway, so she grabbed a shovel and cleared that out. After she was done, Sarah made snow angels and threw snowballs at Peanut who kept dodging them. For about an hour she forgot that she was a widow, she forgot that she'd lost her love, she forgot that she was all alone.

It was the best hour she'd had in a long while. The snow plow had left a massive snowbank at the end of the driveway and within minutes, with her new confidence, Sarah was driving down the long driveway on the tractor to clear the snow. When she got back to the garage, she was soaked but exhilarated.

She actually felt like this was her home and she was solely responsible for looking after it. Maybe she could learn to finish Jack's renovations.

Sarah walked up to the front door and turned. She looked out at the snow-covered world which seemed to end just before the main road, knowing that was just an illusion. She would need to find work. Their savings wouldn't last forever and she definitely didn't want to use it all up. That wouldn't be smart.

She opened the door and called Peanut in, following the little dog inside.

"Well," Hailey said. She was standing in the living room looking out the front window. "The girl isn't totally useless after all."

Sarah turned toward Hailey, and she was about to snap back a snide remark of her own, but Jack's voice in her head told her to leave it alone.

"Nothing to say, as always," Hailey said and walked away. "I hope you wiped down the John Deere. Dad wouldn't be too happy if it went all rusty."

"Hailey, please," Sarah said, sounding more pleading than she'd wanted. "It's Christmas."

Hailey stopped and turned, fire in her eyes. "So? Who cares? Not like Santa Claus is going to bring back Dad. It's a stupid day for stupid kids who believe the stupid bullshit their parents tell them. Wake up Sarah. Santa Claus isn't coming here. There is no Merry Christmas in this house. There's nothing in this house."

Sarah watched her stepdaughter rush up the stairs by twos and couldn't think of a thing to say or do. Just because she'd figured out how to operate a snow blowing tractor didn't mean that she was going to solve all of their problems. Maybe for a few moments while outside she had believed that she could, but Hailey had a way of reminding her of the reality they were living in.

The sweat on her body gave her a chill and Sarah headed upstairs to go take a long hot shower.

Alone.

And lonely.

NINE

Hailey slammed her bedroom door shut and threw herself onto her bed. She was seething. It really irked her that Sarah was taking over more and more of the house, her house. It had been in her family for five generations and now it belonged to a total stranger. What had her dad been thinking, willing Sarah the family home?

He should have willed it to her, his daughter, a real Cormier.

Oh, whatever. She'd be leaving as soon as she was done high school and found a job. College was now out of the question. Although, she did have a college fund and could go somewhere far away, maybe out to B.C. That should be far enough from the wicked stepmother. She wouldn't have to come back here at all. Her uncle and grandparents were out there anyway. She could stay with them.

She didn't hate the idea.

When her grandparents had come down for the funeral, they'd convinced Hailey to finish high school here, with her friends. When her grandparents hadn't stayed at the house for the week they were here, she'd asked them why, and they'd said it wasn't their home anymore, and they didn't want to intrude on

Sarah's grieving. Hailey had seen how hard it had been for her grandmother when everyone had congregated at the house after the service. Losing her oldest son had been extremely difficult, and Hailey had guessed that there was too much of her dad in the house for her grandmother to handle.

No one seemed to care or ask if it was too much for her. It's like everyone else's feelings were more important than hers.

She looked at the time on her phone: 10:34 a.m.

Christmas Day.

Not a single present. No tree to put presents under. Every year she went out with her dad to that place out on Fallowfield Road and cut down their own tree. No fake tree for the Cormiers. Her dad didn't believe in fake trees.

Was no tree better than a fake tree?

Not like she was going to buy anything for Sarah, and she certainly didn't expect or want anything from her.

So, yeah. No tree was better.

In the past, her dad would go crazy with the decorations. If there was a spot to put something, he'd put it there. It took them all day to decorate, between sips of hot chocolate and mouthfuls of shortbread cookies, it was the best day of the year after Christmas and her birthday.

She wanted to text Andréa and Madelaine, but didn't want to be a drag. They were probably unwrapping presents right now— loads of presents, big smiles and big squeals of delight as they ripped the Christmas wrapping off of another box for another gift they'd asked for.

Jealousy turned her face red.

Her thoughts drifted to her mother. She'd been wondering a lot about her mom lately, about what had driven her mother away. It bugged Hailey. She hadn't really cared when her dad was alive simply because being around her dad had left no room for her mother in her thoughts or in her life. And she knew it was probably because she now had a void that she was thinking of her mom, and probably also because she was still looking for a way out of this house that felt less and less like home as the days passed.

Would she have the guts this time around to actually go up to her door and ring the bell if she went back? What would she say to the woman? Her biggest fear was that her mom was going to turn her back on her once more.

Then what would she do?

But what if she didn't? What if she'd always missed her but her dad had kept her mom away? She wasn't sure why this mattered as she was almost an adult. Could it be that she wanted to belong to someone, but not just anyone? She'd seen how Andréa and her mom were together, and she'd had her own bond with her dad, but she now wondered what it would be like to have that sort of close relationship with her mom.

She knew her mom's address; she could drive there in about thirty minutes. Her dad trusted her with the car. They had two Outbacks because he wanted good cars that could handle the bad winter roads. He had made her drive when the roads were awful so that she'd be ready whenever the time came when she'd have to drive on her own. That time had obviously come. She was ready.

Except she wasn't really ready mentally or emotionally.

A soft whine came from the other side of her door and when she opened it, she heard the shower going and figured Peanut wanted some company.

"Hey, girl," Hailey said, and invited the dog into her room. "Let's have a girls' party."

Her bed was too high for Peanut to jump up on, so Hailey threw her pillow on the floor and laid down on the carpet. Peanut found a place in the crook of her arms. She must have been exhausted because, within seconds, the pup was snoring.

Hailey patted Peanut's head tenderly.

She pulled up her hockey schedule on her phone. Next game was on Sunday, in Orleans. It was a two o'clock game so she should pick up Andréa no later than noon. They were playing the Orleans Raiders. The best team in their division. By just one point. If they could pull out a win then they'd be the best team.

Until the next game.

She missed hearing her dad in the crowd. He was always the loudest along with Andréa's parents. Even though Andréa rode in the car with her now, her parents still made it to the games, which was nice. Sarah had tagged along with her dad, but hadn't come since his passing.

Which was fine with Hailey.

She hadn't scored a goal since her dad had died. She was pressing too hard trying to make something happen. And she'd had too many penalties which her coach had not been pleased with. And she was mouthy, talking trash with the other teams, something that had never been her game. There was no body contact in women's hockey, but if she happened to casually push another player into the boards, accidently, it wasn't her fault.

Except the damn referees kept sending her to the penalty box.

She checked Instagram and saw that all her friends were posting pictures of their gifts. She ground her teeth as she scrolled. She wanted to post nice comments but only bitter words formed in her head. She'd read somewhere that Christmas Day had a high percentage of depression and suicide. She had never understood that. Who didn't love Christmas?

She put her phone face down on the carpet and closed her eyes. Peanut's rhythmic breathing was soothing. Hailey envied the little puppy. All Peanut had to worry about was who to give her love to. She was fed, walked, taken care of. Peanut had even adapted to Hailey's dad not being around.

But she sometimes noticed that Peanut would grab a mitten Hailey had left on the vent to dry, one of her dad's mittens that she'd worn. They were a bit big but she didn't care. Hailey would find that mitten in Peanut's bed.

So, maybe the Maltese hadn't quite forgotten her owner.

A knock on her door pulled Hailey out of her daze. Her jerk woke Peanut.

"Is Peanut with you?"

"Yeah."

"Oh, okay," Sarah said. "I was just wondering."

Hailey wasn't about to invite Sarah into her room. She might just keep the dog with her for a while, mostly because she loved the puppy but also to annoy her stepmom. She heard Sarah walk away and a tiny smug smirk crossed her face, though she didn't feel as smug as she thought she would.

She began to cry quietly, burying her face in Peanut.

༺ ༻

Sarah reached the kitchen and realized she hadn't eaten anything this morning, and it was already after eleven. She reached for a bowl and was going to have some Cheerios but stopped herself. This was Christmas Day.

She should make something worthy of the occasion.

She drew a blank.

Hailey loved eggs benedict. Jack would make them every Sunday. Sarah grabbed her phone and googled for some recipes. She hoped there was a Hollandaise sauce package in the cupboard, otherwise that plan was toast. Sure, it was cheating, but she wasn't going to try to make that from scratch.

"Jack, you wonderful man," she said when she found not one, but three packages in the spice cupboard. "This probably won't be as good as yours, but I don't care."

First, she defrosted some English muffins and a package of bacon. She heated a pan, placed strips of half frozen bacon, and cooked them nice and crispy, the way she knew Hailey liked. Then she attempted to poach an egg. Total disaster. Maybe she left it in the simmering water too long.

She threw the mangled egg in the compost bin.

Watched a video five times before trying again. She waited until the first egg started to solidify and then added the second. She turned off the heat, put a cover on the pot, and watched the eggs closely.

She toasted the two English muffins.

Sarah checked the eggs and they seemed okay. She put the bacon down on the English muffin first and, with a slotted spoon, she lifted each egg out of the water and placed each one on top of the bacon. She then poured some Hollandaise sauce over each egg and added a sprinkle of parsley.

Sarah admired the food she had just prepared. It wasn't much but it was the most she'd done in six weeks. Maybe Christmas wasn't about consumable presents this year, maybe it was about something much bigger: learning to live without Jack. As much as she hated the idea, he wasn't coming back.

Jack wasn't coming home.

Peanut came rushing down in a flurry of happy yelps and Sarah lifted the dog into her arms and was subjected to an eager face wash.

"What's this?" Hailey said.

"I made eggs benedict—"

"They look overdone," Hailey said. "Dad's were perfect. The sauce looks watery, and is that bacon? Don't you know you have to use Canadian bacon?"

"I was trying to make a nice breakfast for us," Sarah said. "It's Christmas."

"I'm not celebrating Christmas anymore. It's stupid anyway, the idea of materialistic presents. Most of the time we get stuff we didn't ask for and didn't want."

"I think your dad—"

"Shut up!" Hailey screamed. "You have no idea what my dad would say. Don't pretend to be him. You'll never be him. You'll never be my mother. You'll never be anything to me."

Sarah grabbed the two plates and dumped the eggs in the compost bin and left the room.

"There she goes again, crying and running away," Hailey said. "You're such a mouse. I don't know what my dad saw in you."

Sarah had had enough. She turned and came back into the kitchen. "You're just an ungrateful little bitch who can't see past her own miserable self to show empathy for someone else. This didn't just happen to you. I loved your dad. He was the best thing that ever happened to me. I had a real shitty life before I met him and he showed me how to live and enjoy the little moments. That's all I was trying to do here." She paused. "All I ever wanted was to be your friend."

She didn't wait for Hailey to lash out. She turned and ran up the stairs, Peanut at her heels. She almost slammed her bedroom door on the Maltese.

"Sorry, sorry," she said and let Peanut come into the room. "What an ungrateful . . ."

She let the words die. She'd totally lost it. Her meltdown wasn't going to help the situation or bring them closer. Maybe it was just some unreachable goal. She knew she was trying for Jack, but it seemed hopeless. She was tired of trying.

It was obvious Hailey wanted nothing to do with her. It would be much easier to give up on Hailey and just concentrate on herself. She grabbed the pack of cigarettes which she'd bought while doing groceries a couple days ago, and lit one. She hated to smoke in the house, but right now there was no way she was going back downstairs. Over two years since she'd last smoked and here she was at it again. She knew she was disappointing Jack, and she promised she'd quit again as soon as her life righted itself.

She cracked a window open and the wintry air chilled her.

"Dad wouldn't like it that you're smoking in the house," Hailey shouted from the hallway. "If you think I can't smell that stink, think again."

"I don't care," Sarah said barely above a whisper. "I don't care."

CB EO

Hailey slammed her door and screamed. The woman was so infuriating. To think that she could make some lousy eggs benedict and they'd suddenly become best friends was nuts. And now she was smoking in the house. Dad would be having a bird about that. He hated the smell of cigarettes.

Which made Hailey wonder once again what he'd seen in Sarah. The more she learned, the more obvious it became that her dad had made one big mistake.

And now the house belonged to that mistake.

Six months. Six months before she graduated high school. Six months before she could leave. This was their last year together, her and Andréa and Madelaine. Andréa was going to Queens University in Kingston in the fall, and Madelaine was going to Humber College in Toronto. That was the plan anyway, if they got accepted, which they wouldn't know until May.

Connor was still undecided, and right now any thoughts Hailey might have had of hooking up with him were fading fast. She couldn't see herself living another day with Sarah, let alone six months. Not even for Connor.

Hailey sat on her bed.

Looked at her room.

It felt like a prison. This was the only place that she could hide. It wasn't right. This was her home. The only home she'd ever known and it didn't even belong to her. She wished her dad was here because she had so many questions for him. She had so much anger.

It consumed her.

How could she ever get any sort of closure when the man she was angry with could never be confronted? He'd left without saying goodbye that morning and the last memory of her dad that she had was of him falling asleep on the couch watching a show with Sarah. He normally gave her a hug and a kiss on the forehead when he was heading off to bed, but not that night. She'd just come home from Andréa's—they'd been working on a science project—and her dad had been lights out on the couch so she'd gone to her room.

That was the last time she'd seen him.

She heard the sound of a text coming through to her phone.

What're you up to? It was from Andréa.

Hailey stared at her phone. The first words that came to mind were full of bitterness. What did the girl think she was up to? Not like the Cormiers were celebrating today.

Nothing much.

There was a long pause. Hailey saw the three little dots on her phone which meant Andréa was typing a reply, but nothing came. She waited. The little dots went away. Andréa had probably deleted her reply. Hailey waited some more. The little dots were back.

Today must really suck, she texted. **I'm sorry.**

Not exactly merry.

Another pause. She'd been friends with Andréa her whole life and they'd never struggled for things to talk about. It was her fault. She gave off bad vibes these days. Piss and vinegar as her grandpa would say when she was young and would have a meltdown. It was a little after her mom had left, and Hailey had been having a hard time coping.

Funny how she remembered that. Her grandpa had probably thought she wouldn't understand, and maybe at age five she hadn't truly understood the meaning of his words, but she did now. And yes, she was definitely full of piss and vinegar.

She'd listened to some call-in show last night, Christmas Eve—she couldn't remember from where as she'd found it off the internet—and most speakers were complaining about stupid things, but there was this one boy, his name was Carl, who absolutely hated Christmas. Three years ago, his parents had waited until all the kids had opened their gifts before telling them they were getting a divorce. Minutes later, his dad left carrying a couple of suitcases.

WTF! They could have waited until the next day, or a week. But to tell the kids on Christmas Day.

Hailey had agreed with Carl. That had been shitty.

But losing her dad was shittier.

Not that she wanted people to feel sorry for her, but what had happened to her was way worse. At least Carl still had his parents even if they didn't live in the same house.

Although, she guessed it was possible that Carl didn't see his dad, just like she didn't see her mom.

Do you want to come over?

98 | Francois Houle

She'd forgotten that she was having a conversation with Andréa. She sort of figured her friend had gone off to enjoy her
gifts.

And suck the fun out of your house?

Like yours is a party.

I just don't want your family to feel sorry for me.

Like Marc and Isabelle ever feel sorry for anyone. And Alexi is
too in love to notice anyone else.

True. Her younger brother and sister were too selfish to think
of anyone else. They were constantly trying to guilt Andréa's parents into buying them things. She did envy Alexi, though. Maybe
if she had Connor . . .

I don't want to ruin your Christmas.

We can just hang out in my room, listen to music. We don't need
to talk.

It would be nice to get out for a while. If she stayed here, she
was a prisoner in her room. Sure, she could text with Andréa all
day, and get a group chat going with everyone else, but she'd still
be stuck inside these four walls that seemed to be closing in on
her. And she would need to get out to get some food and chance
running into Sarah. Although, she was pretty sure Sarah was going to hide in her room all day, too. Going to Andréa's would be
a reprieve for both of them. Not that she really cared all that
much about Sarah, but she could use a break.

We could scheme how we'll beat the Raiders on Sunday, Andréa
texted.

We so have to win.

We will.

Hailey felt her spirit lift a little. Talking hockey always brought excitement. She and her dad had always watched the Senators' games. Didn't matter that they weren't that good this year again, hockey season was their special time. Sometimes, Sarah tried to join, but she didn't get the game and usually ended up watching TV in the den.

Or her dad would concede and watch something with Sarah while Hailey grudgingly watched the rest of the game in her room, on her laptop.

Alone.

I'll jump in the shower and be over in about an hour.

TEN

Sarah heard the car start in the garage and she made her way down to the living room to watch Hailey drive away. A sigh of relief escaped her. She could breathe again, not worry about another confrontation. Hailey was getting meaner.

She didn't deserve that animosity.

She understood that her stepdaughter was in pain, like she was, but she didn't have to be so cruel about it.

Sarah went to the kitchen and pulled a can of tomato soup from the pantry and heated it up. She cut a few pieces of cheese and grabbed some crackers, and voilà, Christmas lunch for a queen.

The queen of broken hearts.

She had to stop that, feeling sorry for herself. It wasn't doing her any good. Maybe she'd never be able to patch things up with Hailey, but maybe she could restart her life. Jack had encouraged her to go to school, find a college program. She was old enough that the fact she didn't have a high school diploma really didn't matter. Maybe she didn't need a three-year program. Maybe just a one-year certificate would do. She did love to work with flowers. Maybe she could find work in a flower shop. She didn't need a high paying job. The house was mortgage free, there was plenty of savings—Jack was hard core about having healthy finances. What *she* needed was to feel part of the outside world, have a purpose, feel good about herself.

She ate her lunch with little appetite.

Then she quickly washed the few dishes she'd dirtied and went up to her room to brush her teeth. Her nose curled as the remnants of her cigarette lingered in the air. It really did stink.

On impulse, she grabbed the pack of cigarettes from her purse and crushed them over the toilet. She flushed, and as the remains of her old habit vanished, a small sense of triumph tapped her on the shoulder, as if Jack was encouraging her. She put her hand up in a high-five gesture—something they'd done often to celebrate such mundane things as a great breakfast or spending the day around the pool or making love in the shower.

She could almost swear under oath, if asked, that she had just felt Jack's hand slap hers.

Sarah brushed her teeth and then walked into the walk-in closet. She touched Jack's clothes, inhaled them hoping for any trace of his scent. There was none. Jack was slowly fading from her life.

It felt like someone had just stabbed her in the heart.

It was way too soon. She wasn't ready. She might never be ready. There were no reasons for her to ever get rid of his clothes. It's not like she needed the room. She already had two-thirds of the space. He used to tease her that soon he'd have to move his clothes into the spare bedroom closet—that was before he tore that room apart—and she used to tease back that that would be fine with her. The sooner the better.

Now she couldn't stomach the thought of his clothes being gone.

She spent the next two hours rearranging the closet so that it wouldn't look like such a disorganised space. She then vacuumed the entire house, even Hailey's room. She didn't care if her step-daughter freaked out when she got back. It had been weeks since house chores had been done. By four o'clock it was already starting to get dark as another winter day bowed to the winter night bully.

Sarah looked at the fireplace. It wasn't one of those gas fire-places that you simply had to flip a switch and *whoosh*, the fire lit. This old house had a real fireplace and, once again, it had been Jack's job to get it going.

Sarah closed her eyes and tried to picture her husband going through the process of piling some kindling, then a couple of logs, and some newspaper placed strategically so the whole thing would catch once a match was introduced to the mix.

Her first try died almost instantly.

"Jack, can you help me?" she said to the almost empty room. Peanut was watching her intently, as if cheering her on. "I can do this."

She hated feeling so inadequate, almost childlike. She was a grown woman, after all, even if she didn't feel like one most of the time. Definitely not when it came to Hailey.

Sarah adjusted the kindling and added more paper and struck a match. She put the flame to paper and watched the paper burn, her lips moving as if she were praying to Hephaestus for help.

And then, when the kindling ignited and the logs began to slow burn, she clapped her hands and uttered a small cry of victory.

Peanut barked and twirled in celebration.

"Thank you, honey," she said and hugged the dog, not really knowing if she was saying those words to Peanut or to her dead husband.

CB ∞ EO

Hailey sat down for Christmas dinner at Andréa's place, a mountain of hot and inviting food on the table, but that wasn't what was making her smile internally. It was the small bantering between Andréa and her younger brother and sister (Alexi and her boyfriend Cooper where so into each other that they didn't seem to notice anything going on), her parents' constant refereeing, the festive decoration, and the beautifully decorated tree in the corner of the great room.

And the ripped Christmas wrapping paper littering the floor that no one had bothered to pick up yet.

She stopped herself there. She didn't want to go down pity road and get all emotional. No way was she going to ruin this perfect moment. In her mind, she snapped pictures of Marc making a face at Andréa, of Isabelle complaining that she didn't like no yucky squash, of Alexi and Cooper whispering lovey words to each other, of Andréa's father piling a plate with so much food that his wife was telling him he was going to regret it and he wouldn't have room for dessert.

And there was an assortment: pumpkin pie, pecan pie, yule log, and cherry cheesecake. Hailey was feeling full just looking at it all.

"It's nice to see you smile," Andréa's mother said. "You have such a beautiful face."

Hailey felt her ears turn red, but it was the nicest thing anyone had said to her in a long time.

"Mom," Andréa whined. "Really?"

"It's okay," Hailey said and looked at her friend's mom, not at Andréa when she said it. "Thank you."

"Eat up," Andréa's dad said.

"Yeah, good luck Dad," Marc said and didn't appear to notice that his plate was a little overfilled, too.

Not many words were spoken while they ate, but Hailey noticed that everyone seemed to have big happy grins while devouring the feast. She had a small piece of pecan pie and a sliver of the yule log, and she felt uncomfortably satisfied.

"Thank you for dinner," she said to Andréa's parents.

"We're glad you're here with us," Andréa's mom said and put a hand over Hailey's. "I know this must be hard, but you're always welcome here."

Hailey did her best to hold back her grief.

"Mom," Andréa said with that tone that said *enough*.

"I'm fine," Hailey said to Andréa's mom.

Once Andréa's mom pulled her hand away, Hailey started to help clear the table but Andréa's mother insisted that she didn't need to do that, that she and Andréa could go about whatever they had in mind.

And when Marc and Isabelle took that as their cue to scoot, their mother called them back.

"Not fair," they said in almost perfect rhythm.

"Why don't they need to help but we do?" Marc said.

"Because your mother said so," their dad said.

Hailey followed Andréa back to her room and the complaining faded until Andréa closed her bedroom door and they could no longer hear Marc and Isabelle's whining.

"My mom is great at embarrassing us."

Hailey plopped down on the bed beside Andréa. They were both checking their phones, seeing what was going on in the chat group. It was rather quiet at the moment which probably meant some dinners were still going on.

"I love your mom."

Andréa snorted. "She can be a real pain sometimes."

Hailey didn't reply. She pretended to be doing something on her phone, but right now she was thinking that she'd trade places with Andréa in a heartbeat. She'd rather have a mom that was a bit overbearing at times than have a mom who had no problem leaving. Her dad had often told her that hoping for something to change but that had no chance of ever changing was plain foolish, maybe even a bit mad.

She finally understood.

Her life was what it was, and no matter how she wished it was different, it wasn't going to happen.

"But I guess she's all right most of the time," Andréa added.

"You guess?"

Andréa looked at her. "Yeah, well you're not the one she's after to do your homework, or cleanup your room, or help clear the table. If you weren't here, I'd never have gotten away with it."

"Oh, my heart bleeds for how tough you have it at home," Hailey said, each word biting more than the next. "Are you kidding me? Try having no parents and a stepmom that has no clue how to be a parent."

"I didn't mean—"

"You and Madelaine and Connor never mean to, but I see you all walking on eggshells around me, ashamed to have it so much better than me."

"We just never know when we're going to upset you, say the wrong thing. You're always angry now."

"So sorry for making your life so difficult."

"What are we supposed to do? Stop living? Be miserable like you?"

Hailey's eyes narrowed. "Stop being so *selfish*."

"I wasn't—"

"You were," Hailey said and pulled herself off the bed. Her eyes wandered to the boxes on the floor in front of the closet. "Just look at the mountain of new clothes you have. *Two* new hockey sticks, and that winter jacket probably cost five hundred."

The new jacket was draped over the back of Andréa's makeup chair and the sticks were leaning in the far corner, waiting to be taped.

"I need to go," Hailey said.

Andréa didn't stop her.

Christmas Day was over.

ᘓ ᘔ

Sarah was huddled under a blanket, the fire crackling, a Christmas Hallmark movie on the television. Peanut was sitting beside her but when she heard the car approaching, she jumped off the couch and headed for the front door. She sat and waited.

Hailey came in and Peanut barked joyfully, welcoming her back home. Sarah watched from the corner of her eyes but didn't turn her head.

"Hey girl," Hailey said and bent down. "Did you miss me? I sure missed you."

Hailey walked by without saying a word and Sarah watched her climb the stairs.

"I vacuumed earlier," she said. "Your room, too. It needed it."

She saw Hailey stop, take a beat, and then continue up the stairs without replying. Sarah actually let go of a breath she'd been holding. Peanut came back, jumped up, and cuddled against her.

"She just needs time," Sarah whispered to the dog. "That's all."

In a Hallmark movie, that time would be about ninety minutes before everything turned happily ever after.

CB ED

Hailey threw her jacket on her bed and headed for the bathroom. She looked at the angry face staring back at her, and she wanted to smash it. Andréa didn't understand. How could she? Her life hadn't been shattered like Hailey's—not even once.

And now all Hailey had was Sarah.

She traced the small scars on her left wrist. When Hailey's dad had told her he had asked Sarah to marry him, Hailey had started cutting herself.

To distract herself from feeling abandoned, again.

When her father had noticed the cuts, he'd known right away what she was up to. In his line of work, he saw a lot of ugliness. She had never seen him that angry.

He'd grounded her for a month.

The cutting stopped.

But from then on, she realized that her relationship with her father was never the same. His stare was more watchful, his emotions a little more guarded. She had always blamed Sarah for her dad's slow distancing, but this was on her; he'd turned up his parenting dial and turned down his best pal dial.

Still, if he hadn't married Sarah, Hailey wouldn't have cut herself, and their relationship wouldn't have changed.

Sarah was at the core of all her pain.

Hailey kneeled in front of the toilet, stuck her fingers down her throat, and vomited out all the misery of her life along with Christmas dinner.

There seemed to be no point in anything anymore.

ELEVEN

S unday morning, the day after Boxing Day, couldn't arrive fast enough because the fridge was looking very bare. Sarah hadn't really gotten much in the way of food for Christmas, and she planned to be at the grocery store the moment the doors opened.

A quick weather check on her phone sent a chill up her spine: a frigid minus twenty Celsius with a wind chill of minus thirty.

Bundled up in her winter gear that made her look like the Michelin Man, she stepped outside and instantly her nostrils stuck together. Breathing the arctic air made her lungs ache. She hurried to the garage and started the Outback and turned on the seat warmer.

Best car luxury ever.

She waited a few minutes and then backed out to the road. That little space to the side of the driveway for extra parking, which they used to turn the cars around, was covered in snow since she'd forgotten to clear it on Christmas Day. She waited for a couple of cars to drive by, and then backed onto the main road and headed for the grocery store. She wasn't exactly the first patron, but the store was fairly quiet which suited her fine. She was done in about thirty minutes and then glanced at the new LCBO that had been built just last year. She was out of wine but it wasn't even nine in the morning.

The liquor store wouldn't open for another two hours.

She put the car in drive and headed home. She'd have to return later for the wine. When she got to the main road that led back home, in the spur of the moment she drove past it and instead made a left onto Main Street. She'd had this awful chocolate craving for three days now and she remembered Jack going to this quaint little bakery on Main Street that he raved about all the time. Best bread, best pies, best chocolate walnut brownies.

It shocked her that in the two years she'd lived in Forest Creek, not once had she ventured down this road. It was quaint all right. Lots of little shops. A couple of hairdressers, a spa, a chiropractor's office, and one place that caught her eye instantly.

Flowers by Ruth.

Sarah pulled to the side of the road and put the car in park. She bit her lower lip, her mind trying to put together words that wouldn't make her seem foolish.

Her heart was beating hard.

Sarah killed the engine and walked toward the front door, rehearsing the words in her head over and over again. It had been a long time since she'd asked anyone for a job, and really, the only job she'd ever had hadn't really been too difficult to get.

Her mom had been grooming her for it her whole life.

og ℞

Sarah stepped into Flowers by Ruth and took a deep breath. All the different scents were like a potluck of happiness. The woman behind the counter was a beautiful older woman, maybe around seventy. Her white hair was set in a perfect coif, her eyes behind a pair of reading glasses bright and inviting, her smile contagious.

"Can I help you dear?"

Her voice was like butter and put Sarah at ease instantly. She'd been so nervous about coming in and asking if there might be a position available.

Sarah walked up to the counter. "Beautiful store."

"Thank you," the woman said, her hands working on a blue flower arrangement as if on auto-pilot, like they'd been doing this forever. "Been here since 1970."

Sarah had spent most of the previous day surfing the internet, trying to learn more about flowers, figuring out if she really wanted to pursue this passion. She'd even found an online course that she could start anytime and was just four weeks long. She'd have access to a personal expert and peer support. And it wasn't a lot of money, so if she hated it she could scratch the idea off her list.

Sarah watched the woman work and she was so graceful in the way she moved her hands that she made it look easy.

"There," the woman said. "One order done."

"It's lovely."

If nothing else, Sarah was going to see if she could buy that flower arrangement. Blue was exactly what was needed at home; blue was meant to calm worries and preoccupations, to represent peace and openness and serenity.

Everything that was in short supply in hers and Hailey's lives.

"You wouldn't be Ruth, would you?"

"The one and only. What can I get you?"

"Actually," Sarah said and pulled at the collar of her jacket. "I was wondering if you might have a position open. I've always loved flowers and found that I have a bit of a green thumb. And I need a job before I go stir crazy." She put a hand to her mouth. "My interview skills aren't too sharp, I apologize."

"Don't apologize for being honest," Ruth said. "So, you think you might have a knack for putting together flower arrangements for all sorts of occasions?"

"I think I can be taught."

Ruth nodded. "I don't hear that often from young people."

"I suppose we're the generation that feels entitled."

Ruth smiled again and Sarah felt like Jack had just wrapped his arms around her.

"You know, I just turned seventy last month. My Earl, he tells me every day when I head off to work that I earned the right to retire. I tell him, retire, what's that? Who's going to run the store if I retire?"

"Maybe I could?" Sarah said.

Ruth eyed Sarah, not in a bad way. At least it didn't feel that way to Sarah. It was like she was trying to decide if she could trust the future of her store to Sarah.

"Tell you what," Ruth finally said. "Maybe you could buy the store for yourself. If I keep it, I won't stay away. I'll just show up every day."

Sarah felt her heart jump into the back of her throat. "I wouldn't know the first thing about running a business."

"I have a wonderful accountant. He takes care of all that mumbo-jumbo financial stuff for me. I'm sure he'll be happy to continue with you. And I'd stay on for a while, until I think you'll be fine on your own."

Sarah was lost in a hurricane of fear, thrills, and hope. Could she pull this off? Could she trust Ruth to help her get established?

"Why don't you think about it, talk to your husband?"

Sarah had seen Ruth glance at her left hand. She still hadn't removed her rings.

"I'm a widow," she said and felt tears coming.

Without losing a beat, Ruth came around the counter and put an arm around Sarah's shoulders and guided her to a couple chairs.

"I'm sorry," Sarah said. "It's still recent and I haven't—"

"Don't ever feel you need to apologize for missing your husband," Ruth said. "Been married to Earl fifty-one years and although I could have killed him once or twice over those years, I know losing him would be like losing a limb."

"That's how I feel," she said. "But I'm tired of hiding, of forgetting to live."

"So, that's why you want a job?"

"No. I *need* a job. I *need* to move on. I *need* to prove to myself that I'll be okay."

Ruth patted Sarah's hands. The small contact pumped Sarah full of encouragement and determination. It's as if she had known Ruth her whole life.

"I'm sorry if I put you on the spot," Ruth said. "It's certainly something that was spur of the moment. Hadn't really considered selling this place for another ten years, or if my health started to go."

Sarah watched Ruth head back behind the counter and observed her as she created another arrangement. Her gaze took in the entire store, inhaled all those scents that could belong to her. She could hear Jack in her ear telling her to go for it, that this place was perfect for her. His confidence in her made her believe in herself. She loved that about him, the way he believed in her. The doubts were always hers, not his. He was her biggest fan.

She could do this.

Sarah knew she could use some of the savings for a deposit and she could finance the rest. She could truly put down roots for the rest of her life. Jack had loved this village and this shop would be her connection to him forever, a monument to him.

A bubble of happiness warmed her from her head to her toes. This was meant to be. Why else would she have decided today to take a detour home and cross paths with Ruth?

"So," Sarah said and stood. "How do we make me the new owner of Flowers by Ruth?"

Ruth glanced at her. "Nothing much will happen today, but tomorrow is Monday so I'll call my accountant and lawyer, and see what they say. I don't even know what to sell it to you for."

"I have a little bit of money."

Ruth gave Sarah that grandmotherly smile again. "You remind me so much of me at your age. Excited. Scared. I'd sign the deed over to you for a dollar but I'd never hear the end of it from Earl. Don't worry, we'll figure it out."

Sarah smiled nervously.

"Between you and me," Ruth said. "This place makes a nice little profit every year. You'll do just fine."

Sarah wrote down her name and phone number on a piece of paper. She asked Ruth if she had another one of those blue flower arrangements, and Ruth told her to take the one she'd just put together, that she had time to make another.

And she wouldn't let Sarah pay.

"Thank you," Sarah said and started to walk away. At the door, she turned toward Ruth. The old woman was eyeing her the way Sarah imagined her grandmother would have looked at her if she'd had one as lovely as Ruth. "Bye."

"And if you change your mind when you get home," Ruth said. "It's okay, dear. Don't feel trapped in an old woman's crazy idea."

"Somehow, I don't think I'm going to change my mind," Sarah said and walked out. The cold bit at her face and when she reached the driver's side of the car, she turned her gaze to the sign above the shop door.

Flowers by Sarah.

She liked the sound of that. She liked it a lot. Sarah climbed into her car and put the blue flower arrangement on the passenger seat, and started the Outback.

Serendipity.

She'd watched the movie of the same name the night before and had had to look up the meaning of the word on her phone. Maybe she hadn't met her prince charming this morning—although the way she'd met Jack three years ago certainly felt like karma had intervened—but meeting Ruth was the second-best thing to happen to her after her husband.

Sarah didn't realize that the bakery Jack had raved about was just three buildings over, and she pulled the car into the small parking lot.

She couldn't pull her gaze away from the sign across the façade.

Sarah's Bakery. And underneath: *Forest Creek's Yummy Treasures.*

Serendipity.

Cʒ ʒɔ

Sarah walked into the bakery and fell in love with the warm homeliness that tickled her nostrils. First the calming scents of the flower shop, and now the welcoming smell of fresh baked breads and desserts.

A yearning for Jack overwhelmed her. He should be here with her, her arm hooked in the crook of his arm. He'd probably be making some sort of joke right now—although she couldn't think of what he'd find to joke about here, but she knew Jack—and a tiny smile pulled at the corners of her mouth.

An attractive couple with a little boy took what looked like a loaf of bread and a small box that Sarah assumed was full of yummy treasures.

"Thanks Aunt Cassie," the little boy said—Sarah assumed that's what the little boy said as he was obviously just learning to speak—and she watched him walk away with a homemade cookie in his hand which he was already devouring.

"You're welcome sweetie," the red-haired woman behind the counter said. "I'll see you later."

"K," the boy said, his mouth full.

The couple smiled at Sarah as they walked by and she felt her throat get thick. Although her and Jack had never talked about it, watching that little boy made her realize that she would never have a child with Jack. He already had Hailey, and the subject had never come up. Maybe it would have in time.

But time had run out.

"Can I help you?"

Sarah turned and offered the woman a warm smile. "Cute little boy."

"My nephew," the woman said. "And yes, he's adorable. Do you have any kids?"

Sarah was about to say no, but something made her change her mind. "A stepdaughter."

The woman nodded.

"My husband raved about this place, so I thought I'd check it out."

"I was going to say," the woman said. "I don't think I've seen you around."

"Jack's the one who came." Sarah paused, reflecting. "Not sure why I never came with him, to be honest."

If the woman noticed that Sarah was talking about her husband in the past tense, she didn't let on.

"Let me extend a warm welcome to Sarah's Bakery."

"Is this your place?" Sarah said. "Did you name it after yourself?" She was thinking about the flower shop and how it might look odd if she changed it to Flowers by Sarah, now knowing that three doors down was Sarah's Bakery.

"It was actually named after my daughter's great-great-grandmother. She opened the place in 1918."

Sarah's surprised showed on her face because the woman started to laugh.

"It's been in the family for a few years," the woman said. "So, what can I get you?"

Sarah grabbed a French loaf—she was going to make chili later, something else she'd never tried to make before but seemed unable to get the craving out of her taste buds—and four of those chocolate walnut brownies that called her name, and two pastries that were called cinnamon-date buns.

She'd probably have to devour one the instant she got in the car. Being surrounded by such yummy food was making her stomach grumble.

"See you again," the woman said after Sarah had paid for her purchase and walked away.

"You'll definitely see me again."

Sarah drove away, a piece of cinnamon-date bun in her mouth, her taste buds doing double flips. She slowed and glanced at the flower shop before speeding away, and by the time she parked the car in the garage, she knew that she'd found the rest of her life. The idea excited her. She knew they had a financial advisor. She'd have to dig out his name—there were statements in Jack's office that should have his name on them—and call him.

She wanted a rational mind to bounce this idea off of and make sure she was doing the right thing. It felt right to her. She wanted to do this.

By the time she'd finished putting all the groceries away, and placed the beautiful flower arrangement in the middle of the farmhouse kitchen table, Sarah had started to believe that she could move past the death of her husband.

She heard footsteps on the old and creaky hardwood floor upstairs followed by a door being closed and water from the shower begin to make its way through the house plumbing. She glanced at the time on the microwave and couldn't believe it was already ten thirty.

A reminder on her phone popped up to tell her Hailey had a game at two. Her stepdaughter would be gone most of the afternoon and sadly, she felt relieved. She'd be able to do some research and look at their finances.

Sarah grabbed one of the brownies and as good as the cinnamon-date bun had been, this brownie was like making love to Jack.

The New Year definitely looked promising.

TWELVE

Hailey was standing in the steamed filled shower, the haze so thick she could barely see her hands. The hot stream of water felt like hundreds of tiny massaging pellets that she hoped would loosen her up before the game. Her traps were so tight right now, like she was carrying the stress of the world. She played best when she was loose and relaxed. Way too much tension lately.

She didn't understand why she'd done what she'd done last night, sticking her fingers into the back of her throat so she could puke. She'd never done anything so desperate before, but she'd been so full of anger, again. If it wasn't because of Sarah, it was because of her friends, and if it wasn't them, it was because of her dad.

It had all seemed so hopeless last night.

But today was all about hockey and claiming first place by beating the Raiders. So, she was going to stay in the shower until she loosened up or the hot water tank ran out.

Her thoughts drifted to this past Halloween when her dad had taken her and her friends to the Zombie Adventure at the Diefenbunker Museum, and even though Sarah had also come, it had been a great time. Hailey and her friends had screamed and laughed and teased each other. It was a bit creepy to think that the bunker had been built in the 1950s in case of a nuclear holocaust, but the way the place had been staged for the Halloween fright had been awesome.

She recalled how they'd made fun of the old equipment littering the rooms, looking so archaic now but which had been state of the art back then. Her dad—always one to use any moment as an educational opportunity—had pointed out that today's mobile phone had more computing power then those bulky ancient machines that filled entire rooms.

As annoying as it had been at the time, she could use one of her dad's teaching anecdotes today. It's too bad you had to lose something before its value was appreciated. All the times she'd rolled her eyes or made a *really?* face when her dad was embarrassing her in front of her friends seemed so inconsequential now.

She missed him.

The hockey games weren't the same without his boisterous voice cheering her on above everyone else's. She'd noticed her effort wasn't as great since he'd been gone. So today, she would play for her dad, give him her best game.

Her shoulders and neck felt much better, so Hailey turned off the water and dried quickly before she could get cold. She grabbed a brush but couldn't see in the mirror; instead of wiping it with her towel, she drew a smiley face. Her dad had done that hundreds of times when she was young, back when he used to bathe her, before she got old enough to do it herself. He'd sit her on the counter wrapped up tight and warm in a towel three times too big, and he'd draw happy faces or sad faces if Hailey happened to be grumpy, but no matter, she was always laughing and talking by the time he tucked her into bed.

She knew it hadn't been easy on him, either, when Mom had packed up her things that day and left. Just that stupid note saying she was sorry. Not much of an explanation and no contact information. When dad had tried her mobile phone, it had been cancelled.

Hailey had never seen him so angry. But her dad wasn't the sort of man to explode and scare the people around him. His face would get all hard and stoic, but it was his jaw that Hailey had learned to recognize as the true indication of his anger. He'd clench it so tight she could hear his teeth grinding, and the smile that usually tugged at the edges of his lips would disappear, his sense of humour gone. After her mother left, Hailey had feared he'd never find it again.

But he did. Eventually. But there'd always been something missing, like he couldn't open up all the way to let all the fun out.

Until Sarah.

And that had hurt Hailey, to realize that some strange woman had been able to get her dad to come back to his fun, old self while she'd been unable to do that. She had failed where Sarah, who Hailey was sure hadn't even known that her dad had been a little short on the fun scale, had succeeded just by being there.

It hadn't seemed fair.

Hailey had been there since the beginning, she was his daughter. The two of them had soldiered on after her mother's abandonment, father and daughter. They'd been a team. A strong team. A team who hadn't needed a third wheel.

Except her dad, apparently, hadn't felt the same. He'd needed that third wheel.

At seventeen, Hailey understood the difference between the love of a parent and child compared to the love between a couple—she just had to think of her feelings for Connor lately; but that was proving to be way more effort than it was worth because the boy was blind or maybe he wasn't into her after all—but she had been fourteen when her dad had met Sarah and she hadn't wanted to share him.

Sarah was a ten.

She made Hailey feel like a five, maybe a five minus. Resentment had exploded inside of her the moment her dad told Hailey he was going on a date. At fourteen, she'd balled like a baby, yelled at him that it wasn't right, that he shouldn't do that. What if Mom wanted to come back?

Until that day, Hailey had held on to the thinnest of hope that her mom might just walk through the front door at any time, showing up unexpectedly just like she had left years ago unexpectedly. Why, after ten years, she would still hope for her mom to come back didn't make much sense to her, especially since she had never had that thought until Sarah started to weasel her way into her father's life, and hers. She barely remembered her mother anyway. Truthfully, she just hadn't wanted to give any part of her dad to anyone else.

That first time she'd met Sarah when her dad had brought her over for a barbecue, Hailey had been standoffish. She had tried to engage her dad in conversation with things that Sarah knew nothing about, but her dad had seen through her and had only needed to give her a *look* that said, give Sarah a chance. The only chance Hailey had been willing to give Sarah that day was *a fat chance of that happening.*

But then Andréa had come over and Hailey had forgotten about Sarah being there. Until her dad spoiled it.

"Sarah and I have some good news," he'd said at dinner.

Hailey had barely looked at him.

"We're getting married."

Hailey's face had felt like it had dropped to the ground. She'd looked at Andréa and had seen the same look of shock on her friend's face. She'd left the table and had run to her room, Andréa right behind her.

What a way to meet her future stepmom.

And now her dad was gone and she was stuck with his perfect-ten wife.

Good thing Hailey had hockey today. She could focus on that and tune out everything else around her.

CB ED

In her room, Hailey combed her wet hair and then put it in a tight pony tail. She slipped her favourite old t-shirt on—it was a worn Ottawa Senators t-shirt that used to belong to her dad which she'd claimed as her own about four years ago—and then covered it with a long sleeve shirt that she'd take off later when she got to the arena and donned her hockey gear.

The old t-shirt would stay underneath; her lucky charm.

She slipped into sweatpants and didn't bother with makeup. She knew some girls never played without making sure their faces were well painted, but she never saw the point considering they wore the full facial cage and there was no one who could see them. And if you played as hard as she did, that makeup didn't have a chance, anyway.

Her dad had always said she didn't need it, but at seventeen, she picked her occasions now. Not always, and definitely not on game day.

She left her damp towel on her bedroom floor and headed down to the kitchen for her protein shake. There was a time when she loaded up on oatmeal and eggs, and considering what she'd done last night it might not be a bad idea to load up this morning, but she didn't want to change her routine today.

Sarah was standing at the sink, her back to her. She was rinsing kidney beans and Hailey didn't bother to ask.

She grabbed a banana from the fruit bowl, pulled fresh strawberries from the fridge and cut off the heads on five of them before putting the rest back in the fridge, poured ten ounces of milk into a blender. She scooped a big helping of protein powder, added the fruit, a pinch of nutmeg, and blended her breakfast.

Since there was no cup big enough, she simply drank straight from the blender. She knew it annoyed Sarah, and Hailey didn't really get it. Really, the blender was just an oversized glass so why not drink from it.

"I'm going to make your dad's chili for dinner," Sarah said. "I've been craving it. And I got you one of those brownies from that bakery on Main Street."

Hailey noticed the box on the counter but didn't say anything. Definitely not part of her pre-game meal. But maybe later.

She finished her shake but since Sarah had taken over the sink, she left it on the counter and walked away without saying a word. As she headed down to the basement to get her gear, she couldn't stop feeling annoyed at Sarah for trying to make her dad's chili. Didn't she know that there was something her dad added that he didn't write down on the recipe? She would never be able to do it as good as his.

Hailey stuffed her gear into her bag, zipped it, and carried it up to the front door. She checked the time on her phone: 11:32 a.m. Almost time to go get Andréa.

She went upstairs to brush her teeth, grab her jersey that she'd laid out on her bed earlier, and went to put on her winter jacket.

"It's bitterly cold," Sarah said. "Have a good game."

Hailey's skin between her brows creased. Why was Sarah trying so hard this morning? It was grating on her nerves. She really liked it better when they didn't say anything to each other.

Hailey shrugged into her winter coat and slipped her Ottawa Senators tuque on, grabbed her leather gloves, snatched the car keys from the hook on the wall just below the front hall mirror, and opened the front door.

The arctic air slapped her across the face and stole her breath. After a moment, she pulled her bag out, closed the door, and headed for the garage. She threw her gear in the back of the older, blue Outback, started it, and left.

Ten minutes later, Andréa was sitting beside her and they were on their way across town to take on the Raiders.

CB &O

There was noticeable tension in the car. Hailey could tell something was bugging Andréa because she wasn't her typical hyped up self right now. Normally, Hailey couldn't get a word in, but there definitely was a wall between them.

"Remember their goalie likes to go down early and leave a five-hole big enough to drive a car in," Hailey said.

"I know," Andréa said but didn't look at Hailey.

They drove in silence until they reached the highway and once Hailey was comfortably cruising, she glanced at her friend.

"What's going on?"

Andréa eyed her for a brief second and then stared straight ahead. "You were a bit of a bitch Christmas night."

They had never minced words.

"I know," Hailey said. "I got in a mood. Sorry."

"I know it's been hard losing your dad," Andréa said. "I can't imagine losing mine. But don't shut me out. I know I was babbling, but sometimes I see this anger in your eyes and I get uncomfortable. I don't know what to say or do."

Hailey reached for her friend's hand and gave it a squeeze.

"I just want us to be like we've always been."

Andréa shifted to the left. "We're not kids anymore, Hail. In nine months, I'm off to Kingston. I want us to have the best nine months of our lives. Probably not realistic considering what happened, but I don't want to look back on this time and only remember my best friend being mad all the time."

"I know."

"If I say or do something that upsets you, then tell me," Andréa said. "Don't just leave and look at me as if I'm your enemy."

"I'm sorry."

"I know you," Andréa said. "You keep everything bottled up until you explode. And you've been exploding. Lately, you're scaring me."

"Scaring you?"

Andréa rubbed her hands on her thighs. "If your eyes aren't filled with anger, they're full of something worse."

Hailey glanced at her friend for a second or two before returning her attention to the road.

"Worse?"

"Yeah." Andréa looked out the side window before looking at Hailey again. "Like you don't give a damn about anything anymore, like . . ."

Hailey did a shoulder check as she merged from highway 416 to highway 417. Another twenty minutes or so before they'd be in Orleans.

"Just promise me you won't do anything stupid, like ever. Okay, Hail?"

Hailey gave her friend a quick, somewhat fake smile. She hadn't realized she'd become so transparent, that her emotions were really that easy to read. Certainly, when it came to Sarah, but around her friends? She thought she was under control.

And then she remembered how she'd fallen to pieces that day at Charlie's. But that was weeks ago, just after her dad had died. Maybe she'd become a horrible friend and hadn't realized it. Maybe she'd scared Connor away. Maybe that was why he hadn't made any sort of move.

No boy wanted to date the crazy girl.

"Nothing stupid, I promise," she said.

⁂

Sarah followed Jack's chili recipe to a T, and while it simmered on the stove she went into the den and sat in the big plush leather chair. She felt tiny and insignificant sitting in it. This had been

Jack's space where he handled all the family finances. She had paid so little attention to it, mostly because she was too afraid to get involved. What did she know about money?

Only that she'd never had any.

Ironically, she saw a twenty poking out from under the laptop and wondered what it was doing there. Strange that Jack would have left it there. She couldn't help but feel like she was stealing from him when she pulled it out and stuffed it into her pocket.

What else was she going to do with it? Leave it?

She powered up the laptop and waited. Jack had a beautiful old desk made of hard maple. She realized she hadn't been in the den since his passing. His book case was full but it was the pictures of Hailey that drew her eye. They were all of her dressed in hockey gear. In one, she smiled a toothless grin. He must have had one picture for each year. The last one looked like it must have been last year's.

Hailey had so much of Jack in her.

Sarah looked away and noticed that the password prompt was waiting for her on the screen. She typed in what he'd told her it was.

Thankfully, he hadn't changed it without telling her.

There were thousands of emails, mostly junk. One caught her attention as it had come on Christmas Day, from their financial adviser. A Christmas wish addressed to her, and a note that he was there to answer any questions she may have. But she didn't need to worry, Jack had left her and Hailey in great shape.

That made her breathe easier.

She didn't have to bother trying to go through Jack's papers to find their advisor's number. His signature had all she needed.

Maybe she'd send him an email, telling him of her plan. He'd be able to tell her if she was making a mistake.

Suddenly, she felt faint and her breaths became shallow and strained. She felt cold then hot, then cold again. And the shaking started innocuously enough but quickly took over completely. She felt like she was going mad, that this was just too much for her.

She couldn't pull this off.

She knew nothing about running a business. She would lose all their money. The idea was insane. She hadn't been thinking. Ruth's optimism had been infectious but now that she was back home, surrounded by the reality Jack's passing had left behind, her doubts ruled.

With an iron fist.

She was just some stupid girl who knew nothing about life and had trusted Jack implicitly. She told herself it was because she had loved him unconditionally, and she had, but she'd also been too happy to let someone take care of her for a change. All her life she'd waited for her mom to do it, but in the end her mom had been incapable of caring for herself, let alone her daughter.

Sarah closed her eyes. She didn't want to think about how her mother had failed her. She didn't want to remember what Axel had taken from her while her mom slept in the next room. Her mom had come into her room the next day and, after Sarah had told her what had happened, held her to her breast and told her what a brave girl she was, that this was the best they could do, that it was better than being homeless.

Sarah suddenly found it difficult to catch her breath. There was a sharp pain behind her left eye and the pounding at the back of her head made her feel nauseated. Her past always did that when she dared to think about it. Mostly, it was her anger toward her mother and the fear Axel had put into her that made her feel like her world was imploding.

Her mother had failed to protect her. Her mother had failed to take care of her. Her mother had simply failed.

Jack had been everything her mom had not been.

Jack protected her.

Jack believed in her.

She needed him so much right now, to whisper in her ear that she wasn't making a mistake, to give her that big kid grin that she loved so much because it made her forget all of her doubts and insecurities.

Like the ones she had when it came to Hailey.

If only Sarah didn't doubt herself so much when it came to her stepdaughter. Maybe it was her fault. The two of them had never really talked about anything, Sarah had never revealed herself to her stepdaughter. Either the moment had never felt right, or when Jack was alive there had been no real need, but all that was different now.

At least, for Sarah it was.

She knew Hailey wouldn't bend and meet her halfway. This was all going to be on Sarah's shoulders to forge whatever friendship would be allowed to flower, if at all. She had to try, really try, and if in the end they just resolved to be strangers to each other, Sarah could accept that because she would have made an effort.

Suddenly, Sarah felt drained and no longer had the energy to email her financial advisor. She'd call him tomorrow instead. Sarah closed the laptop lid and walked away. She noticed the framed picture of her, Jack, and Hailey sitting on the middle shelf of his bookcase, just below all the hockey photos. It had been taken last summer in the backyard. Jack had invited his fellow firefighters and their families over for the annual Cormier barbecue, and someone had snapped a picture of the three of them standing close enough together to look like they'd actually posed for it. Jack and Sarah were both laughing and staring into each other's eyes, and even Hailey's features were soft and relaxed, like she was having fun, too.

Sarah tucked away that memory close by, hoping to pair it with more such moments in the uncertain future which faced them. Just before leaving the room, she grabbed the picture and brought it back with her. She placed it on the mantel, beside Jack's urn.

He'd want his family close by.

Suddenly her throat closed, and before she lost it, again, she turned and went to check on her chili. It sure smelled wonderful.

Hopefully it tasted just as good.

THIRTEEN

Hailey parked the Outback and the two girls unloaded their hockey gear and made their way inside the arena to the dressing room. They were first to arrive, as always, so they went to check out the game currently in progress—mostly to soak in the vibes and get their heads in the game. Hailey liked to picture the plays she was going to make, the no-look passes to Andréa because they knew where the other would be on the ice at any given moment.

It's what made them the most dangerous duo in the league. It's why they were sitting on top of the scoring chart. And it's why Hailey felt confident they were going to win today and own first place for the rest of the season.

A girl from the Raiders came and stood a few feet away from them. She stared at Hailey and Hailey recognized her as their top player, number twelve. Hailey knew number twelve tried the occasional push in the back or slash across an opponent's calves, and always got away with it. The girl gave Hailey a knowing smile and then walked away.

Hailey was itching to get on the ice and teach that girl a lesson. Today, this wasn't going to be a friendly girls' game. How she yearned for body contact to be allowed. Why was it that just the boys had all the fun? The girls should also be allowed to have some contact.

Maybe number twelve was going to get a little taste of her own medicine today. Hailey watched number twelve walk out from the ice area, probably heading to her dressing room.

"Let's go," she said to Andréa.

෴

Sarah put her face over the pot and inhaled. The chili made her mouth water. Her taste buds were flipping in anticipation. Maybe she could just take a spoonful and try it, just to make sure it did taste as good as when Jack made it.

She grabbed a small bowl from the cupboard and ladled a tiny helping into it, and waited for the chili to cool a bit. She checked the clock and noticed it was nearly one-thirty and her thoughts turned to Hailey. She hadn't been to a game since Jack's passing, mostly because she wasn't much of a hockey fan and didn't really get the game, but also because she knew that Hailey didn't want her there and she'd only be a distraction if she did go.

It was best to stay away from the one thing Hailey was truly passionate about.

Sarah scooped some chili with her spoon and brought it to her lips, blew on it, and then tasted it.

Bland.

It tasted like ground beef. It had no flavour. Frantic, she grabbed the recipe book and went over all the steps Jack had written out and mentally checked them off. She'd followed it exactly. So, why didn't it taste like when Jack made it? Panic gripped her again. Something else Hailey would ridicule her about, belittle her for. She'd be right in her face with that mean smirk she loved to thrust at Sarah, telling her how useless she was. She couldn't even follow a simple recipe that was all spelled out for her.

Sarah took another spoonful and it was just as tasteless. She threw her spoon in the sink and felt her shoulders begin to quiver and her eyes start to burn as her anger boiled out of control.

Her husband had died and nothing could change that. And she was beginning to think that all the effort she was putting into trying to survive without him, continuing with the wonderful life he'd been so kind to share with her, would prove to be as much of a waste of time as tossing pennies into a wishing well.

CB EO

Hailey and Andréa got back to the dressing room and most of the players were in now. There was a lot of pre-game bantering going on, the girls pumping each other up for the big showdown. They all knew first place was at stake. Even if the season was barely half over, and there were a lot of games left, grabbing that top spot early was always the goal.

Hailey slipped on her gear and tried not to get too worked up this early. She knew a couple of the girls always talked a big game in the dressing room, but then didn't follow it up on the ice and that drove Hailey nuts.

Coach told them ten minutes until they hit the ice.

Time to lace up the skates.

"Did you see number twelve?" Hailey said.

"I saw her," Andréa said. "I know she can get under your skin, so don't let her."

"She just thinks—"

"So, don't let her," Andréa said again. "Just stay focused on your game. You're miles ahead of her. But, let her into your head and you become distracted. It's a game she plays. Ignore it."

"You're right," Hailey said.

"Look at me," Andréa said. "Don't do anything stupid."

Hailey laced up her other skate. "I won't."

The two friends had a way of keeping each other accountable to each other and to the team. Hailey was captain and Andréa assistant captain for a reason. They were the leaders and the others took their cues from them.

Hailey appreciated what Andréa was doing, trying her best to take Hailey's dad's place by making sure Hailey used patience and common sense. Right now, her dad would have been talking to her in his even keeled tone to make sure she wasn't too jacked up before the game, that she didn't explode onto the ice on her first shift and have nothing left for the rest of the game.

Hailey closed her eyes and pictured her dad talking to her, calming her. She missed him. So damn much. The worst was the void in the crowd. She was always listening for his cheers but couldn't hear them anymore. His encouragement had always helped her reach that other gear that pushed her above everyone else, but she hadn't been able to find it since his accident.

"Game time, girls," the coach shouted.

The room filled with the excitement that always preceded hitting the ice as, one by one, they filed out of the room, the goalie first followed by the rest of the players. Hailey was always the last one.

Andréa tapped her on the knee and the two of them got up and headed out of the dressing room and onto the ice. The moment her blades touched the ice, Hailey closed her eyes for a second and smiled. She didn't need to see where she was going. This was her ritual, her mind conjuring up that first time her dad had taken her skating—it was shortly after her mom had left and he told her years later that it was the first thing that had popped into his head, to get her skating, wanting to distract her for a while. She fell a bunch of times on that first outing, but got up each time and persevered. She still didn't know why she'd been so stubborn about not just learning to skate, but excel at it.

And then she became obsessed with hockey. She started watching the games with her dad whenever the Senators played and soon she was bugging him to play.

He'd signed her up the following fall.

Hailey opened her eyes and picked up her pace. In just a few strides she was blowing by everyone. She was ready to play.

CB ED

Sarah panicked. She couldn't let the chili be ruined because she'd missed something, so she added more herbs and spices, desperately trying to turn this bland simmering impostor into Jack's masterful chili.

But the more she tried, the worse it tasted.

"I ruined your chili," she said, her eyes burning. "I can't even make some lousy chili, Jack. I'm so stupid to think I could run my own flower shop when I can't even make your chili."

She stood in the middle of the kitchen, the pot of chili on the stove mocking her, her frustration draining away her determination. She should have asked him to teach her how to do these things instead of just watching him, sitting at the island enjoying a glass of wine and enjoying even more her man own the kitchen like a world class chef. She'd been so happy to just feast her eyes on him, feeling so lucky that this wonderful man had not given up on her when she'd told him she couldn't go out with him, like ten or twelve times. He kept coming back to watch her do her show and ask her out, and he was so relentless, so determined, so damn handsome that she'd finally given in. Selena had convinced her to just go out with the guy, get him to buy her an expensive meal and expensive wine, and then stow away the memory if it was worth it, or just trash it if he wasn't worth remembering.

There hadn't been an expensive meal or expensive wine, but that Beaver Tail after skating the canal was the best memory she'd ever stowed away.

A fairy tale. That's what he'd told her on their wedding night. She was living her fairy tale and she had believed him. She had never imagined anything like that could happen to her, but it had and she had bought in to her happily ever after.

But seven weeks ago her perfect ending had been torn to pieces, and she had no idea how to put it back together. Whatever she tried didn't fit properly, left jagged edges poking out everywhere, left scars that wouldn't heal. It was just one failure after another. Made her feel small and incompetent, like the twelve-year-old who'd cried herself to sleep for months after that asshole Axel was done visiting her during the night; until that one time when she'd been waiting with a pair of scissors tucked away under her pillow, and when he'd showed up that night and crawled in beside her, she had pulled the weapon out from its hiding place and stabbed him in the arm with all the strength she'd had. He had screamed and backhanded her across the face, which had left a black eye for a couple of weeks, but by then he'd kicked them out of his apartment and they were back on the streets—homeless, cold, and hungry.

But she'd worn that black eye with pride.

"I'm sorry, Jack. I ruined your chili," she said as she sat on the kitchen floor with her back against the fridge door, her knees drawn up to her chest and her arms wrapped around them while frustration left wet streaks down her cheeks. "I ruined your chili."

⚜

The period ended in a zero tie, but the Raiders scored two quick goals in the first three minutes of the second and suddenly Hailey was pressing too hard. She was trying to do everything herself, and she and Andréa were yelling at each other on the bench.

"It's a team sport," Andréa said.

"Then get open," Hailey said.

"I was on that last play," Andréa shouted back.

"Girls," the coach said. "Leave it on the ice. I need the two of you at your best."

Hailey and Andréa eyed each other coolly and then jumped on the ice as the third line came off. Instantly, the Raiders' top line also jumped on the ice and a battle began. Number twelve bumped Hailey along the board, which should have been called interference, but the referee turned a blind eye. Andréa stole the puck from the Raiders' right winger and started up the ice, but Hailey was too eager and the lineman blew an offside.

Hailey and number twelve lined up for the faceoff.

Hailey won but got one of those slashes on the calf and she started yelling at the ref to keep her damn eyes open. All she got was a stern glare from the ref and a stupid grin from number twelve. She was going to have to wipe that grin off number twelve's face.

The left defence on the Lightning's team shot the puck deep into the Raiders' end and Hailey pursued number twelve into the corner to get the puck and smashed her into the boards hard. Number twelve grabbed the back of her knee as she crumpled to the ice.

"Seventy-seven," the ref yelled. "You're done." She pointed to the far gate.

"Are you kidding me?" Hailey said. "What about all the times she slashed me!"

The ref pointed to the far gate again. "Game misconduct. Go take a shower. You're done."

Hailey skated by the referee and eyed her with a hard, cold glare. As she reached the other end and neared the goal, she raised her stick and smashed it against the crossbar. The one-piece composite stick exploded in multiple pieces and Hailey just left the remains on the ice. That stupid ref could pick them up for all she cared. This wasn't fair. Stupid number twelve got away with all sorts of shit and Hailey got tossed just because number twelve couldn't handle a little push into the boards.

Someone opened the gate and Hailey stepped through the opening. She could barely see through her tears. She slammed the dressing room door against the wall and threw her helmet against the far wall, pieces of plastic flying in all directions.

She fell to her knees. "I hate everyone," she whispered. "Dad, this wasn't my fault. That girl, she asked for it."

The assistant coach came in and Hailey just stayed on her knees.

"You okay, Hailey?" the assistant-coach said.

"I'm sorry," she said and stood. "I got carried away."

"I know, but you know the rules," the assistant-coach said. "She may have torn an ACL or an MCL. If you're lucky, it's just a bruised knee."

"What's going to happen?"

"You could be suspended for a few games, or maybe the rest of the season if she's really hurt."

Hailey sat on the bench. "You know, she's always getting away with stuff."

"Yes, but she doesn't run other players into the boards," the assistant-coach said. "You looked like you were trying to kill her, Hailey. I know you've been through a lot, but you can't do that. It's a game, only a game. What you did showed poor sportsman-ship and a complete disrespect for a fellow player."

"I'm really sorry," she said.

"I know," the assistant-coach said. "Take a shower or get dressed. We'll talk about it after the game."

Hailey waited until the assistant coach had left and then put her sweats back on, packed her gear, and texted Andréa that she'd decided to leave and if she could just get a ride back home with her parents.

FOURTEEN

Hailey got into her car and sat there for a moment, key in hand, trying to convince herself that it was time she take care of this. She knew it was going to burn a hole inside of her if she kept ignoring it because all she really did was obsess over it. If today wasn't a direct result of her frustration, of her need to get answers, then she'd become completely mad.

Time to pay her mother a visit.

She started the car and plugged her mom's address into the GPS and headed off. She drove in silence, her thoughts a jumble of doubts that put pressure at the base of her neck and shoulders. She tried to crack her neck but it wouldn't give. The harsh winter sun heading west made her squint and she swore under her breath for forgetting her sunglasses on her dresser at home.

She eased off the Queensway and made her way down Bank Street until she reached her mother's street. She crawled along the narrow neighbourhood road and found an empty spot about three doors down from her mom's house.

She parked and killed the engine.

And waited.

Hailey could feel her mouth go dry. Minutes passed and she didn't move. A woman came out of the house but Hailey didn't think it was her mom. It had been thirteen years since she'd last seen her mother so it was possible it was her, but this woman seemed too tall and had long, blonde hair. She also looked about ten years younger than what her mom would be now.

Hailey closed her eyes and steeled herself. The idea had seemed easy back at the arena, but actually sitting here, in a car that was getting colder by the second, planning to confront her mom and get answers, made her doubt herself. Her gut told her this was going to be a waste of time. She knew her mom wasn't going to throw her arms around her and invite her in so they could talk and forgive each other. You didn't cut all contact for all those years if you still cared about the other person. And that's what Hailey was scared about. To find out the truth about her mom leaving.

Actually, she knew the truth. What Hailey wanted, needed, was to find closure, to hear it from the woman herself.

But then again, not hearing it let her keep that bit of hope and did she want to lose that?

Her phone made that sound that she'd gotten a text. It was Andréa asking her if she was all right.

Was she all right?

She didn't really know. What exactly was being all right? How did someone who was all right behave? Did someone who was all right purposely run another player into the boards wanting to hurt her? Did someone who was all right sit in a car in front of her mother's house, wondering what the hell she was doing? What exactly was she hoping to find?

Hailey couldn't remember the last time when she'd been really all right. The day her dad died definitely seemed to be the day she stopped being all right, but maybe the reason she was sitting here in the car, getting cold, was because she had stopped being all right the day her mom left. So, maybe she hadn't been all right since then.

She didn't text Andréa back because she couldn't honestly answer that question and she didn't want to lie to her friend. She could always pretend her phone had died and she'd left her power cord at home.

Please don't do anything stupid, Andréa texted.

The space between her brows folded. Was confronting her mother after all these years Andréa's idea of doing something stupid? Hailey didn't think so. She was pretty sure Andréa was telling her not to hurt herself, physically at least. Emotionally, Hailey was a real mess and confronting her mother wasn't going to improve that. So in that sense, maybe Andréa's concerns were dead on.

Hailey slipped her phone inside her jacket pocket, stepped out of the car, and walked toward her mother's house.

C3 80

Sarah poured the chili into a strainer over the sink to drain all the liquid from the solids, and then dumped all the meat and beans and other solids onto some newspaper which she then rolled up and placed in a composting paper bag. She then placed the bag inside the green bin in the garage.

No chili for dinner tonight.

Her attempt had been a complete bust. It would have been best to just leave it bland because the more she tried to salvage her mistake, the worse it tasted until it literally wasn't fit to give to a dog. No way was she going to feed that crap to Peanut.

She went to the cupboard where they kept the wine and her shoulders sagged as she remembered the last bottle had been enjoyed before Christmas. The idea of going out into the cold didn't appeal much to her, and she was starting to get a headache.

Instead, she plugged the kettle in and made a cup of tea, grabbed a box of crackers and peanut butter from the pantry, armed herself with a knife, and parked herself in front of the television to pass the rest of the afternoon watching her personal vice: a Hallmark movie.

She smothered a cracker with peanut butter, stuffed it in her mouth, pushed it down with a sip of tea. She repeated the process a dozen times before starting to feel a little peanut buttered out. Out of nowhere, she had a craving for something chocolaty now and went to get the brownie Hailey hadn't bothered to eat. She smiled when she saw there were still three left. She'd forgotten she'd bought four of them so she could satisfy her craving—at least she didn't have to feel guilty about taking Hailey's piece now. After all, she'd gotten them so if she wanted to eat them all, that was her prerogative. She grabbed one and took a big chunk and once again felt like Jack had just wrapped his strong arms around her and was whispering sweetness into her ear. She took another bite, and another, and then a last one.

Her brownie was gone and so was Jack.

Sarah got dressed and headed out to the liquor store.

03 80

Hailey walked up the steps to the front door, feeling the cold bite at her flesh while she tried to ignore the dread in the hollow of her stomach that made her want to puke. She didn't know how long she stood in front of the door trying to find her courage, but then the blonde-haired woman was standing in front of her talking to her, but Hailey didn't hear a word.

"Can I help you?"

"I'm looking for someone I think lives here," Hailey said. Up close the woman wasn't that pretty. Her mouth was too big and her eyes too wide apart, and that dye job was bad. She definitely wasn't her mother.

"Who are you looking for?"

"Natalie Cormier."

The woman nodded. "Can I tell her who's asking?"

"Her . . . friend."

The woman didn't seem to buy it but she told Hailey to wait out here. Being so cold, the least she could have offered was for Hailey to wait inside. It seemed like a long time before anyone came to the door, and Hailey was about to give up when the door opened and Hailey was staring at an older version of her mother.

There was a long silence as the two women just eyed each other, neither wanting to be first to acknowledge what this moment might mean.

"So, this is where you've been hiding," Hailey said, surprised by the bitterness of her words. "Actually, I knew that. I came last summer but didn't have the guts to knock."

Her mother crossed her arms and Hailey could tell her mom was trying to figure out how to best handle this intrusion by her daughter. It was obvious she wasn't welcome.

"You shouldn't have bothered," Natalie said.

"To come?" Hailey said. "Yeah, I'm sensing that you're not giddy with me being here."

"You've grown."

"Kids tend to do that when you abandon them at four."

Her mother said nothing. Just cautiously scrutinized Hailey which made her look away. Hailey knew this had been a mistake, that she wouldn't get any answers here. They were strangers to each other, their only link a man who had died a few weeks back.

"Dad died."

"I heard."

Nothing else. No, "I'm sorry," no "he was such a good man." Only indifference, like she hadn't loved the man once, loved him enough to have a child with him. Maybe her mother had never loved her father, and she'd been a mistake that her mother had needed to get rid of. Now, that made sense. It hurt like hell, but that's the only thing that made sense now.

An older woman came up behind Natalie and put her arms around Hailey's mom. "Who's this?"

"No one," her mom said. "She got the wrong house."

"We're waiting for you upstairs," the woman said and walked away.

Hailey then noticed all the paintings everywhere, hanging on walls, leaning against furniture, sitting unfinished on easels. Most were of naked women. Some almost looked pornographic.

"So, I'm no one to you."

"You should go."

"Did you paint those?" Hailey remembered her mom trying to paint before she left. Didn't look like her mom had gotten any better. "Woman porn?"

"Call it what you want. I paint people." A long silence. "I was never meant to be with your dad. I never wanted kids."

Hailey felt her face melt away. "You never wanted me?"

"You or any other kids," Natalie said. "Your dad wanted at least three kids and I couldn't bear the thought of having to devote my life to strangers I didn't want."

Hailey fought back the burning at the back of her eyes.

"A stranger you didn't want to take care of," Hailey said. "That's what I was to you?"

"What did you expect to find here?" Natalie said. "Have I ever done anything to make you think I wanted you to find me?"

"We missed you for years," she said. "We waited for you. But Dad got tired of waiting. He found someone else."

"I'm sure she's better than I ever was."

"I hate her."

"You're almost an adult," she said.

"What's that supposed to mean?"

"I can't help you," her mom said. Someone called her from upstairs. "Coming."

"Why did you have me if you never wanted me?"

"I never wanted to be a mother," she said. "I thought I loved your father, and maybe I did, but I hated the life he wanted, the life he'd trapped me in. I tried for as long as I could, but then I had to save myself. Leaving was the most unselfish thing I could have done."

"Unselfish?"

"You would have come to hate me even more if I had stayed."

"Oh, I hate you quite a bit right now."

"Go home. Forget about me."

"Gladly," Hailey said while staring disgustedly at the woman who had given her life. This wasn't her mother. This was a complete stranger. "I won't bother you again."

Hailey turned and walked away. She heard the door close behind her, and although she wanted to look back, she didn't. There was nothing there for her. There never had been.

She was all alone.

ርሜ ዜ

Sarah saw couples everywhere. Walking down Franktown Road, coming out of Tim Hortons with coffees and boxes of Timbits or bags full of delicious donuts, in and out of the grocery store with carts full of food, and in the aisles at the liquor store. Young, old, somewhere in middle-age, tall, short, thin, and big, it didn't matter. Some were barely talking while others were overly loud in their laughter and conversation.

She had never been more aware of her oneness, that her entire social circle had been Jack's circle of friends, colleagues, and acquaintances. She had enjoyed their company and joined conversations, but she had never truly formed her own friendships with any of the other women. There never seemed to be any sort of burning desire to do so, and now she realized that that had been a mistake.

How could she have known that Jack would leave her a widow so soon? She wasn't even thirty yet.

"It's a good one."

Sarah glanced at the man standing beside her, looking faintly familiar. He was pointing at the bottle of Apothic Dark that she was holding in her hand, which she couldn't remember picking up.

"Yes, my husband loved this one," she said. "But he passed away last month."

She had no idea why she was telling this stranger her sad story. Maybe because she was missing human contact so badly and he'd showed her some sort of compassion.

"I'm sorry," she said. "I have no idea why I said that."

"Losing someone is never easy," he said. "I lost my mother two years ago and there are still days when I feel like giving her a call and I need to remind myself that I can't. It will take some time."

"He was a firefighter. Died trying to save someone."

"You must be proud."

She was, but she would have preferred that Jack hadn't been so damn daring all the time. "He was a wonderful man."

"I'm sorry for your loss," he said. "I can see you loved him very much."

Sarah nodded. She didn't trust her voice.

"I didn't mean to intrude," he said and started to walk away. She watched the man catch up to that lady she'd seen at the bakery with that little, cute boy. That's why he'd looked familiar. They were such a gorgeous couple those two, both tall and so together.

Reminded Sarah of her and Jack. That's the way Jack had looked at her all the time, the same way that man was looking at his wife right now, like there was no one else he wanted to be with.

Sarah grabbed two more bottles, paid, and headed home. Maybe she was trying too hard with everything, trying to fill Jack's shoes. Maybe she should give Hailey time to come around. Maybe she never would, but someday she might. She was only seventeen, still full of teenage angst. Give her space and if one day she came to her, she'd be there. That's really all she could do.

In the meantime, she had to start her own life again. And maybe she'd crash and burn trying to run her own flower shop, but at least she would have the satisfaction of having tried. Sure, it scared the crap out of her, but Jack wouldn't be too proud of her if she didn't even try, let her fear take over.

When she got home, she poured a glass of wine and then went into Jack's den—her den—because she decided to send her financial advisor an email after all about her plans for the flower shop.

It was time she took control of her life.

Should have done that long ago.

She was no longer that twelve-year-old girl who'd waited too long to stand up for herself.

FIFTEEN

Winter in the capital region of Ottawa can be both beautiful and enjoyable with all the different activities like skiing, tobogganing, and skating the canal, or deadly cold and unforgiving. It's not unusual for the temperature to dip below minus thirty Celsius and have a wind chill factor of minus forty, or worse. Frostbite warnings come quite frequently during those dreaded winter months, and the few shelters available that rarely get filled during the rest of the year can become overwhelmed by the homeless seeking a little warmth for a night.

When she walked away from her mom, Hailey didn't turn toward her car. Instead, she headed in the opposite direction, confused and hurt, just needing to walk and clear her head and figure out what to do. She wasn't really paying attention; she just walked and took a turn here and a turn there, and before she'd realized it, she was completely lost. She was not that familiar with downtown and the day was already running out even though it wasn't quite four-thirty in the afternoon.

She stopped.

Looked around.

Started to get a little panicky.

A chill ran through her and she pulled the hood of her winter coat over her head. It wasn't as warm as her toque would have been, but it was better than nothing. She wished she hadn't left her gloves in the car because her hands had become quite numb.

And she was hungry.

The man ahead of her seemed to be having an argument with himself. Hailey slowed and noticed that people were going out of their way to avoid him. She watched a group of boys, probably about her age, walk by and make fun of the guy, saying he must be off his meds. When she looked back at the man, though, he'd turned around and had started heading her way. She freaked, startled, and went to cross the street without looking when a horn blast made her jump backward and into the guy off his meds. He started yelling and grabbing at her. Hailey screamed, tried to back away, and slipped on the icy sidewalk. She broke her fall using her hands but both knees of her sweatpants were instantly soaked.

Why had she not gone back to her car and driven home after her conversation with her mom? She'd probably be in her room now where it was warm and safe. Instead, she was downtown, out of her element, afraid.

She wanted her dad.

The thought was cut short when the guy made a weird sound, like too much phlegm in his throat, and seemed to be coming for her. Hailey quickly got to her feet and started to run deeper into the downtown core, getting more and more disoriented. People were now giving her a wide birth and she wanted to tell them that she wasn't the crazy one, but when she finally stopped and looked back, no one was chasing her. She stood, motionless and shocked, looking around and finally noticed the street signs: Sparks and O'Connor.

What she would give right now for Connor to be here with her. She felt so alone and lost. And she was so cold. She pulled her phone from her pocket and wanted to cry—she'd let the battery run down to one percent and now her phone was totally useless.

But she must have been standing there longer than she realized, or maybe she hadn't actually run that far, because the crazy guy was back. He was sitting across the street on what looked like some sort of air vent and he was staring right at her, looking eerily like Gollum. And then she understood why he was sitting there. Hot air from the subway escaped through those vents.

She wanted nothing to do with him. She turned and started to walk down Sparks Street and found a Tim Hortons. She ordered a hot chocolate, a chicken wrap, and found a table at the back. She would eat her food and then find her way back to her mom's place to get the car, and head home.

To Sarah?

The thought made her want to cry. Her life had become a pathetic nightmare. A mother who'd never wanted her and a stepmom she hated. And she'd gotten lost downtown on the bloodiest coldest night of winter. Her phone was dead. She couldn't even call for an Uber without her phone.

Hailey stayed in the Tim Horton's long after she'd finished eating, mostly to stay warm, but also because it was dark outside now and she was scared. Nothing much ever happened in Forest

Creek but she was in downtown Ottawa and something bad always happened. It was on the news every morning how someone got stabbed or shot or mugged. And that guy had really freaked her out.

"Excuse me, miss," one of the Tim Horton employees said. "You can't just stay here all night."

"What time is it?"

"Almost six thirty."

If only she could remember the name of the street her mom lived on, she could ask for directions, but she'd trusted the GPS to get her there so remembering the street name had not been a priority.

"Thanks," she said. "I just need to use the washroom."

Ten minutes later, bundled into her winter coat, she left the warmth of the store only to be assaulted by winter's unrelenting bitter cold. She had never been downtown on her own before, and she didn't know which way was which and she didn't trust anyone. People were all hidden behind winter gear, everyone was walking with purpose to stay warm or get out of the frigid arctic air. No one but the unfortunates roamed the streets on a night like this.

She managed to get back to the corner of Sparks and O'Connor and decided to head right because she was pretty sure she'd come that way. She crossed Queen and then everything went wrong.

She saw the crazy guy and decided to avoid him by turning into what was a narrow alley full of garbage containers. She realized it was probably the back of pubs or restaurants as she could hear music coming from inside, figured it'd be safe enough at least to get to the other side.

Big mistake.

She turned and a huge lump lodged itself in the back of her throat. The crazy guy was following her, coming straight for her. She froze. Didn't know what to do. It didn't even occur to her to scream for help until he'd slammed her into a wall. Her head hurt. She could feel something warm and wet on her lip and when she drew her fingers away, she saw blood.

It made her woozy.

Then she felt a fist against her cheek and it really hurt. Tears filled her eyes along with the bitter cold, making things even more blurry—she could barely see.

"Leave me alone," she said but it sounded weak and helpless. "Please."

He punched her again, in the left eye this time, and she couldn't believe how painful it felt. Her face was numb. She doubled over and he shoved her hard against one of the garbage containers. She fell to the ground, winded. She tried to scream but nothing came out. She was too afraid to look up.

"You're the devil's child," he shouted, "and you must be punished for your sins."

"Fuck you," she said weakly.

That seemed to anger him and he kicked her in the ribs. She couldn't catch her breath. She was going to die here, in a back alley, in minus twenty-degree weather, alone.

He slammed her against the garbage container again and then it all went dark. When she came to, she couldn't remember where she was.

She couldn't remember who she was.

Her left eye was throbbing and she could barely see out of it. Her ribs made every breath feel like she was being stabbed.

And she was cold.

She tried to stand but the pain in her chest was too much. She stayed on all fours and waited for it to pass. Then she started to crawl out of the alley, toward O'Connor, toward people.

She needed help.

03 80

Sarah selected everything with the cursor and pressed the delete key. Her thoughts sounded anything but coherent and she kept having to start over. Finally, she decided to stop trying to sound like she knew what she was talking about and sent a very brief email asking to meet with him that week to discuss buying a flower shop here in town.

There was no point pretending to be someone she wasn't. She just wasn't that sophisticated.

Sarah sat back in the big leather chair and took a sip of wine which didn't seem to taste as good as she remembered. Kind of upset her stomach a bit.

Nerves. She'd been on edge too long. The tension between her and Hailey was draining. Speaking of which, Hailey should have been home by now. Then again, not like she would bother to tell Sarah if she stayed at Andréa's for dinner. And tomorrow wasn't a school day, so chances were good she'd be home pretty late, if at all if she decided to sleep over at her friend's house. Just would be nice if Hailey would let Sarah know.

That way, she wouldn't worry.

It didn't matter how much Hailey didn't care about her, Sarah still cared about Hailey. She had no real reason to, except that when she'd married Jack, she had accepted in her heart the responsibility of caring for Hailey, and even though the girl pushed her away every chance she got, Sarah was going to do everything she could until Hailey was a legal adult. At that point, if Hailey wanted nothing to do with Sarah for the rest of her life, then so be it.

Sarah had eight months to win Hailey over. Not a lot of time, to be sure, but it would feel like forever if they continued the way they were.

Sarah took another sip of wine and grimaced. She walked back to the kitchen and covered her glass with plastic wrap. Maybe she wasn't in the mood for wine right now.

The home phone rang which caught Sarah by surprise. The last phone call on the home phone had been from Hailey's school the day Jack had died. She'd actually been meaning to cancel it, since neither she nor Hailey used it. When she looked at the on-call display, she saw Andréa's name. Maybe Hailey's phone had died and she was calling her to let her know she was staying over Andréa's tonight.

"Hello?"

"Hi Sarah, it's Andréa."

"Oh, hi," she said tentatively. "I thought maybe it was Hailey calling the home number."

"No," Andréa said, sounding concerned. "Isn't she home? I've been texting her for two hours and I thought she was just ignoring me because of what happened at the game today. I know she was mad, but I didn't think she was mad at me."

"Sorry," Sarah said, a frown creasing the skin on her forehead. "What happened today? Are you're saying Hailey isn't with you?"

"No, she's not," Andréa said. "Isn't she home?"

"She never came home," Sarah said. "What happened at hockey? Did she get hurt?"

Andréa told Sarah what happened at the game, and how by the time she got back to the dressing room, Hailey had been gone.

"And she never told you where she was going?"

"No," Andréa said. "Just a text asking me if I could get a ride home with my parents. I assumed she was too upset to wait for me and just wanted to get home."

"Not exactly the place she loves to be these days."

"I know," Andréa said. "Give her some time. I'm sure she'll come around. She can be hard on people."

"I only want us to get along, you know," Sarah said, not sure she should be telling this to Hailey's best friend. Then again, if anyone might be able to influence Hailey, it would be Andréa. "I know I can't be her mother, but is it so wrong to want us to be friendly to each other?"

"She's a good person," Andréa said. "She had a hard time when her mom left, and now with her dad gone—"

There was a pause.

"Do you think she might have tried to find her?" Sarah said. "I believe she still lives in Ottawa."

There was another longer pause. "She does know where her mom lives," Andréa said. "We went last summer, but she never actually met with her. I think she was too scared to find out the truth."

"Maybe today she changed her mind?"

"I guess she could have," Andréa said. "I just wish she'd answer me so I could stop worrying."

"Now you've got me worried." Sarah thought of something. "Do you think you remember where her mom lives?"

"Not really sure," she said. "Down in the Glebe, but I don't remember the street or the address. I wasn't really paying attention. Sorry."

"It's okay," Sarah said. "Hopefully she'll be home soon."

"I hope so," Andréa said. "Can you let me know when she does?"

"Of course," Sarah said. "And if you hear from her, please do the same. I hope she didn't get into an accident. It's really cold tonight."

"Should we call the police?"

"I think a person has to be missing for at least twenty-four hours before they bother."

"I think I'll look at Google Maps and see if I can find where her mom's place is. Never know."

"Good idea," Sarah said.

They said goodbye and hung up. Sarah made her way to the front of the house, and stared out the living room window. All she saw was the dark night. She stood there a long time, Peanut at her feet until Sarah scooped the puppy into her arms, waiting to see car lights turn into the driveway. Worry made her shoulders tense and her stomach tighten. She could feel the cold coming through the window, and she hoped that Hailey wasn't out in it. It always made her feel bad when she heard frostbite warnings on the radio, knowing that for some homeless people, nights like this could be their last.

Where are you?

An hour went by. No car lights turned up the driveway.

॥ ॥

Hailey was shivering and crying, and when someone tried to help her up she began to scream and tried to crawl away, but only got as far as the wall that led down the alley. She shook violently with fear and from being cold, and she couldn't see. Her left eye was swollen shut and her right eye was just a blur from tears which had frozen over her eyelashes.

"Just leave her," a man's voice said. "She could be dangerous. She obviously doesn't want your help."

"I can't just walk away," a woman's voice said. "She's hurt. She needs help."

"There's a homeless shelter by Ottawa U," the man said. "It's a bit of a walk. We can't force her to come with us."

The woman hunched down in front of Hailey and offered her a sincere smile. "Are you homeless? Is there someone we can call for you?"

Hailey felt dizzy. And her head was hurting really bad.

"What's your name?"

Hailey bit her quivering lip. After a moment, she shook her head.

"You don't remember your name?"

Hailey shook her head again.

"Her face looks like it took a beating," the woman said to the man. "Can you see if you can get a blanket somewhere? Anything to keep her warm."

"All the shops are closed," he said. "We should just call 911."

"Yeah, do that. But we wait with her until someone comes. Maybe she has a concussion. I think she got mugged or something."

The man called 911 and told the operator the little he knew.

"They're sending someone right away," he said. "We're going to be late for the show," the man said.

"We're not leaving her."

The man hopped from foot to foot. "It's frigging cold."

"Really, Steve," the woman said. "She's only got a thin hoodie on, and you're complaining about being cold. I wish she'd let me hold her, try to keep her warm."

"Just be careful," he said. "You don't know that she was mugged. She could be dangerous. My sister Tracy was attacked years ago when some crazy woman thought she was part of her hallucination and started punching and clawing at her face. Tracy still has that scar above her left eye."

"Someone is coming to help you," the woman said. "My name is Janet. I'm not going to hurt you. Any chance you can tell me your name."

Hailey just shook her head.

"It's okay," Janet said. "Someone will be here soon, and I'm sure they have blankets so you'll be able to get warmed up. I know you're cold. Just hold on a bit longer, okay?"

Hailey nodded, or maybe she was just shivering.

"My head really hurts."

"You probably have a concussion."

"I want to go home."

"Do you know where that is?"

Hailey shook her head.

"I'm sure you will soon," Janet said. "You don't have a phone or driver's licence?"

"I don't know."

Janet gave Hailey a sad face. Suddenly, the red and white hue of flashing lights became more and more prominent and then the paramedics pulled in front of them.

"Over here," Janet said. "I think this girl was attacked. She doesn't know her name."

"Thank you for staying with her," the lady paramedic said. She had a thick blanket in her arms while her male counterpart held a backboard. "She wouldn't have lasted long in this cold."

"She wouldn't let me hold her," she said. "To help keep her warm."

"Well, in a case like this, it might not have been safe for you to get too close anyway."

"That's what I said," Steve added.

Janet glared at him.

"Do you need us for anything?" Steve asked the male paramedic.

"No, you two can go," he said. "We'll take care of her now. But thank you. You'd be surprised how many people would have just ignored her."

"I'm a school teacher," Janet said. "I couldn't just walk by and pretend she didn't need our help."

"You folks enjoy your evening."

The lady paramedic hunched down in front of Hailey and turned to her partner. "We should lay her down on the backboard, just in case. Her left eye looks pretty swollen. There's some dried blood above her eyebrow. Probably a laceration on her head."

The paramedics told Hailey everything they needed to do to make sure she was all right. They also put on a neck brace and, once Hailey was secured on the stretcher, the lady paramedic covered her with the blanket.

"We're going to bring you inside the ambulance now," the female paramedic said. "I want to get you warmed up and then examine you."

"My head really hurts," Hailey said. "And my ribs."

"Looks like you had some head trauma," she said. "Maybe you fell against something which might explain why your ribs hurt, too. Do you remember anything?"

"No," she said, close to tears.

"We'll take care of you," the female paramedic said and with the help of her partner, they lifted Hailey up and brought her inside the back of the ambulance.

"Montfort or CHEO?" the male paramedic asked.

"Montfort is closer," the female paramedic said. "If they figure out she's under eighteen and want to transfer her afterward, they'll do that."

The male paramedic closed the doors and the few onlookers who'd gathered started to disperse once the ambulance pulled away.

SIXTEEN

S arah glanced at the clock on her night table for the tenth time in as many minutes, and sighed heavily. She could feel Peanut staring at her from her bed on the floor beside the dresser. Jack had loved Peanut but he hadn't wanted the dog to sleep with them. Even though Sarah could have changed that rule now, she hadn't.

"Can't sleep either," Sarah said to her Maltese. She pushed the covers back and swung her legs over. It was after midnight, and Hailey had not come home yet nor had she heard from Andréa. She slipped into her silk bathrobe Jack had given her last Christmas and headed down to the kitchen, Peanut at her heels.

She plugged the kettle and put a tea bag in a cup and waited for the water to boil. She gave Peanut a treat. Cut one of the remaining brownies in half and nibbled on it. The water was ready so she poured it into her cup and let the bag steep for a couple of minutes.

She sipped her tea.

Nibbled the brownie.

Worried.

She glared at the clock on the microwave. The bright red numbers changed to 12:23 a.m. Her stomach was in knots. She wanted to call Andréa but she knew Andréa would call her if she heard from Hailey.

Something must have happened. Maybe she got into a car accident. No, the police would have called. They would have used the licence plate to find out who it belonged to and where she lived. Maybe she was dead and they had all sorts of procedures to follow before they could call. No. She couldn't lose another person in her life. She'd lost too much already. But what else could it be?

She fought for air. She started to shake. The urge to make herself small down on the kitchen floor against the cupboards called to her. She remembered crawling into a cupboard more than once to hide from Axel when her mom wasn't around or had passed out on the couch. She was a grown woman. With big kid fears.

Where are you?

What Sarah would give to have that sourpuss of a stepdaughter up in her bed right now. The waiting, the not knowing, the fearing the worst, was murderous. What could have happened? Could Hailey have found her mother after all and decided to stay the night? That wouldn't explain why she was ignoring Andréa. Even if she was mad at her friend, Hailey would have gotten in touch with Andréa, wouldn't she?

Wouldn't she?

Sarah grabbed her phone. She was done waiting. She would call every hospital in Ottawa until she found Hailey. There weren't that many. At least, she'd be doing something other than waiting and worrying.

She'd be doing what any mother would do.

Find her child.

CB 80

Hailey was lying on a bed in emergency, her chills finally gone. A couple of doctors had come to see her, and assessed that the nasty cut on the side of her head had been caused by some blow to the head, either a punch or slammed against something. The cut was closing nicely, though, and they hoped her loss of memory would be temporary.

Her black eye would take a few days to heal.

As would her bruised ribs.

"How are you doing?" a nurse asked as she checked Hailey's chart.

Hailey shrugged. "Where am I?"

"Montfort hospital," the nurse said. "Do you remember why?"

"No," Hailey said. "My head and chest hurt."

"You have a concussion," the nurse said. "And some badly bruised ribs. At least none are broken. We'll be keeping a close eye on you."

"Can I have more water?"

"Sure." The nurse came back with a cup of ice water. "If you remember anything, let one of us know, okay?"

Hailey nodded. "Will I stay here until then?"

"For now."

"How long have I been here?"

The nurse checked her watch. "A little over five hours."

Hailey seemed to think of something. "Do you know who I am?"

"You came in without any ID."

"Oh."

The nurse touched her reassuringly on the arm. "We'll take good care of you until we figure out who you are."

"Thank you."

The nurse started to walk away.

"Excuse me?" Hailey said. "Did I have a phone?"

"Unfortunately not," the nurse said. "We probably would have been able to contact someone if you had."

"Maybe I didn't have one," Hailey said.

The nurse smiled. "A teenager without a phone? Must have lost it. Get some rest. I'll be back in a little while." The nurse paused. "You're wearing an old Ottawa Senators T-shirt. Does that mean anything to you?'

"No," Hailey said. "I don't even think I like hockey."

C8 80

Sarah's first call was an exercise in frustration. She was put on hold, transferred, transferred again, put back on hold, and disconnected. It took nearly an hour and a lot of begging and explaining to be finally told no one who appeared to be her stepdaughter had been admitted at the Queensway-Carleton hospital.

It was just after one in the morning.

She called CHEO. Not quite as long, but Hailey had not been admitted into the children's hospital. She then tried the General, and again no sign of Hailey. By then it was almost two-thirty and she was beat. Her eyes were heavy with sleep.

Two more to call: Civic and Montfort.

Civic took forever. Maybe because it was the middle of the night now and staff was at a minimum, but Sarah was not getting anywhere. She could barely stay awake and the clock was inching past three when someone confirmed that her stepdaughter was not at the Civic.

One more.

Sarah endured the same long process until she got the right person who put her on hold for almost ten minutes.

The woman's voice sounded far and thin and it took Sarah a moment to realize she wasn't holding her phone against her ear.

"You there, ma'am?"

"Yes," Sarah said groggily. "I think I was falling asleep. It's been a long night."

"We had a young female admitted around 7:46 last night. It looks like she has a concussion and can't remember who she is and she has no ID on her."

"Long dark hair, green eyes, about five foot eight or nine. She's quite tall and athletic. She was last seen playing hockey."

"Seems to fit except for the hockey," the woman said. "She doesn't think she likes hockey although she is wearing an old raggedy Sens T-shirt."

"That's her dad's. She wears it for every game and she had a game yesterday afternoon."

"What did you say her name is?"

"Hailey Cormier."

"Age?"

"Seventeen."

There was a pause while Sarah heard the woman typing on a keyboard. "I think we might have our Jane Doe. I'd recommend you come and identify her as soon as possible."

"I'm on my way."

03 80

Sarah felt bad about leaving Peanut home but she couldn't take the dog with her. Where she'd been falling asleep a short while ago, adrenaline was keeping her wide awake now, which was good because the drive to the Montfort was almost forty minutes.

At least at three in the morning there was no traffic, so once she hit the 416, she pushed her speed to 125 km/h, hoping it might cut a few minutes off her tense drive.

All sorts of worries filled Sarah's thoughts. What had happened at the hockey game and what had Hailey done afterward? Where had she gone? How'd she get the concussion? Why didn't she have any ID on her?

A lot of questions that she hoped would be answered once she got to the hospital. Thankfully, Hailey was safe. Sarah had found her. There weren't a lot of murders in Ottawa, but they did happen. Just a few years back a Carleton University student was found dead near the campus.

Sarah pushed the thought away. Hailey was alive. Concussions were nasty but they did heal, and soon her stepdaughter would have her memory back. Sarah felt sure of that.

Would Hailey recognize her?

Good thing she'd been smart enough to grab the picture of the three of them that sat on the mantel above the fireplace, beside Jack's urn. As she was heading out, she'd turned to his urn to let him know she'd found Hailey and had seen the picture. It could prove useful, especially if Hailey didn't know who Sarah was. The hospital wouldn't release her to Sarah's care until they felt sure Sarah was actually her parent.

What if the picture wasn't good enough?

She'd worry about that if the time came. Right now, she just wanted to get her stepdaughter and bring her home. What happened after, they'd figure it out.

Sarah parked the car and hurried to the emergency department where it took nearly fifteen minutes before someone finally brought her down to see Hailey. When she saw her stepdaughter's black eye, a hand covered her mouth and she felt a sting in the back of her eyes. It probably looked worse than it was, but still, it wasn't something she'd been prepared to see.

"She'll be fine," the nurse said. "Our biggest concern is her memory loss. We'll need to keep her here until we can confirm you are who you say you are."

"Even though I have this picture?"

"Unfortunately," the nurse said. "For everyone's safety."

"Of course," Sarah said.

"You can have a seat," the nurse said. "I'm sure it's been a long night."

"The longest."

The nurse left and an awkward silence settled between Sarah and Hailey. At least it wasn't filled with anger and hatred. It felt more like they were strangers with nothing to talk about.

"I'm glad you'll be okay," Sarah said.

Hailey gave her one of those cautious nods typical between people who didn't really know each other. The silence started to put Sarah to sleep and when her eyes sprang open, it was almost seven thirty.

She'd fallen asleep and now had a horrible kink in her neck. She stood and tried to stretch it out.

"It's better if you pull your opposite arm over your head," Hailey said.

"Hey, you remember that," Sarah said sounding hopeful. "Do you remember anything else?"

"No," Hailey said. "Not sure why I even know that."

"You do a lot of stretching before hockey."

"Hockey?"

Sarah did a couple more stretches and actually felt a bit better. She moved closer to the bed and put her hands on the rails.

"You play hockey," Sarah said. "And you're really good."

"Seriously?" Hailey said, a frown on her face. "I'm so not athletic."

"Actually, you really are," Sarah said. "But hockey is your passion. You've been playing since you were five, I think."

Hailey didn't seem to believe her.

"How's your eye?" Sarah said. "The nurse said it will probably be a week before the swelling starts to go down. I'm really sorry this happened."

"Do you know what happened?"

"No," Sarah said. "You don't remember anything do you?"

Hailey shook her head. "I'm not even sure where I live."

"Forest Creek."

Hailey concentrated on that. Sarah could see she was really trying to make sense of that.

"You don't know where that is?"

"No," Hailey said, frustrated. "Why can't I remember anything? I want to know what happened to me, why my head feels like someone hit me with a baseball bat, and why my ribs feel like I was hit by a train? Apparently, I lost my phone and I had no winter jacket."

Sarah put a hand on Hailey's and was pleased when her step-daughter didn't pull away.

"My things are in that plastic bag."

Sarah looked and all there was was a debit card.

"Your wallet isn't there," Sarah said. "You probably had your driver's licence in it, and your health card. I'll call to cancel your phone. We'll need to reapply for your driver's licence and health card."

Hailey looked like she wanted to cry.

"I know this is frustrating," Sarah said. She handed Hailey the photo. "That's us. You, your dad, me. Last summer. In the backyard. We were having our yearly barbeque with all the other firefighters and their families."

"Why isn't my dad here?"

Sarah felt her heart break. How could she tell Hailey that her dad had died less than two months ago, and that since then their lives had become a horrible mess? She looked into Hailey's one good eye and could see how scared she really was, how little she appeared at this moment. She looked like she wanted Sarah to make everything all right, but Sarah had never been able to make anything all right, certainly not since Jack's accident.

"Your dad died a while ago."

Hailey looked stunned, like she couldn't process what Sarah had just told her. What she would give for Jack to be here with them. He'd make everything right.

"I'm sorry," Sarah added. "I know none of this is making any sense."

"And my mom?"

"Your parents have been divorced a long time," Sarah said. "She left when you were four."

"Is she dead too?"

Sarah pulled in her emotions. "No. But you haven't seen her since she left. As far as I know."

"So, you're all I have?"

"Your grandparents and your uncle are out in B.C."

Sarah could see Hailey trying to make sense of everything she was learning, the frustration on her face heartbreaking.

"So, you're my stepmom and you're all the family I have here?"

"Yes," Sarah said. "And you're all the family I have. My mom died, I don't know my father, and I have no siblings."

"At least you remember those things."

Sarah reached for Hailey's hands again. As bad as she felt for Hailey, she was enjoying the conversation and the lack of tension between them. This is how she wanted their relationship to be. To stay.

"What happened to Dad?"

"He was a firefighter and he died trying to save someone."

"So, he's a hero?"

"I wish he hadn't been," Sarah said before she could stop herself. "Then he might still be here."

"You love him?"

"Very much," she said. "And he loved us."

"What was he like?"

Sarah looked at the picture in Hailey's lap. Both love and anger battled inside of her.

"He took too many damn chances," Sarah said. "I really think he believed that nothing bad could happen to him, but he was wrong. Something horrible happened and we're paying the price for that stubborn heroism."

Sadness filled Hailey's good eye.

"He was my love," Sarah said. "He was my prince. Until I met him, I didn't live. I just made it through each day, hoping for something better, never believing it would ever come my way. When he looked at me, he made me believe that I was special, that my past didn't matter. When he held me, I believed nothing bad could ever happen to me."

She looked at Hailey. This would not have happened if Jack had been around.

"He was the most wonderful father," she said. "He would have done anything for you. When he looked at you, I could tell his heart was breaking he loved you so much. He hated when we . . . didn't get along."

Hailey glanced at her. "Did we not get along?"

"Not always," Sarah admitted.

"Why?"

Sarah's gaze fell on the other bed. It was empty at the moment, though the emergency area was abuzz with activity. The nurses were non-stop, back and forth, in and out of rooms, as were the doctors in attendance. Sarah admired these health care professionals. They were truly amazing.

She wouldn't last a day here.

"I don't know," she said. It was a small lie. Hailey didn't need to be told that she hated Sarah for reasons that were really just known to her. The pre-concussed Hailey anyway.

"When can I go home?"

"I don't know," Sarah said. "Do you remember anything?"

Hailey looked at Sarah, and shook her head.

"I should let Andréa know where you are," Sarah said and pulled her phone to text Andréa. "She's been worried."

"Who is she?"

Sarah looked sad. "Your best friend. Maybe she can come see you and it'll help you remember things."

"Maybe," Hailey said, not convinced.

Sarah texted back and forth with Andréa for a few minutes, told her where Hailey was and that it would be great if she could come visit, and then excused herself to go to the bathroom.

"Andréa should be here in a while," Sarah said when she returned. "I'm going to go get something to eat," Sarah said. "There must be a cafeteria somewhere."

"You'll be back?" Hailey said, sounding a bit panicky.

"I wouldn't leave you, honey," Sarah said. "I'm just starving. Do you want me to bring you back something?"

"Sure."

One of the nurses told Sarah that the cafeteria was just down the hall and there was also a coffee shop on the first floor. She got a couple of cinnamon bagels and a coffee for herself. She wasn't sure if there were any dietary restriction for Hailey. She forgot to ask.

She ate her bagel and drank her coffee while she wondered what would happen when Hailey got her memory back. It was so nice to be having a conversation with her stepdaughter, and the longer this went on the harder it would be when things went back to the way they were.

Because she knew that they would. Hailey's memory loss had to be temporary.

SEVENTEEN

Hailey had started to doze when the nurse came back to check on her. She took her blood pressure, looked into her good eye, and asked her the same questions as earlier. She asked the nurse when she thought she could go home and she got the same response as before.

Hopefully soon.

The nurse left and a teenage girl that looked a lot like her, minus the black eye, came toward her. The girl's smile died quickly when she got a good look at Hailey.

"Ohmygod!" the girl said. "This is so much worse than I expected." She stopped by the railing, not knowing what to do with her hands. She appeared to want to lean in and hug Hailey, but wasn't sure. "How are you doing?"

"I'm okay," Hailey said, uncertain. "It looks worse than it is." She paused. "Are you Andréa?"

The question appeared to upset the girl, as she covered her mouth with a hand. "You don't remember me?"

"Sorry," Hailey said. "But the doctors say my memory should come back anytime, as quickly as it went away."

Andréa reached for Hailey's hand. The touch felt familiar to Hailey, like they'd done this thousands of times. Maybe this was the beginning of the return of her memories. She wouldn't mind. She was tired of being a hostage in this hospital bed. She wanted to get her life back, go home.

"Sarah warned me, but seeing you like this . . . I wish you would have waited for me." Hailey stared blankly at Andréa. "After the game. You left when you got tossed out. We could have talked about it."

"Why did I get tossed out?"

"You took number twelve into the boards pretty hard," Andréa said. "You're lucky she didn't get hurt badly. Probably just a bruise because she was back in the game after a few shifts."

Hailey shook her head. "I don't remember."

"Doesn't matter now," Andréa said. "I'm just glad we were able to find you. Sarah and I were pretty scared last night when we realized you were missing. She really cares about you."

"I know."

"You do?"

"Well, I could see it when she was here earlier," Hailey said. "She does seem nice."

"You need to remember that," Andréa said.

Hailey frowned.

"Trust me on this," Andréa added. "You've not always thought that."

"Why?"

Andréa seemed to think it over. "You've disliked her since the day your dad told you he was going on a date with her. You never gave Sarah a chance."

Hailey was surprised to hear that. She wondered what had happened to make her feel that way. Seemed so unlike her. She really hated not remembering her life. It's like there was this big void where her memories should be, and the more she tried to find where they'd all gone the greater the void grew. She had never realized how much her memories defined who she was.

Without memories, she really was just an empty shell, void of personality, unattached to events and people that should mean the world to her.

"Without my memories," Hailey said. "I don't even know who I am. Do you know how scary that is?"

"I think I can imagine," Andréa said and touched Hailey's arm. "I wish I could do something."

"Tell me who I am."

"You're my best friend," Andréa said. "We met in JK. Your dad walked you into the classroom and spoke to the teacher, and you wouldn't let go of his hand when he tried to leave. You cried forever. Our teacher—can't remember her name—made me go sit beside you. I did not want to be sitting beside a crybaby. I was four. I wasn't a baby."

"You remember that?"

Andréa shrugged. "I know my parents told me the story plenty of times. Our teacher probably told them. I can't be sure if I really remember it all."

"And what happened?"

"I asked you why you were crying and you said your dad didn't want you anymore, so he'd left you at school and you were never going to see him again."

"Really?"

"I laughed," Andréa said. "And you got so mad at me. You said I was stupid and walked away from me. Fine. I went and played with some other girl who wasn't such a crybaby."

"Thanks."

"But Mrs. Whatshername forced me again to go play with you and I eventually went, reluctantly, and started to play with some dolls and I kept trying to give you one but you kept throwing it back into the bucket with the others, and I was getting so annoyed. And then I yelled at you."

"You what?"

"I told you to stop being such a baby, that your dad was coming back in a little while, just like mine was, and we'd get to go home until tomorrow."

"And?"

"You cried even more because you didn't want to come back tomorrow, or the tomorrow after tomorrow. You never wanted to come back at all, ever."

"So how did we become best friends?"

Andréa shook her head. "I have no idea. I didn't play with you again for a long time. I hated you."

"Is any of that true?"

"All of it," Andréa said. "Like I said, my parents told me the story so many times that I think I remember it. Anyway, by the end of JK we'd become inseparable and have been since."

Hailey looked at her friend with her good eye. She didn't remember any of that. She wanted to because this Andréa girl seemed to be really nice, like the sort of friend she'd want, but she had no recollection of knowing her. She was getting really frustrated. She wanted things to speed along so she could get out of here and get back to her life.

"It wasn't until years later that I understood why you'd cried so much," Andréa said. "Your mom had just left and you were afraid your dad was doing the same."

"Sarah said I haven't seen her since I was four, so that would be about the same time we started JK." She paused. "What am I like now?"

"Well, without that shiner, you're gorgeous. All the boys love you but they're also afraid of you. You have this *'don't mess with me'* kind of vibe."

"Me?"

Andréa looked uncomfortable. "Yeah, you kind of do. It's really since your dad died. You've become a bit unpredictable. Angry. Mean."

"We're still friends?"

"Yeah," Andréa said. "I know you're really just a crybaby under that armour. You don't scare me."

"I like you," Hailey said.

"I know."

"Do you think I'll go back to being mean when I get my memory back?"

Andréa hesitated. "I'm not a doctor, but probably. I'd think you'll be back to who you were."

Hailey thought about that. "And Sarah and I didn't get along?"

"It's more you than her."

Hailey stayed quiet. She didn't look at Andréa, instead she was looking at Sarah who was standing quietly behind her friend. She didn't know how long Sarah had been there, but probably long enough to have heard some of the conversation. Was that why Hailey didn't like her? Because she was a sneak? Because she spied on Hailey?

ভ ৎ

Sarah hadn't wanted to intrude, so she'd remained in the background, but she saw how Hailey was glaring at her and she figured her stepdaughter might be remembering how things were between them.

She had so hoped to have that tension between them stay forgotten. It had been nice to speak with Hailey earlier, to be able to show her stepdaughter she cared.

"Hey, I got you a cinnamon bagel with cream cheese," Sarah said and handed it to Hailey. "You love them."

"Oh."

"You do," Andréa added. "We wouldn't lie to you."

Hailey took a bite and found that she did like it. She devoured the rest in five bites.

"I was starving," she said.

"No kidding," Andréa said.

"I hope I didn't interrupt?" Sarah said. "I saw the two of you talking and it was so nice. I didn't want to stop it. I wasn't eavesdropping."

She was looking at Hailey.

"No big secrets were being told," Andréa said. "I was just telling Hailey things about herself, hoping it might help with her memory."

"Did it?" Sarah said.

Hailey shook her head. "No. I still don't remember Andréa being my best friend or you being my stepmom. Or my dad dying."

"It's been hard on us," Sarah said. "He meant a lot to the both of us."

Even if you didn't like sharing him with me, Sarah thought. *I loved him and losing him has been the worst thing in my life.*

"I'm sorry for fighting with you," Hailey said.

Sarah offered a soft smile. How long had she wanted to hear that? Too bad it wasn't the Hailey she knew who was saying those words. It was nice, but she was fairly sure they'd be short lived.

She did her best to hide her doubts.

"Me, too."

"Can we go home?" Hailey said.

"I'll go ask," Sarah said and left.

Minutes later, a doctor came to check on Hailey, and since the hospital had been able to confirm that Hailey was who Sarah and Andréa claimed she was, and they also had confirmed that she did live at 1025 Rushmore Road in Forest Creek, and there didn't appear to be any brain swelling, they released her into the care of Sarah.

"Is it okay if I come over?" Andréa asked.

"I think that would be a good idea," Sarah said to Andréa before they headed in different directions to their respective cars. She and Hailey climbed into their Outback. "Buckle up."

Hailey figured it out.

"You okay?" Sarah said.

Hailey put on a brave face. "I guess."

"The doctor said it could take a few days."

192 | François Houle

"Or weeks."

"Hopefully, it won't take that long," Sarah said and backed out of her parking spot. "Hopefully."

C3 80

When they pulled into the long driveway, Hailey tried to coax out any memory that would tell her this was her home, but there was nothing but emptiness. It was a nice-looking farmhouse, that seemed to have a big addition on the left side and a two and half car garage, but none of it looked familiar.

"Nice place."

"It's been in your family for a long time. Belonged to your great-grandparents, if I remember."

Hailey gave her a look.

"Sorry," Sarah said and pulled the car into the garage. "Well, you're home."

"Home," Hailey said and stepped out of the car. She followed Sarah to the front door. When they stepped in, she stood in the foyer and took it all in—stairs to the basement straight ahead while stairs to the second floor seemed to curve around the railing that surrounded the basement stairwell. To the left, a spacious living room. To the right, a huge closet and then a den. Across the way she could see a magnificent stone fireplace in a great big room.

Something on the floor barked at her.

"Ohmygod!" she said and bent down. "You are so adorable. What's your name?"

"Her name is Peanut."

"Fitting," Hailey said. "Can I pick her up?"

"I'm sure that's what she's waiting for."

"How long have we had her?"

"Your dad brought her home last summer," Sarah said. "She's about nine months."

"She's so adorable."

"Yeah," Sarah said. "She sure is."

Hailey stood with Peanut in her arms who was going crazy licking her face.

"I guess she likes me."

"She does," Sarah said. "She was pretty sad all night long. She could tell I was worried that you weren't home."

Hailey looked at Sarah. "I'm sorry."

"Not your fault," Sarah said. "I'm just glad it wasn't worse."

"What do you mean?" Hailey said. "This is pretty bad."

"I'm just happy you're alive."

"Oh," Hailey said. "I guess whoever hit me could have killed me."

Sarah touched Hailey's arm. "You're home and that's all that matters."

"Thanks," she said. "Can I see my room?"

"Yeah," Sarah said. "Up the stairs. It's the room at the end of the hallway, before it goes left."

"Can I bring Peanut?"

"Of course." Sarah watched Hailey move tentatively about the house, like someone who didn't feel completely comfortable. It was sadly cute.

Minutes later, Andréa arrived and Sarah let her in.

"How is she?"

"Like a lost puppy," Sarah said. "It's just so nice to have her not hate me."

"I know," Andréa said. "Maybe that part of her memory will stay lost."

Sarah looked forlorn. "That would be only getting a part of her back."

"The nice part," Andréa said and headed up the stairs.

Sarah watched her go. She couldn't deny that it wouldn't be unpleasant to only get the nice part of Hailey back, but she knew it didn't work that way. When Hailey's memory returned, she'd have to deal with whatever came with it. She had been for the last two years. She would handle it for as long as she needed to. This was her home, her future.

And Hailey was her family.

 C3 80

Hailey was sitting on her bed when Andréa let herself in. They looked at each other, Peanut desperately trying to escape Hailey's grasp.

She put the dog down and she ran to Andréa.

"Guess she knows you."

"Been here once or twice," Andréa said. "So, seeing your room, does it bring back anything?"

Hailey did the visual tour. She frowned at all the hockey paraphernalia on her wall, the trophies on her bookshelf, the poster of Brady Tkachuk on the back of her closet door, as if she was hiding a dirty secret.

"Okay, I get it. I'm into hockey."

"Yep."

"But why does all the furniture look homemade?"

"Because your dad loved to make things."

"I thought he was a firefighter?"

"He was," Andréa said. "And firefighters have a lot of time on their hands."

"Oh."

"He built your furniture, built the deck around the pool, built the huge shed in the backyard. He's been fixing this house since forever. He'd finish one thing and start another."

Hailey just took it all in. It felt rather strange that Andréa knew her dad better than she did. Andréa knew her whole life better than she remembered.

"You look tired?"

"I guess," Hailey said. "It's just . . . do you have any idea how this feels? Like it's someone else's life that I just stole. I have no idea who this Hailey was. None whatsoever. It's really kind of freaking me out. What if my memory doesn't come back? I know you're my friend, best friend, but to me, right now, you're really a stranger. And so is Sarah. And even this cute little dog. I don't remember any of it."

Andréa sat beside her. "I know it's got to be weird."

"It's beyond weird. It's freaking me out."

"There is a bright side."

Hailey glared at her. "I don't see how."

"It's giving you a chance to get to know Sarah without prejudice."

Hailey didn't say anything to that. It just made her wonder what sort of relationship she'd had with her stepmom. She also wondered what sort of father her dad had been, why her mother had left, and why she was afraid of getting her memory back.

She didn't sound like she'd been very nice.

EIGHTEEN

The police phoned three days later to tell Sarah that they had a car registered to a Jack Cormier out on Third Avenue in the Glebe. Neighbours had complained that it had been there for days and was taking a parking space away from them. If the car was still there in two hours, it would be towed.

She got the address, and since she couldn't have Hailey drive the car back home—other than the fact that she'd lost her driver's licence, with her concussion she wasn't allowed to drive because there was no knowing if she remembered how—Sarah texted Andréa and she agreed to go with her get the car.

"This looks familiar," Andréa said when Sarah turned onto Third Avenue. "Corpus Christi Elementary School. Oh, I know where we are."

Sarah glanced at her in the rear-view mirror. "Where?"

"Hailey's mom lives here."

Sarah had had a feeling. What other reason would Hailey have had to park the car here? She spotted the older Outback and pulled behind it.

"My mom lives here?" Hailey said as she looked at the house the car was parked in front of.

"I don't think it's this house," Andréa said. "I think it was the second one from the corner."

Both Sarah and Hailey looked that way. It was a well-maintained house. They all were. Glebe people were almost of another class. Houses weren't on the cheap side here, many creeping past a million, some hitting two million.

"Why would I do that?" Hailey said. "Was I looking for her?"

"Only you can answer that," Sarah said. She had to admit she didn't really care to be this close to Jack's ex-wife. As rocky as her relationship with Hailey was, she didn't want Hailey to have any sort of contact with her mother. Not after what Jack had told her about the woman. Hailey was better off staying away. Except, it was a bit late for that.

Sarah looked at Hailey and couldn't help but feel a little jealous. She wondered if Hailey had actually met her mother before her memory loss, but then felt stupid because even if Hailey had, it must not have gone well. Why else would her stepdaughter abandon her car and end up downtown where she was assaulted?

ભ ૪૦

Hailey took the passenger seat while Andréa sat behind the wheel. Since her and Hailey were the same height, Andréa didn't need to adjust anything. She started the car and pulled past Sarah. They were going to try and follow each other but if they got separated by traffic, they agreed to just meet back at the house.

"D'you remember talking to your mom?"

Hailey was looking out the side window, completely lost. She had no recollection of ever being here. If she could at least remember things before the concussion, something from her past, she wouldn't feel like such of a stranger in her own skin. But there was nothing.

Nothing.

That was scary. How could you lose all the memories that made up your life? That's what we really were, the sum of our experiences and memories. Right now, she was hollow, a big void of nothingness.

She wanted to scream.

Being nothing made her skin crawl. This morning, she had looked in the mirror after her shower, and she hadn't recognized her own face. The harder she'd looked, the less she'd seen.

"I don't remember being here. If I did talk to her, I have no idea what she told me."

"Must have upset you quite a lot."

Hailey turned her head quickly toward her friend. "I don't remember, okay? I don't remember a damn thing and you keeping on asking will not make me remember any more. It's like someone carved out my brain and left this big empty lunchbox."

"I didn't mean to upset you," Andréa said. "I'm just trying to help."

"It's not helping," Hailey said in a weary and frustrated voice. She closed her eyes and let the car rock her into a semi-coma. She was tired of trying to remember. "I just want to go home."

Andréa made a right on Chamberlain Avenue, drove under the Queensway, made a left on Catherine Street and another left on Lyon before merging with the westbound traffic on the Queensway.

"We'll be home soon," she said. "Have a nap."

"I'm sorry," Hailey said. "I know you're my friend and you're trying to help me. It's just so frustrating, you know, not to remember. I just want to remember. I just want to feel normal again."

"I know."

"If I hadn't gone to find my mother, none of this would have happened," she said. "Why else would the car be there? I must have gone to find her, talk to her. After the hockey game, right? But why? Why did I want to find her now? And what did she do or say to me that I ended up getting attacked."

"Do you remember being attacked?"

"No," she said and winced. Her head was throbbing and her ribs still hurt. "Not the actual attack, but I know that I was by looking in the mirror."

"I'm sorry I wasn't there for you."

Neither said more. Hailey watched the buildings along the highway pass by in a blur. She needed answers. Not knowing, not recognizing someone who's supposed to be her best friend, was driving her crazy. It had been four days and not a sign of recognition had even come close to flirting with her. Next week, Christmas holidays would be over, but how could she go back to school when she couldn't remember anything they'd been learning? She'd be like a five-year-old in a grade twelve class.

The thought horrified her.

And all those strangers staring at her, expecting her to know who they were. There's no way she could go back until her memories returned. What if it took months? She'd lose the year and have to redo grade twelve. The thought appealed to her about as much as getting a lobotomy. The irony of her thoughts didn't escape her. Still, the longer this ordeal went on, the worse her life would be.

The scenery changed to forests and fields. The traffic was lighter.

"Where are we?"

"Heading south on the 416," Andréa said. "We'll be home in about fifteen minutes."

Hailey had no idea where she was. She'd lived her whole life in the Ottawa region, and right now she might as well have been in Russia. She closed her eyes and felt her body shake. This was so bad it was funny.

She wanted to cry.

She thought of Peanut. At least she could remember the little dog's name, so that must be something. Maybe she wasn't going to lose the new memories she was making. It wasn't much, but for now it gave her some comfort. Before she had left the hospital, the doctor had told her baby steps, to have a bit of patience. She could wake up one morning and have all of her memories back.

She didn't want baby steps, she wanted those memories back right now. Maybe if she bumped her head again, they'd all suddenly come back. Didn't that happen in movies?

But life wasn't a movie.

It should be. A snap of the fingers and all would be back to normal.

Hailey let out a loud frustrated breath. Andréa eased the car onto the exit ramp and at the light, she turned right. They drove past farmlands. The road was very bumpy, full of potholes. The traffic light changed and Andréa slowed down quickly and some yahoo behind them honked his horn. Hailey glared at him and the moron made all sorts of hand gestures.

She flipped him the finger.

Andréa laughed. "At least you remember what that means."

Hailey grinned. "Guess so."

The light changed and Andréa turned left and followed the Jock River. They drove right through Richmond and five minutes later the Forest Creek sign came into view.

"Almost home," Andréa said.

Hailey remained quiet. It was pretty here. But it didn't look familiar at all. Which was weird because just a couple hours ago they'd come the other way. But maybe that was why she didn't recognize anything. They'd been going the opposite way.

When Andréa pulled into the long driveway, Hailey recognized where she was.

"Home."

ᝯ ᝯ

Sarah tried to follow Andréa but the girl had a bit of a heavy foot and Sarah was woolgathering. She was worried about Hailey. Losing her memory like that must be scary. She tried to imagine not recognizing where she lived, the people she should know, even her little Peanut, and she got chills.

She also wondered what could have happened at Hailey's mom's? It couldn't have been good otherwise Hailey would have stayed with her mother and none of this would have happened. Sarah was pretty sure that Hailey was going to be devastated when she remembered what she talked to her mother about.

Sarah was also thinking about the flower shop. She was meeting her financial advisor Friday morning. He was coming by the house at ten. She was excited but also quite nervous. She kept telling herself that Jack would be behind her one hundred percent, so really, she was the one holding herself back. She had never done anything this big before.

Exciting.

Scary.

And there was a little bit of Hailey's angst in Sarah right now. She almost wished her mother were still around so that she could show her how she'd managed to make a life for herself regardless of the shitty circumstances her mom had trapped her in.

Her mother was her fuel to be better. This was the reason why she wouldn't give up on Hailey, no matter how bad it might get when she got her memory back. It would come back. She believed in what the doctor had told them. It was just a matter of time. The trauma had to run its course, her brain had to heal, and Hailey would be back to her old self.

Sarah just had to believe that Hailey's angst wasn't personal, that deep down it wasn't Sarah she hated. It was her own mother. And she was hoping that once Hailey did remember what had happened Sunday, that she would stop projecting her anger at Sarah and direct it at the person who deserved Hailey's wrath.

She knew it wasn't going to be that simple. She knew the two of them were in for some more tough times. She knew that if she could be the strong person Jack always told her that she was, she and Hailey would come out of this eventually.

Eventually.

That seemed so open ended. Sarah wanted an expiry date, a target she could focus on. She wanted to see the light at the end of the tunnel.

As long as it wasn't a runaway train.

Sarah shook her head. She was becoming a little melodramatic. She'd always been a black and white sort of girl. Hadn't known anything else. Until Jack.

He'd painted colours into her world.

Oh, Jack.

He'd made her believe in a better life. No, he'd shown her what a better life was. She was living that better life. No, it wasn't full of monetary riches, although she was grateful there was some money. His love, his good heart, his belief that there was good in everyone if you looked deep enough.

He'd found it in her.

And she'd found that she could trust again. All she had to do now was show Hailey that she could trust Sarah to always be there for her.

That's really all Sarah wanted.

She pulled the car into the driveway, parked it in the garage, and went to see if Hailey had made a miraculous recovery on the drive home.

NINETEEN

The following Monday, Hailey knocked on Sarah's bedroom door and let herself in once her stepmom told her to come in. She looked a bit out of sorts and paced back and forth across the room, pulling on the ends of her pyjama top, biting her lips, twirling her hair.

"What's the matter?" Sarah said. She had been reading in bed.

"I have school today."

"Right," Sarah said and put her book on the night table, beside the framed picture she'd taken to the hospital with her. "You probably shouldn't go yet."

"I have no idea what we've been learning," Hailey said. "How am I supposed to pick up where we left off before Christmas?"

"I'll call the school and explain what happened," Sarah said. "We'll tell them we don't know when you'll be back."

"I'd appreciate that," Hailey said. "It's not that I don't know anything. I know how to add and multiply, and I can spell. But I have no idea what I've been learning in grade twelve. I'm not sure about any of my high school years. I don't even remember Andréa and we've been friends since JK. So basically, I remember nothing."

Sarah swung her legs over and stood. She hesitated a moment and then hugged Hailey, who let out a small cry.

"Sorry," Sarah said and pulled away. "Your ribs are still tender?"

"Yeah," Hailey said. "The hug was nice."

"I wish I could make it all better," Sarah said. "Over the last two years, I've really come to think of you as my own daughter."

Hailey studied Sarah. "You're still a stranger to me."

"I know."

"Maybe if you told me about you, I'd feel like I know you a little. I do seem to remember new things."

Sarah shifted her weight, a feeling of discomfort folding the skin of her forehead into a frown. "Why don't I call the school and then make breakfast. You love cheese omelettes and I've been getting better at making them."

"Sounds yummy," Hailey said. Then she made a face. "A seventeen-year-old probably doesn't talk like that."

Sarah smiled. "Don't be hard on yourself. And it does sound yummy. I'll toast some English muffins and we can smother them with peanut butter."

At the sound of her name, Peanut started to bark, her way of letting them know that she was here, too.

"Can you take her down and let her out while I go to the bathroom?" Sarah said. "And I'll call your school right after."

"Yeah, no problem."

"And give her some fresh water and a scoop of her food. It's in the pantry."

"I remember from watching you."

"Great."

"Come little Peanut," Hailey said and left the room. "Let's go get some breaky."

Peanut yelped with the enthusiasm of a puppy who had just scored the biggest, juiciest bone in the county. Down in the kitchen, Hailey let the dog out and cleaned out her bowls and refilled them with water and food, and then she went to the fridge and took out some eggs, milk, and cheddar cheese. She grabbed the grater and grated a good helping for the omelettes. She cut up some tomato slices, found the English muffins in the fridge and carefully cut them so they could be toasted, and sat at the island waiting for Sarah to come down.

She liked Sarah. She was nice.

Her phone chirped and she looked at the text that had just come. It was from Madelaine.

Who was Madelaine?

Hailey started to text Andréa. They'd been texting all weekend, and although she still couldn't remember their old friendship, the new friendship was going along pretty well. Sometimes Hailey thought she could remember when she and Andréa were a lot younger, like in elementary school, but she couldn't be quite certain.

Do I know Madelaine?

Yeah, she's one of your new friends from this year.

She wants to know what I'm wearing.

She's all about fashion.

I'm just wearing PJs. Waiting for Sarah to make omelettes.

I guess you're not going to school?

Sarah is going to call the school and tell them. I'm just going to be lost.

I guess you would be.

Maybe you can tell everyone what happened?

I'll tell them. Don't be surprised if you get a bunch of texts from people you don't know.

Maybe just tell them not to bother.

Sure. They probably won't listen.

What do I tell Madelaine?

Just tell her you're not feeling well and won't be at school today. She'll probably pester you with a bunch of other texts but the old Hailey would just ignore her.

Oh. Okay.

I'll come over after school and relieve you of your boredom.

Okay.

Hailey texted Madelaine and Andréa was right, Madelaine sent five texts one after the other, obviously not waiting to get answers from Hailey. She wasn't sure she liked Madelaine. She seemed needy.

Oh, well. Andréa had told her that the old Hailey would just ignore Madelaine, so that's what she was going to do. She turned her phone face down on the counter and started to get a little impatient waiting for Sarah.

She was starving.

ℭ ℬ

Sarah went to grab another roll of toilet paper from the bathroom cupboard when a little box of tampons caught her attention. She grabbed the toilet paper, but kept staring at the tampons.

She couldn't remember the last time she'd used one. So much had happened in the last two months, could it be possible her periods had been thrown off schedule? She could see maybe missing one, but two? She got on the scale and waited for the numbers to appear.

Six pounds.

She'd gained six pounds since Jack's accident. She knew she'd been binging on carb heavy foods, and her chocolate cravings were enough to drive her crazy lately, but that didn't mean anything.

Nothing at all.

But she was pretty sure she'd gained another pound since Christmas.

Six pounds?

She was just eating too much. Because of the stress. That's all it was. Stress.

Sarah replaced the new roll of toilet paper, looked at herself sideways in the mirror, and left a reminder on her phone to pick up a pregnancy test kit next time she was out.

Rule it out before she started to obsess over the possibility that she might be pregnant. She'd still been on birth control when Jack had died, but now she couldn't remember if she'd missed some in the haze that followed Jack's death.

And she remembered that last morning together.

A knock on the bathroom door. "Sarah, will you be much longer?"

"Sorry I'm taking so long."

"Did you call my school?"

She crunched her face. "I'll do it right now."

"I got cheese grated and English muffins in the toaster," Hailey said, sounding tired.

"Are you okay?"

"I have a bit of a headache."

"Don't do too much," Sarah said. "I was reading up on concussions, and they can last a long time. I appreciate you helping out, but just go lay down and I'll finish breakfast in a minute. After I call your school."

She waited to hear Hailey walk away and then phoned the school. Just before leaving the bathroom, she glanced once more at the cupboard where her tampons were and tried to deny that she was getting excited about the possibility that might exist.

She put a hand on her stomach.

Switched the light off and headed down to the kitchen to make omelettes. She hoped that the food might just trigger something in Hailey.

"Talked to Mrs. Charbonneau at the school office and explained what's going on. I promised we'd keep them up to date with your recovery."

"Thanks."

Sarah saw that Hailey had everything out and ready so she picked up where her stepdaughter had stopped, and within ten minutes they were sitting at the island devouring the best omelettes Sarah had ever put together.

"I appreciate everything you're doing for me," Hailey said.

Sarah took Hailey's hand and was grateful these moments of closeness weren't being shunned. If only things could stay this way when Hailey got her memory back.

Maybe if Sarah was pregnant, it would change a lot of things. She needed to go get that kit soon because if she didn't find out, it was going to drive her nuts. And what would she do about the flower shop if she did find out she was carrying Jack's baby?

A baby certainly would change everything. She had no idea how to care for one. And she'd be doing it on her own, without her husband's help. If Sarah was pregnant, it would all be up to her to do everything. She couldn't count on Hailey. Her stepdaughter was a ticking time bomb.

A matter of when she got her memory back.

Her enthusiasm waned a bit. A baby now wouldn't exactly be great timing. Not when she'd finally made up her mind about getting her own business. That would be too much work to care for a baby at the same time.

"You look sad?" Hailey said.

Sarah feigned a smile. "I'm just worried about you."

"Afraid I'll be back to my old self when I get my memories back?"

Sarah shrugged.

"Andréa told me we don't get along."

"It's been hard since your dad died."

"She said I wasn't really nice even before Dad died."

Sarah looked at Hailey, compassion filling her eyes. She was really trying to make amends and Sarah wanted to grab it and stow it away, but she knew that wouldn't guarantee they'd be the best of friends when the time came. On Friday, when she'd met her financial advisor and he'd supported her plan—they just needed to know what kind of money Ruth would ask for and then her advisor would be able to prepare a complete financial plan—Sarah had entertained the idea that maybe Hailey could help her at the flower shop after school and next summer. Maybe the shop would bring them closer.

It had been a silly thought, she knew. She couldn't expect Hailey to feel any sort of enthusiasm for the shop, or feel any sort of obligation to help Sarah. She'd probably argue that the store wasn't her idea so why should she help?

Sarah knew Hailey wouldn't be wrong to think that way, but it didn't mean she couldn't hope for them to bond somehow, so why not around the business? She had never bonded with her mother, but they hadn't had the kind of life to find anything to bond over. Ironically, Sarah had followed in her mother's footsteps, but she knew she hadn't had any real choice. A girl who didn't finish grade ten didn't have many options.

That life seemed so long ago now, like it had happened to someone else, someone Sarah had known but couldn't quite remember.

"You're a teenager," Sarah said. "It's your job to make adults miserable." She smiled tenderly at Hailey. "Don't worry about it."

"I didn't make my dad's life miserable?"

No, you didn't, Sarah thought. But voicing those thoughts wasn't going to score her any points. She recalled many times when it had taken her all the willpower she could summon not to retaliate toward Hailey, not to let herself act like an angry teenager. She had wanted to, mostly because she hadn't had the luxury of doing it when she was Hailey's age. She'd been too busy surviving the streets or some other asshole her mom happened to shack up with. So many times, Sarah had wanted to tell Hailey about her shitty life so that her stepdaughter could just stop bitching about how horrible hers was. She had no idea what real hardship was.

Well, maybe she did now. Sarah knew that losing her dad was extremely difficult on Hailey, and she wondered, as she sat and eyed her stepdaughter, if part of her memory loss might not be some sort of psychological barrier Hailey had erected to forget her father's accident. Maybe Hailey just didn't want to remember because those memories were just too painful.

She was no shrink so she let that thought simply dissipate like smoke.

"You loved him."

"I think I remember him being funny, like he loved to tell jokes. Is that true?"

Sarah lost herself in something that happened last summer. Not exactly a joke—Sarah was horrible at remembering jokes— but a really great moment one Saturday afternoon by the pool. Hailey had invited Andréa, Sylvie, and Jessie over and they'd played games of volleyball in the pool for hours. Jack had cooked chicken kabobs on the barbecue for them all and after the girls had all turned in for the night, she and Jack had sat around the fire pit in the backyard and she had looked at the star-speckled sky and had known she had never been this happy. And with her friends around, Hailey had been spectacularly wonderful.

"He had a kind and gentle heart," Sarah said. "He loved to do things to try and get us closer. We were his two girls and he loved us so much."

"I miss him."

Sarah looked at Hailey, wondering if her stepdaughter was really missing him because she actually remembered her dad, or she was just saying it in rote.

"I think," Hailey added, as if talking to herself. She turned to Sarah. "Can I miss him if I don't quite have any recent memories of him being around?"

Sarah shrugged. "You must have some memories."

"Not really sure."

"Just don't get too discouraged," Sarah said. She'd done a little internet searching and had memorised a few things. "People generally don't remember certain events, or chunks of time. Like, it might make sense that you can't remember the last three or four years, but you'd remember the years before that."

"I want to remember everything now."

"I know, but try not to let it upset you," Sarah said. "Maybe if you could talk about things you do remember, that it might speed up your recovery. Maybe once you start to think about things, it might be like a snowball effect and your amnesia will go away."

"That's dumb," Hailey said but looked unsure. "Isn't it?"

"I don't know," Sarah said. "Maybe I shouldn't be reading things on the internet."

"I do know what that is," Hailey said. "And I know how to use my phone and text. I knew how to grate cheese and cut up the English muffins."

"You're doing those on auto-pilot."

"Maybe," she said. "But it's because I know how to do them. So, maybe you're not wrong. I do remember some things, just not what happened in the last few years."

"Can you think of something?"

Hailey tried hard to remember something, anything. Sarah thought Hailey looked like a kid who was constipated and tried her best not to laugh. Laughing would not be taken kindly, she was sure of that.

Still, Hailey looked years younger as she tried to pull a memory from the depth of her amnesia.

"You guys got married here, in the backyard," she said, awe filling her eyes. "And you asked me to be your maid-of-honour."

Sadness toyed with Sarah. The only reason Hailey had agreed was because Jack had given her a stern talking to and he'd told her she'd be grounded for weeks if she ruined their wedding day.

The weather, unseasonably warm for early November, had done what Hailey couldn't. Just when they were about to say their vows, the sky opened up and chased everyone inside. Sarah's dress was soaked and her hair had flattened against her scalp. She'd been so devastated until Jack, being Jack, had joked that God was such a crybaby and a sucker for a beautiful wedding that he'd started to bawl like an old lady. Seeing as most of the guests were firefighters, their wives and families, as well as Jack's parents, his brother, and his brother's then-girlfriend, had all erupted in laughter. The reverend had quickly run through the vows so that Jack and Sarah could peel off their wet wedding clothes as soon as they could before catching a chill, and the day had actually turned out pretty decent.

Hailey had disappeared into her room and hadn't even been present to hear the vows.

"I did."

"And it rained like crazy," Hailey said. "We all got wet."

"We did."

Sarah saw a shadow of shame cross Hailey's beautiful face and her stepdaughter turned away. Of all memories, this was the first one to come back. Sarah wondered why? Was it the day Hailey decided she hated her new stepmom? Was it the day that filled Hailey with anger? Was it the day that had left the biggest negative impact on Hailey's life?

Jack had assured Sarah that Hailey would come around, but he'd been wrong. He hadn't been wrong very often, and she knew he'd wanted to believe that his daughter would eventually accept that he'd met someone who made him happy, that he loved.

Jack had desperately wanted them to be a family, a close and loving family.

Sarah pressed her lips into a tight line. Would all of Hailey's memories come crashing in like unstoppable ocean waves now, a fury of nature that couldn't be stopped?

The thought left Sarah unsettled. It had been so nice to enjoy her stepdaughter's company, to sit and talk like they were good friends, maybe even mother and daughter.

She should be happy that Hailey might be getting her memories back, but a feeling of uneasiness settled into the pit of her stomach.

Sarah got up and started to clean up the dirty dishes.

TWENTY

H ailey was sitting on the floor with her back against the end of her bed while Andréa was lying face down on the bed above her. She could almost feel her friend breathing on top of her head, which wasn't entirely pleasant.

Andréa had come over after school like she'd promised and Hailey had asked Sarah if she minded finishing the Hallmark movie they'd been watching on her own while she and Andréa went up to her room.

"Of course not," Sarah had said.

After her memory of the wedding had come and intruded between her and Sarah, Hailey had felt awkward. She'd felt bad about ruining her dad and Sarah's wedding day, and although she'd had nothing to do with the bad weather, she hadn't stuck around to make the day as special as it should have been for them.

She'd only been thinking of herself.

Something between her and Sarah had turned a little uncomfortable, even a little icy as they'd settled to watch the movie. Neither had said much.

Sarah had mentioned she needed to go out, but had made no effort to get dressed and actually go do her errands. Instead, her stepmom had parked herself on the couch and found a movie; Hailey had eventually made her way from the kitchen to sit beside Sarah. She'd wanted to talk about her memory, about what had happened at the wedding, but in the end Hailey hadn't been able to find the right words and had chosen to say nothing.

And now she was sitting on the floor in her room, wondering what might come next. She wanted her memory back, all of it, and soon. She hated to be imprisoned in not knowing who she was, who Sarah was, who her friends were. She wanted to remember her dad.

She wanted to know what had happened to her that Sunday she went looking for her mom and ended up in the hospital with a big black hole in her life.

Most of all, she wanted to know the girl who looked back at her in the mirror. She had tried to explain to Andréa what it was like to see a stranger staring back at her, but she knew her words had fallen short of making her friend really understand the gripping malaise that turned her stomach every time those beautiful green eyes asked the same question.

Who are you?

She was an attractive seventeen-year-old high school student who was an amazing hockey player, had lots of friends, and whose dad had been a firefighter.

Those words should describe who she was, but instead they were words without context, words lost in a void of amnesia, floating aimlessly like big fat snowflakes looking for a place to land in a vast landscape that sprawled endlessly.

"I remember that it rained when my dad and Sarah got married," she said, uncertain. "But I also saw the wedding picture on the mantel in the great room so I can't be really sure if it's a true memory of the day or not."

"Can you see that it's raining in the picture?"

"No," she said. "I guess it was taken before."

"Maybe you do remember then."

"Maybe."

They remained quiet for a few minutes more. Hailey could hear Andréa fiddling with her phone so she assumed she was texting someone, probably Madelaine, telling her not much was happening over here.

"Do I have a boyfriend?"

Andréa put her phone down on the bed in front of her and a hint of a grin toyed with her lips. "No, but you sure wished Connor would ask you out."

"Is he cute?"

"He's tall and has unruly sandy blonde hair that just barely touches his shoulders. He's got a birthmark on his neck which looks like he's got a permanent hickey. He's smart, but I guess not when it comes to reading you."

"Oh," Hailey said.

Andréa grabbed her phone and flipped through some pictures. "Here."

Hailey took Andréa's phone and looked at the picture. She flipped through a few others. I guess they were her friends.

"He is kind of cute," Hailey said. "But I'm not sure he's my type."

Andréa burst out laughing. "Oh, just wait until you remember."

"Really?"

"Really."

Who was this other Hailey? Or better yet, who was the Hailey that was currently sitting on the bedroom floor of a room she barely remembered? This Hailey must be an impostor, a fraudulent impersonator who was doing an awful job of filling in while the real Hailey took her sweet time drifting through the land of amnesia . . . as if she was on some holiday of discovery.

More like a trip through the bowels of hell. She remembered reading The Gunslinger series by Stephen King a few years back and . . . she remembered how creepy those worlds The Gunslinger kept falling into were.

She remembered.

A hint of a headache put pressure at the back of her head and she felt slightly nauseated.

But she was remembering.

That was just before her dad had met Sarah. She was sure of that. It was her horror phase and her black phase—a thirteen-year-old who was no longer a geeky kid but wasn't a true teenager yet. She was trying, like all the other kids in her grade, but she could see the older teenagers laughing at them and shaking their heads. Too old to play with the children, but too young to fit in with the older crowd.

The wasteland of adolescence.

That's why she'd taken to The Gunslinger series. She was The Gunslinger, lost in the badlands of her life, never knowing what horrors awaited her at every turn.

Like her dad falling for a girl who was way too young for him. Like Hailey falling for a guy who was too immature for her. Like her dad going to work one day, a day like any other day, and never coming home.

A wave of dizziness made her pause. The headaches and dizzy spells had become common since her attack, and when they happened, she usually just crawled into bed and curled up under her covers until they passed or she fell asleep. With Andréa here she couldn't do that, so she just sat on the floor, her eyes closed, waiting for the dizziness to go away.

The headache would linger as it always did.

But today was a bit different. She could feel memories rushing to the forefront of her thoughts, things she'd had trouble remembering just yesterday, like getting that phone call from the fire chief the day her dad died and feeling the weight of his loss collapse her world. But other things were still a mystery, like her relationship with Sarah and what had actually happened two Sundays ago.

And she still didn't feel anything for Connor, even though Andréa kept telling her she *really* liked him. He still didn't look like the sort of guy she'd go for, but then again, she had no idea what sort of guy she would go for. Maybe her memory would just trickle a little bit at a time, like a leaky faucet, a drop here and a drop there. An old memory followed by a newer memory, followed by a long gap while the next one tried to find its way in the maze of her brain, looking to find that elusive door back into her consciousness.

"Maybe I'm into girls?" she said once the dizziness passed.

Andréa chuckled. "You're not into girls. You're into Connor. Just don't worry about it. He's not going anywhere. No one is going to steal him while you recover."

"I'm not feeling it."

"Then ignore it for now," Andréa said and came to sit beside Hailey on the floor. "It's no big deal."

"Not for you," she said. "You're not the one with the great big hole in her life."

"Indirectly, I am."

Hailey glared at her.

"You're my great big hole," Andréa said. "I miss my best friend. You're an okay stand in, but—"

"That's not funny," she said. "It's not like I'm doing it on purpose. Trust me, I wish none of it had happened. I wish I hadn't been thrown out of the game and gone to find my mother, and then got my life mysteriously knocked right out of me. It's not been a party to live in my head this past week. I hate not remembering who I am or who you or Connor or Madelaine are. At night, I lie in my bed and stare into the darkness of my room and it's like looking into the nothingness of my memories. I hate it."

Andréa took her hand. "It's only been eight days."

"Eight long days," Hailey said, close to tears. "I feel like my life is on hold, like I'm not in control of anything. Someone is pulling strings and I'm just a dummy without a brain."

"You're no dummy."

"Maybe not normally, but right now it seems to fit."

Andréa pulled Hailey into her arms and Hailey let her. She had no idea if this was normal in their friendship, but she sure needed to feel someone comfort her and help her carry this burden. Even if her ribs were killing her.

She couldn't do it alone. Alone was a very lonely word.

"It will work out," Andréa said, sounding motherly. "Things always do for Hailey Cormier."

"Do they really?"

"Yeah, they do."

Hailey wasn't sure if Andréa was being serious or not, but she didn't care at that moment. If it took a lie from her best friend to keep her going, then Andréa really was her best friend. Only a best friend would lie to you when it was the only way to help you.

CB ED

Sarah was sitting on the toilet holding the pregnancy test stick in her hand, unable to decide how she felt.

After the movie had ended, she'd thrown on a pair of jeans and a thick cozy sweater, and had driven to the drug store and bought the kit. She'd sneaked passed Hailey's room and closed her bedroom door, and then had sat on the toilet for fifteen minutes before peeing.

She stared at the stick.

She had no idea how she felt, how she should be feeling, what she wanted to feel. Relief? Excitement? Concern? Fear? Disappointment? Anxiousness?

She wished Jack were here. He'd be able to tell her how she should feel. Things would be so different if he were here. He'd find the right words. He always did.

She longed to hear his voice, his strong and calming voice. It was fading from her memory. Funny how she'd heard it every day for almost three years and only two months after his death, she was beginning to forget what he sounded like. Shouldn't it take years?

Why did he have to get killed?

He should have been thinking about her and Hailey before playing the hero. He should have considered if saving someone else was worth it. But she knew firefighters made split second decisions, that they were totally immersed in the moment, in the task at hand. They didn't have time to debate whether they should or shouldn't go up to the third floor of a burning building. If they could save a life, they'd do everything they could to save that life.

At the risk of their own.

He'd told her all of this just before he'd proposed, to make sure she knew what she was saying yes to. Being a firefighter wasn't a job. It was the very essence of who he was and would always be. It's what she had loved about him, the way he cared about people as if every stranger was a close personal friend. She had never known that sort of genuine care from her own mother let alone from a man she'd only known a few months. How could she have said no to that?

She had no regrets. Loving Jack had been a privilege she would hold close to her heart forever. She recalled how the other firefighters had talked about Jack the night she'd met him on his birthday. They loved him. She knew every one of them would have risked everything to save him. He was a brother to them.

Sarah missed being loved by him, being touched, being kissed, being held. She missed the way his lips brushed hers as they made love, the gentleness of his touch on her body, the grin on his face when she reached orgasm.

It pained her to think that each of those memories would fade over time until they became something she sort of remembered but couldn't quite relive. In that sense, she could understand Hailey's predicament and frustration. Those memories defined the life she had lived, but more importantly, the person that she was.

Unfortunately, the sound of his voice couldn't survive the passage of time like other memories. The human brain simply couldn't store sound into its collective awareness.

Thank goodness she'd saved a message from him from last summer on her phone. She should transfer that sound byte to the laptop in the den, and make a backup of that, too. It was the only reminder of what Jack had sounded like.

A priceless treasure.

Sarah wrapped the stick in toilet paper and hid it at the bottom of the trashcan. She flushed, washed her hands, and went down to the kitchen to get her phone which she'd left on the counter. She played the message seven times, her tears coming harder and thicker with each listen, the sound of him a blanket she wanted to stay wrapped in forever.

I love you, Jack.

Sarah looked around and spotted the grapes she'd bought earlier in the week sitting in a bowl on the counter, unwashed. She brought them over to the sink and gave them a rinse, and then stood in front of the sink staring out the window, popping red grapes into her mouth one after the other. Jack had loved grapes and had insisted that they have grapes in the house at all times. She hadn't really cared for grapes before she'd met him. They were expensive, and it wasn't something her mother had been able to afford.

Sarah had never been much of a fruit eater before Jack.

She popped another grape between her lips and loved the way their sweetness exploded inside her mouth. These grapes were incredibly sweet and crunchy. It's the only way a grape should be. She hated it when they looked sweet and crunchy and she bit into one and it was soft and bitter.

Soft and bitter was a bad combination.

For everything.

TWENTY-ONE

The rest of the first week back to school went by uneventfully, the glimpses of memories Hailey had had on Monday had pulled a Groundhog Day and were seemingly hiding until spring.

She had so wanted to return to normal, and even had hoped to get back to school and her friends, but as Friday afternoon inched toward dinner time, a feeling of despair refused to leave her alone.

"We should go get some sweets at the bakery," Sarah said. "For after dinner."

Hailey had been moping on the couch, surfing through the television channels so quickly she couldn't possibly guess if any of the shows were worth watching. It was just something to do to kill time.

And she had plenty of time to kill. She was bored out of her mind. The pun didn't go unnoticed.

"Sure," she said and pulled herself off the couch. "Give me a minute to brush this rat's nest on my head and go pee."

She climbed the stairs leisurely, thinking about what she was in the mood for. Problem with the bakery is that everything looked and smelled so good that it was impossible to settle for just one thing. Maybe she could grab something for tomorrow, too. She didn't think Sarah would mind.

Sarah had been pretty good this week, not really bothering her much. They played a game of Scrabble on Wednesday—something she'd done with her dad often but never with Sarah, and although her words were simple, she was just happy she could actually remember how to spell—and a couple games of Yahtzee, but mostly Sarah had seemed preoccupied and had spent a lot of time in her dad's old den.

On Thursday morning, Sarah had told her that she had a doctor's appointment and asked if she was going to be all right by herself for a while. Hailey had said not to worry. She could watch something on TV or read. She'd gotten the ebook *The Alice Network* from the library onto her eReader and was really liking it. She couldn't remember if she'd already read it but if she had, maybe it would jog her memory if it started to become familiar.

It hadn't so far.

But she couldn't read for hours. She got antsy. And after a while she would feel the beginning of a headache. Which was why she'd been horizontal on the couch desperately trying to find something worthwhile to watch. After a while, TV got boring, too.

Everything was boring her.

But she didn't know what she wanted to do. She was still trying to figure out what interested her. She'd watched the hockey game last night and had enjoyed it for the most part, but she'd felt she should have loved it, not just enjoyed it, and she really hadn't if she was honest with herself. The trophies in her room told her she should love hockey.

Andréa had told her about her three-game suspension and Hailey hadn't been upset at all. Like everything else, she wasn't sure if she wanted to play right now, and she knew she'd probably be just a shadow of the player she had been so maybe the suspensions were a good thing. Andréa had told Hailey that she'd told the coach what was going on and that she had no idea when Hailey would be back on the ice.

The coach had phoned Hailey and they had talked for about ten minutes, but Hailey had had no idea who the coach was and had felt like they were talking about someone else, not her.

She managed to comb out the knots in her hair—she hadn't washed it all week and thought that she probably should sooner or later—and then realized she couldn't go out with her left eye looking like this. Although she'd been able to open it for a while now, there was still a bit of a yellow ring below her eye. Better than the purple it had been until just a few days ago. She did her best to hide it with several layers of foundation, then she peed and was about to leave the bathroom when she heard Sarah call up to wash her hands. Especially since they were going someplace where they served food. Sarah could be such a mom sometimes.

"Ready," Hailey said when she reached the front door and grabbed her old jacket from the closet. It was a bit small.

"We should probably go shopping for a new coat," Sarah said.

"I guess I won't be getting mine back?"

"I wouldn't count on it."

"Did I like it?"

"Yes. We can see if we can find another like it," Sarah said. "Good job on the eye."

"Didn't want to gross out anybody."

Peanut was standing in front of the door, wagging her tail, hoping to tag along.

"Sorry," Sarah said. "You stay and keep an eye on the house."

Peanut walked away with her head down and gave a big groan when she laid down.

Hailey bent down and gave the Maltese a loving rub. "We'll be back before you miss us."

Sarah locked the door behind them and five minutes later, they stepped into the bakery.

"Well, hello stranger," the lady behind the counter said to Hailey. "Haven't seen you and your friends all Christmas break."

Hailey looked at Sarah.

"Do you know Hailey?" Sarah asked the woman behind the counter.

"She's been coming here with her dad for years," she said and then looked at Hailey, "and you usually come in here at least twice a week with your friends. I see a lot of you."

"She's had a really bad concussion and lost some of her memory."

"Oh, you poor thing," the woman said.

"I'm Sarah. Hailey's stepmom."

"I'm Emily. Emily Knighton. I own this place. And I'm sorry about your husband. Everyone in town loved Jack."

"Thank you."

"Funny we've never met."

"Jack was the one who always came here," Sarah said. "I think he tried to keep me away because he knew once I came, I wouldn't be able to stop."

Emily smiled and turned to Hailey. "Hopefully you'll get your memory back soon."

"We're hoping," Sarah said.

"What can I get you ladies?"

Hailey shrugged and looked at the display cases. The apple strudel looked delicious, especially if they heated them and plopped a scoop of French vanilla ice cream on top.

They got two of those, two of the chocolate walnut brownies Sarah was becoming addicted to, and some homemade specialty called Emily's Pecan square.

"Hope you feel better soon," Emily said.

"Thanks," Hailey said.

They left. Once again, Hailey felt awkward at not recognizing someone she should know. When she got in the car, she was very quiet.

"You okay?"

"My head really hurts," she said and burst into tears. "Are these headaches ever going to go away?"

Sarah reached for Hailey's hand which turned into a hug. "I'm sure they will."

"That woman knows me, says I come here all the time with my friends, and she looked like a complete stranger to me. I'm tired of this, Sarah. Why did this have to happen to me?"

"I don't know," she said after pulling away. "Everyone heals differently when it comes to concussions."

Hailey wiped her tears.

"Here," Sarah said and handed Hailey a pecan square. "A bit of a treat can't hurt."

They ate in silence while the car radio played an old Big Wreck song from the 90s.

"God! That was delicious," Sarah said after licking her fingers. "I think my taste buds are having a party right now."

Hailey laughed softly, the pressure in her head still not gone. "That's something Dad would have said."

They both looked at each other, surprise on Hailey's face, sadness on Sarah's.

"That's definitely something your dad would have said."

"You miss him?"

This time it was Sarah's turn to shed some tears. "Every day." Sarah blew her nose and started the car. "I feel like we deserve a big greasy pizza from Gino's."

"Perfect Friday night food," Hailey said. "And we need to get some French vanilla ice cream."

♋ ♌

Sarah was lying in bed, full of pizza and apple strudel and French vanilla ice cream. This had been a great evening with Hailey, possibly the best they'd had together, but now she was tucked under the covers in a king-size bed that felt much too big and lonely.

She needed to get in touch with Ruth and ask her if she'd come up with a number for the shop so that she could get back to her financial advisor. Maybe if Ruth wanted too much money then Sarah's decision would become obvious.

She'd been spending a lot of time taking that online flower course and was really loving every second of it. Her confidence was growing and if it wasn't for the distraction Hailey was throwing her way, she'd be all into her new business venture.

Which brought her back to tonight.

She hated herself for thinking this, but Hailey's amnesia was a bit of a blessing. They were really spending time getting to know each other beyond the parent/stepchild relationship; they were getting to know one another as two women who were both learning to move on after a devastating loss. And Sarah could see a lot of Jack in his daughter which made Sarah want to get close to her even more.

And that scared her.

What would happen when Hailey's memories returned? That was a question she was afraid to get an answer to. Could any of the quality time they were spending together trump the return of the old Hailey?

Sarah knew that time would come eventually and she worried that when it happened, the old Hailey would completely overshadow the Hailey she was getting to know. It sure would be nice if the new Hailey didn't completely disappear but stuck around. Sarah would love it if Hailey helped at the flower shop, make it theirs and not just hers.

A family business.

Of course, the plan had been for Hailey to go to university come next September, but what if her amnesia went on for months and she didn't graduate high school? Sarah told herself not to jump to conclusions, to hope for the best. Nine months was a long time.

She turned on her side and stared at the space that should have been occupied by Jack. There were so many things she wanted to talk to him about. He was great at listening. Even better at offering an opinion; but he always let her make the decision. It was like he'd been preparing her for the possibility that he could be gone someday.

Her hand touched the bed sheet where his body had left a bit of an indentation in the mattress. He was a big man. A solid man. She had loved to cuddle into the strength of his arms as they lay in bed.

Hailey had fallen asleep on the couch and Sarah had watched her sleep for a few minutes, loving the peacefulness in her stepdaughter's face and the tiny hint of a smile that had played on her lips. Maybe she was dreaming. Sarah had reached for Hailey's face and gently moved the hair that had fallen over her eyes. The makeup had smeared and Sarah had noticed how yellow the skin around the eye was. It had looked so tender.

Hailey had stirred and looked at Sarah for just a second, and had mumbled something that had warmed her heart.

Goodnight Mom.

The words had been spoken so softly that Sarah wasn't sure they'd been spoken at all. She was pretty certain that in Hailey's sleepy state she might have been thinking of her real mother, but she would hold on to that moment, stash it away to cherish forever because there was no telling if it would ever come again.

Mom.

Quite a lovely word. Not a word she'd ever expected to own. How could a high school dropout and former stripper ever be good enough to be anyone's mother? Maybe that's who Hailey had seen and why she'd disliked Sarah instantly. She had seen the fraud that she was while her dad had been blinded by stupid love.

Hailey's hatred had been a warning to Sarah that she was on to her, that she would expose her, make her dad see he'd made a huge mistake.

I'm not a fake.

She had to admit that, at times, she was jealous of Hailey. Her stepdaughter had no idea how lucky she was to have had such a loving father who provided for and protected her. Maybe if Sarah's mom had done the same for her, she wouldn't have grown up feeling worthless, feeling that the only choice she had was to follow in her mom's path and become a stripper like her. It had been so easy to fall into. When her mom had died, she'd had nothing. The other girls had known her because she'd been hanging around backstage for years, and it was Selena who'd convinced her to join them. Selena was five years older and sort of took her under her wing. She showed her how to dance, how to tease, but Sarah hadn't really needed to learn. She'd watched her mom her whole life, sneaking glimpses from backstage and at home. It was the only thing her mom had known how to do— to please the assholes she shacked up with.

Her first time, Selena had gotten Sarah totally drunk. She'd been awful—the bar owner had told her as much. But she got better, much better, and soon she was the main attraction. She packed the Gentlemen's Lounge.

And that's where she'd met Jack.

TWENTY-TWO

O n Sunday morning, two weeks since the events that led to her concussion and amnesia, Hailey got up just after ten and felt something was different. She looked around her bedroom, at her hockey trophies, her Ottawa Senators paraphernalia, and then stopped at her closet door.

Where was the poster of her new favourite Senator? Where was Brady Tkachuk? Had Sarah done something to her poster? This wasn't her stepmom's room. She had no right to touch anything. And what was this on her night table? Whose phone was that? It looked like the phone she'd had two years ago. Where was her new iPhone?

What the hell was going on?

Her phone—that prehistoric piece of junk—chirped and she glanced at it. Andréa. Oh, she didn't have time to get into a long conversation with her right now. She had to find out what had happened to Brady. Her closet door looked all wrong without number seven smiling back at her. He was only four years older so it wasn't unrealistic that she could end up dating him. After all, they were both hockey jocks so they'd have a lot in common.

The conversations they could share about their love of the game could fill years.

Why would Sarah take down the poster?

Probably just to piss her off. That was so like Sarah to do shit like that. God, that woman was a real pain. And now she was stuck with her until she went away to university. Nine long months. Might as well be a life sentence.

She had to find Brady.

Hailey remembered when she'd gotten that poster. It was at the end of last season. Her dad had gotten tickets to the last game of the year—they weren't making the playoffs—and he'd gotten great seats just four rows behind the Sens bench. Close enough to hear the guys jostling and talking trash, close enough to smell his sweat. She was sure at one point when she'd yelled his name that he'd turned around, spotted her, and winked.

They were practically engaged with that wink.

If Sarah threw out her poster, she was going to go crazy. How dare she do that? This wasn't her stuff. It was so like her to do something to spite Hailey. It was like she was always trying to provoke her. Not like Sarah could tell her dad anything now that he was gone, so why would she continue to antagonise her?

Her phone chirped again. Another text from Andréa asking her how she was doing today. She was goddamned pissed right now because her annoying stepmom had stolen her beloved poster of Brady Tkachuk, that's how she was this morning.

Pissed. Off.

Since when did Andréa text her to ask how she was doing? What was with that? Didn't sound like the Andréa she knew. And she had a bit of a headache. Probably why she was in such a foul mood.

And her ribs ached for some reason. Had she gotten hurt during the previous hockey game?

She should tell Andréa what Sarah had done to Brady. She could tell Andréa anything and often vented about Sarah to her friend. True, Andréa had mentioned a few times that Sarah really wasn't that bad, and those might have been the only times the two friends had disagreed about anything. But she was sure once she told Andréa about Brady going missing and that Sarah had probably trashed the poster, Andréa would see Sarah the same way Hailey did.

An instigator busy body who pulled this sort of childish nonsense just to anger Hailey. It's like the woman was purposely trying to pick fights with Hailey.

Why had her dad married Sarah?

Hadn't he met her in a strip bar? She remembered asking him on several occasions and he'd been elusive for a long time, but he'd finally come clean not long before he died. She'd been shocked. Who the heck went to a strip bar to meet someone? What was her dad doing in a place like that anyway? When she'd asked him, he'd said the guys—meaning the other firefighters—had taken him out for his birthday.

Such a guy thing to do.

So, her dad had fallen for a waitress who worked in a strip joint. Not exactly high class. It was the only time Hailey had been disappointed with her dad. It was probably why she'd never been able to accept Sarah.

240 | François Houle

At least she hadn't been one of the strippers. That would have really made Hailey question her dad's common sense and might have caused her to respect him a little less. The worst thing was that he was no longer around, so she couldn't chastise him about his poor choice, and now she was the one stuck with that woman.

Who now owned the house.

Another thing Hailey was mad about. Why had her dad made Sarah the beneficiary of the family home? She wasn't real family. It should have gone to Hailey, or at least back to grandma and grandpa.

She loved this house. Dad had been renovating it for years but it still kept that classic farmhouse essence, except with modern amenities. Mostly. Dad had never changed the water regulator in her shower because he would have needed to tear the wall down, which would have led to a bathroom reno and he hadn't been ready for that yet. Or so he'd told her numerous times.

Her phone chirped again.

I'm peachy keen, she texted back, hot under the collar. One of her favourite expressions when she was angry or annoyed. Never better.

That doesn't sound like the Hailey of the last two weeks, Andréa texted back.

What the hell did that mean? Who else would she sound like?

Who else would I be?

You sound angry.

That's because my poster of Brady Tkachuk is gone.

Want me to come over?

Not now.

Looks like you're remembering more.

A long pause.

What?

Two Sundays ago, you got a concussion and lost your memory, Andréa texted. Sarah and I went to get you at the hospital. You didn't recognize either one of us.

Hailey stared at her old phone. She sat on her bed, trying to understand what she'd been told. She didn't remember getting a concussion. What she remembered was being thrown out of the hockey game because she'd taken number twelve into the boards hard and then she'd gone to find her mother who pretty much told her that she'd never wanted Hailey. After that, Hailey didn't remember a thing. She assumed she'd gotten in the car and driven home.

That conversation with her mom had really kicked her in the gut. All these years she'd missed her, had wanted her mom to come back, but turns out the woman had escaped a life she'd never wanted and there was no way she was ever going to want it back. Which meant she never wanted to have anything to do with her own daughter, one she'd apparently wished she'd never given birth to.

Now she understood her dad's anger.

And that anger had led him to Sarah. Why couldn't he just have dated her for a short while and then moved on? The first few times Sarah had been at the house, the woman had smiled way too big and laughed way too much. She'd been trying way too hard to get Hailey to like her, and that had made Hailey dislike her even more.

Being told by her dad that they were getting married the first time Hailey met Sarah hadn't help much either.

Besides, Sarah had seemed too simple for her dad.

Maybe that was the attraction? The complete opposite of her mom. Although, her mom hadn't looked all that sophisticated when Hailey had gone to her house. Sarah was sweet while her mom was bitter. Sarah appeared to want to get to know her while her mom didn't want to know anything about her. Sarah had looked at her dad like she'd found the love of her life while her mom hadn't loved either one of them.

Hailey hadn't wanted to share her dad. Plain and simple. Because she hadn't wanted him to be happy while she remained stuck by herself in her anger, her anger that she transferred toward her dad's new girlfriend.

I don't remember any of that, she texted back to Andréa.

I guess you don't remember being home these last two weeks?

I haven't been going to school?

You didn't think you'd understand anything.

You're being serious?

Yes. No one knew when you'd get your memory back.

I've been home with Sarah this whole time?

Yes.

And?

And nothing. You've been getting along great.

You're kidding?

You two have been playing games, watching movies, talking.

Hailey had no idea what to say to that. There's no way she would have made friends with Sarah unless, like Andréa had just said, she'd lost her memory and had no idea who Sarah was.

Had no idea she didn't like Sarah at all.

And while Hailey had been nice to Sarah, she'd sneaked around in her room and stolen her Brady Tkachuk. That was pretty pathetic, even for Sarah. But then again, Hailey shouldn't be surprised. Now that her dad wasn't around, Sarah probably felt she could treat Hailey horribly all she wanted.

That definitely doesn't sound like me.

CG &O

Sarah pulled the car into the parking lot of Flowers by Ruth and killed the engine. She took a deep breath, stepped out of the car, and walked to the door.

A little bell above the door announced her arrival.

"Well hello, Sarah," Ruth said with that voice that sounded like liquid gold. "It's nice to see you, dear."

"It's nice to see you, too," Sarah said and made her way to the back of the store where Ruth was working on a yellow flower arrangement. Sarah smiled as she recalled yellow meant happiness, the celebration of friendship, the taste of success. That course was teaching her a lot. Now she needed to spend time with Ruth to learn how to make the arrangements as perfectly as she did. It's what her clientele had come to expect and if Sarah was going to succeed, she'd have to uphold that same standard of quality.

"Sorry I haven't gotten back to you," Sarah said and explained what had happened with Hailey. "It's been a difficult two weeks."

"I hope she'll feel better soon," Ruth said. "And don't you worry. You take all the time you need."

Sarah put her purse on the counter and watched Ruth work. Her hands moved around expertly, like synchronized figure skaters.

"Did you decide on a price?"

Ruth stopped working and looked at Sarah. She wanted this place so badly it almost hurt. She knew she had a lot of decisions over the next few months to make, but she'd figure it out. This shop would be the first thing in her life that truly belonged to her.

"My accountant suggested its worth is somewhere between a hundred fifty to two hundred thirty thousand. I was quite shocked, as I see you are." Ruth pulled something from behind the counter and placed a brown envelop on the counter. "It's all in there. Is there someone you can go over this with?"

"Yes," she said. "My husband had a financial advisor."

"Good," Ruth said. "Show him this. Take your time."

Sarah turned and wandered to the front of the store, imagining this place as hers. *Hers.* She glanced out the front window. For a Sunday morning, the traffic was quite steady. Of course, there was a new housing development farther south, just past the Jock River bridge, and the big development on the west end of the village. She'd talked about that with her advisor. Those were all good signs for her business.

She turned and walked back to the counter. "You mentioned before you weren't in any hurry to sell."

Ruth nodded. "What's on your mind?"

"Would you wait until fall?"

"I don't see that as a problem, dear. I'm really in no hurry."

"Thank you." Sarah grabbed her purse and the brown envelop. "I've been doing this online course on flower arrangements. It's really interesting."

"The more you understand the meaning of each flower, the better you'll serve your clientele. You're a smart girl."

"I'll get back to you once I hear from my advisor."

"If he has any questions, just ask."

"Talk to you soon," Sarah said and left.

Being so close to the bakery, she grabbed a couple of those apple strudels Hailey seemed to love and a French loaf of bread—she was going to make beef stew for dinner, which she hoped would turn out better than her attempt at making Jack's chili.

She drove home, the tunes on the radio blaring while she did her best to sing along. The car smelled wonderful, like a bakery on wheels.

TWENTY-THREE

S arah put the bread and dessert on the kitchen counter and went looking for Peanut. Usually, the puppy would be waiting for her at the front door, curled up under the small bench in the foyer, but the Maltese hadn't been there when Sarah came home. She figured Peanut must be upstairs with Hailey. It was almost noon, so she assumed her stepdaughter was probably just lounging in her room with the dog at her side.

Sarah climbed the stairs, the last song she'd heard on the radio still playing in her head, filling her with good vibes. She reached the second floor and saw Hailey's bedroom door open, but no sign of either Hailey or Peanut. She stuck her head into the spare room doorway but didn't see them in there either. She made a mental note to come clean up the room. Maybe hire someone to finish the work.

"Peanut, you in here?" she said as she stepped into her bedroom. "Peanut?"

She heard the little darling bark, which sounded like she was in the closet, but when she pushed the door open, she saw that Hailey was in there, too, going through her things.

"Hey," Sarah said, trying to sound casual. "Looking for something?"

When Hailey turned, all that happiness Sarah had been basking in this morning quickly vanished.

Hailey's eyes were full of fury.

CS &O

After she stopped texting Andréa, Hailey burst out of her room, annoyed and angry that Sarah had taken her poster. What right did she have to take her things?

Hailey wasn't going to put up with that. Her room was private and Sarah needed to stay out. If her dad had been here, she'd have talked to him, but since he wasn't she was going to stand up for herself. Sarah might own the house, but Hailey's room was off limits, as were her things.

Hailey walked toward the master bedroom and saw that the door was open but that her stepmom wasn't in it. She went down to the main floor but didn't find Sarah anywhere.

Oh, well, she thought and headed back to the master bedroom to see if she could find her poster. It was hers, and if Sarah had hidden it in her closet it was her own fault that Hailey was invading her privacy.

Totally justified.

She looked under the king-size bed, in the wooden chest at the foot of the bed, and rummaged through the huge walk-in closet but couldn't find her poster.

Where could Sarah have hidden it?

Hailey was getting really frustrated. Wait until Sarah came home. Hailey wasn't going to put up with her stepmom's bullshit.

No way.

And then she heard Sarah call out for Peanut and turned to see Sarah standing in the open doorway, trying to look all happy and easygoing, but Hailey saw right through her façade.

Sarah looked as guilty as someone who knew she was busted.

Hailey felt her face become hot.

ෆ ෨

Sarah wasn't as concerned about Hailey going through her things as she was with the look in Hailey's eyes. Something seemed off, and she wondered if Hailey was having one of her terrible headaches. She'd noticed that when they got really bad, Hailey looked totally different, like out of it.

But there was more to the way Hailey looked right now that worried Sarah. The last two weeks had given the two women time to get to know each other, to sort of bond. Sarah had grown accustomed to Hailey asking her questions, making conversation.

Sarah had started to feel like Hailey was accepting her. And Sarah had begun to develop feelings of attachment.

Hailey's amnesia had been wonderful, for both of them.

Not a great thought.

But still.

So much better than the animosity that had ruled their relationship before the amnesia.

Sarah felt an unpleasant tightness in her chest. She really didn't want to let go of the new Hailey. She wanted to reach out to her stepdaughter and hold her, like she had done that day outside the bakery, but the ferocity in the girl's beautiful, lawn-green eyes made Sarah hesitate. Hailey had the look of someone who had been wronged.

Sarah took a deep breath. There had to be a reason why Hailey was searching her closet. It might not be as ill-intentioned as she feared. And it wasn't like she had anything to hide.

But it was the principle of the fact that Hailey hadn't asked— okay, Sarah hadn't been home, but Hailey could have waited. She was sure whatever her stepdaughter was looking for wasn't that pressing.

Then again, everything was pressing at seventeen.

Still, this was her room and Hailey needed to respect that. She would have to make that clear. The agreeable Hailey of the last two weeks would have understood, but Sarah had her doubts about the fiery Hailey standing in front of her.

Truthfully, the girl that was staring at her scared her a bit. She didn't think she should ever feel scared in her own home, afraid of someone she actually really cared about. Sarah knew the old Hailey didn't want her stepmom to care about her, that her stepdaughter didn't want Sarah to be here at all.

Hailey definitely had a lot of resentment, and Sarah understood her better than anyone ever would. Problem was that Sarah had never told Hailey her life story because she'd been too ashamed of it. She had made Jack promise that he wouldn't either, and as far as she knew he'd kept his promise. But now, Hailey was almost an adult and maybe it was time Sarah opened up. It could be the link they were missing.

Or it could be the catalyst that would totally tear them apart.

Sarah watched her stepdaughter and she felt that doing nothing, saying nothing, would be worse. She had to try and reach the girl. It's what Jack would have done. She was the parent, so it was up to her to change this.

"I can see you're upset," Sarah said.

"You have no idea."

Sarah crossed her arms and noticed that Hailey's fury seemed to intensify. Maybe that had been the wrong thing to do, but she'd hoped it would show Hailey that she wasn't going to be intimidated and was going to stand up for herself. She was done being the one to cower. She wasn't that little girl whose mom's deadbeat boyfriends had taken advantage of. She'd been abused far too long and wasn't going to let Hailey abuse her.

Those days were gone.

"Why don't you tell me what's got you so upset?"

෬ ෨

Hailey stood just inside the walk-in closet, her anger growing and becoming more unpredictable. She was tired of being walked on, first by her mother who didn't give a shit about her, and now Sarah who used childish behaviour just to get Hailey upset on purpose.

Without her dad, she had no one left.

Andréa had told her she'd had a concussion for the last two weeks, but she couldn't remember any of that. She knew her friend had no reason to lie, and she honestly didn't remember what had happened two Sundays ago, but right now she didn't care. She wanted her poster of Brady Tkachuk back and Sarah was the only one who could have taken it.

Her dad had bought her that poster. It was one of the last presents he'd gotten her before he'd died. He was never going to buy her anything else.

Ever.

He was gone. Forever. He'd taught her how to drive. He'd taught her how to play hockey, to dominate the ice. He'd driven her to all her practices at six in the morning or ten o'clock at night. He'd taught her how to work out properly so she'd have an incredibly strong core and lower body. Only then did he teach her how to stick handle a puck with finesse. You didn't need to shoot a puck at one hundred miles an hour to score goals. What you needed was the ability to beat the goalie, and a perfectly placed wrist shot was really the best option.

And patience.

On the ice, she had the patience of a hunting lioness, and she owed that skill to her dad. She wouldn't be who she was without him.

Without him, she was lost.

Hurting.

Angry.

She wanted her poster back. She needed that poster back. She couldn't lose more of her dad. His stupid job had stolen him from her. Even the smell of him was gone from the walk-in closet. She'd put her nose to his clothes while looking for Brady Tkachuk and couldn't smell her dad. He'd only been dead for two months, but traces of him were already gone. That didn't seem right. Shouldn't his scent be held hostage in his clothes for longer than two lousy months? How could her dad's existence only last two *fucking* months?

Two months.

It hardly seemed fair. The man had given his life to save others, and Hailey couldn't even remember what he'd smelled like. Lately, she had a hard time remembering his booming voice, the one she used to hear over everyone else's at her hockey games, or calling her for dinner. She'd even settle for his angry voice, which could be really scary, but then he'd always come and apologize later and she would cry into his shoulder and promise she'd do better and so would he. They weren't a perfect family of two, but they'd been a family, her and her dad.

He'd been all she'd needed.

But he'd needed more. She understood that now, but she'd been too angry with him to give Sarah a chance. She didn't see the point in giving her a chance now. Soon she'd be an adult and would never need to see her stepmom again. She'd be fine on her own. Or she'd go live with her grandparents out west. There wasn't anything left in Forest Creek for her. Not once all her friends went off to college or university.

Staying behind would make no sense.

This wasn't her home anymore. Another reason why she was angry with him. And with Sarah. He'd probably never considered that he wouldn't be around, or probably believed that he and Sarah would be here until they were old and grey and Hailey was out in the world living her life, but none of that had happened and now he'd given the house to his wife and left his daughter trapped or homeless.

So much had changed in just a few minutes on that dreadful morning of November fifth. She had lost more than just her dad that day, she had lost herself.

"You stole my Brady Tkachuk poster."

ଓ ଓ

Sarah stood a few feet away from Hailey just by the end of her bed, the back of her legs touching the chest, and she could feel the skin between her eyes tightening. Is this what this was all about, why Hailey was looking at her as if she'd committed murder? And who the heck was Brady Tkachuk and why would she steal his poster?

If it weren't for the deadly glare she saw in her stepdaughter's icy green eyes, she might have been tempted to laugh this off. But she didn't think that would be a good idea. It would just antagonize Hailey, which didn't seem like a smart thing to do right now.

Jack's daughter looked capable of bloody murder. When she had left Flowers by Ruth, Sarah had thought that this was going to be a wonderful day. She wanted to make that beef stew for dinner and had thought that maybe she and Hailey could take Peanut—who had come out of the closet and was sitting patiently at her feet—for a short walk since the day didn't appear to be too cold, but none of that was going to happen.

"I what?"

"You stole my Brady Tkachuk poster, the one Dad bought me last year."

"I have no idea what you're talking about," Sarah said, the exasperation in her voice noticeable. "Who's this Tkachuk guy?"

"You're hopeless," Hailey said with venom. "He's my favourite Senators hockey player."

"You don't have to belittle me," Sarah said. "You know I'm not into hockey like you and your dad. Which proves my point."

Hailey narrowed her eyes and shook her shoulders.

"Why would I want a poster of a hockey player?"

"I don't know," Hailey said. "You stole it from my room to piss me off."

Sarah made the mistake of laughing just a little. This was absurd.

"This isn't funny!" Hailey yelled. "Dad bought me that poster. It means a lot to me and I want you to give it back."

"I can't give you something I don't have," she said. "Something I never took."

"You're such a liar."

Sarah rubbed her face with both hands. There was no reasoning with Hailey right now. She wasn't listening. She couldn't listen. All she saw was red. It didn't matter what Sarah said to her. She wanted a confession, but Sarah couldn't give her one. There was none to be given.

She had not kidnapped Brady. There was no conspiracy against Hailey to deprive her of her favourite hockey player. Sarah could care less about hockey. No matter how many times Jack had tried to explain it to her, she didn't get it, didn't enjoy watching it, didn't see the point of wasting almost three hours of her life three to four times a week glued to the television cheering for a game she didn't understand.

Sarah took a deep breath. She had to remain the adult here and diffuse the ticking time bomb that stood just a few feet from her.

She wondered what Jack would do? How would he handle his daughter right now? He'd simply look at Hailey the way Sarah had seen him do many times, with that intensity in his eyes, that stern glare on his face that said *I will not put up with this.*

Fat chance of her pulling that off.

First off, Sarah had to look slightly up at Hailey. Not by much, but her stepdaughter was still taller. And probably outweighed her by a good fifteen pounds. Which was all muscle. The girl had shoulders Sarah envied and legs as hard as rocks. Sarah had no chance if Hailey got physical. And right now, Sarah was standing between Hailey and the bedroom door.

Probably not an advantage. In fact, she felt like she was standing in the way of a rabid animal's only escape route and unconsciously began to move over to the left a little, just in case.

"I have no reason to lie."

She could see that Hailey didn't believe her. Where was the beautiful teenage girl whose company she'd enjoyed these last two weeks? How could she be so completely different, so full of hostility where none existed just yesterday? Her memories weren't a blessing, they were a cancer.

Killing them both.

"Just tell me where it is."

"Hailey, honey—"

"You don't get to call me that," she said through clenched teeth. "Only Dad called me that."

Sarah felt her stepdaughter's pain. This was far more than just a missing poster. It had to be. There was so much hurt in those green eyes that Sarah could see Hailey drowning in her grief. If only Hailey would let her in, she could comfort her, maybe not like her dad used to do, but she'd do her best. Sarah wanted to love her like the daughter she wanted Hailey to be. Why was this so damn hard?

So damn impossible?

She wasn't vicious like those men her mom had hooked up with. Sarah wasn't going to hurt Hailey like she'd been hurt. She knew all too well about that sort of pain, and it was the last thing she wanted Hailey to have to live through on her own. But she couldn't break through that wall her stepdaughter kept fortifying.

"I'm sorry he's not here," Sarah said. "I know you miss him. I miss him too. But we have each other."

Hailey laughed but it sounded cold and full of sharp edges, like broken glass. "You're really stupid if you think we have each other. We'll never have each other."

TWENTY-FOUR

H ailey was getting tired of this. Why was Sarah stalling? Why couldn't she just tell her where she'd put the poster? Was it because she'd thrown it in the garbage and she didn't have it anymore? That better not have happened.

She had no idea what she'd do if Sarah had actually trashed her poster.

Hailey glanced at poor Peanut. She was lying closer to Sarah than to Hailey and that kind of saddened her. Even the dog wasn't really hers. Nothing in this house was hers.

Except what was in her room which included the poster of Brady Tkachuk. This was so goddamned childish of Sarah. She was supposed to be an adult.

Yeah, right.

There was a time a few years back, before her dad had met Sarah, when he'd taken her to see the Sens in Montréal to play the Canadiens. They'd left early in the morning and driven the two hours. They'd checked into one of the fancy hotels beside the Bell Centre, spent the afternoon shopping for new clothes that she couldn't find in Ottawa—Montréal always seemed to be

260 | François Houle

ahead of the curve when it came to fashion—and she'd tried her first lobster for dinner. Hailey couldn't remember the last time she and her dad had done something like that, just the two of them. That trip to Montréal might have been the last time.

The memory pulled a tiny sad smile on her lips. At least her dad still lived inside her memories. That was something that Sarah couldn't steal.

Hailey glared at Sarah, loathing her presence. Her dad had kept asking her to be nice, told her that once she got to know Sarah she'd see what a wonderful person she was. He'd been blinded by stupid love, so of course he'd thought Sarah was the most magnificent thing in the world. Hailey didn't know how Sarah had managed to turn her dad into putty, but she had and she'd turned him against his own daughter. Those last few months before her father had died, it was as if Hailey was invisible. They hardly did anything together. He was always with Sarah.

The sneaky manipulative wench.

Hailey stared down at Sarah. She knew it wouldn't take much for her to hurt the woman. She was delicate. Pretty. She understood why her dad had been attracted to Sarah. Full lips, perfect thin body, pretty eyes that melted your heart.

"What did you do before you met my dad?"

C3 80

Sarah was trying to find the right words to reach Hailey when her stepdaughter totally threw her off with a question that came out of nowhere. If she recalled correctly, Jack had told his daughter that he and Sarah had met in a bar. But she couldn't be completely certain. It's not something they'd really discussed because she had expected him to be here if Hailey ever had questions.

"I worked in a bar." It almost sounded like a question.

Hailey had a bit of a sinuous smirk on her face, like someone who knew the real answer.

"Wasn't it a strip joint?"

A wave of panic made Sarah take a step back while her mind worked to find the right explanation. She didn't know why she was feeling so ashamed at the moment. It's not like she'd done anything criminal. She'd survived, paid the bills, put food on the table.

"Yes."

"Why did you work there?" Hailey said. "Wasn't it weird to be around women who stripped for a bunch of dirty men? Or maybe you got off on it, like you wanted to be one of them? They probably made a lot more money than you did."

Sarah had trouble breathing. Hailey was toying with her. She was looking for Sarah to come out and tell her, no, confirm, what she probably already had figured out. Jack wouldn't have told her when she was just fourteen that her future stepmom was a stripper. Had Hailey overheard them talking? Sarah didn't think she and Jack had ever talked about her former life in the house or near Hailey. In fact, the only time they'd come close to talking about it was on their fifth date when he'd told Sarah that he didn't care why she'd become a stripper, but if she ever wanted to tell him, he'd listen and never judge her. What he did care about was whether she would quit if he asked her to. He didn't want the woman he loved to work in such a place anymore.

Love?

That's all she'd heard in that conversation. The man, whom she'd only known for all of five dates, had told her he was in love with her. Not like she didn't hear that every night from drunken patrons, but they were out at a small café, sitting on the patio on a beautiful spring night, and she'd known Jack hadn't been drunk.

Why had she agreed to go out with him? Selena and a couple of the other girls had coaxed her into it. What harm could there be? The man was a hunk and she should go out and have a good time. It wasn't normal for any of the girls to go on dates with patrons, but they'd also told her that not too many opportunities ever came their way in the form of a gorgeous rock of a man who'd actually turned red when Sarah had gone to dance for him on his birthday, courtesy of the guys in his unit. Just a bunch of firefighters out for a good time.

Polite and kind and respectful.

Not a combination the girls often had the opportunity to experience. And they'd paid her three times the normal fee for a dance.

Jack had looked everywhere but at her until he'd finally locked eyes with her. He'd apologized profusely afterward, confessing that he hadn't been in a place like this since he was twenty and it now made him feel uncomfortable. He thanked her and told her she was absolutely beautiful, which turned his face a darker shade of red than it already was.

He'd looked so awkward and innocent and for some reason she could never find an answer for, she'd leaned in and kissed his cheek and told him he was sweet and any girl should be so lucky as to find a man like him.

He'd been waiting for her at the bar when she'd finished, which had made her a little nervous. Fraternising with customers wasn't encouraged. He'd offered to buy her a drink but she'd turned him down saying she was tired and just wanted to go home. Fact was that she was already drunk—guys bought her drinks all night long and there were some nights when she needed to feel nothing and just pretend she wasn't there, just her body doing its thing—but when she saw the disappointed look in his eyes, she had sat beside him and ordered a club soda.

They'd talked until the bar closed and she had revealed more to this stranger than she'd ever revealed to any of the girls. And when he'd asked to walk her to her car, she'd laughed.

"See that car over there?" she said.

"Is that an Uber?"

"That's the car I can afford."

They'd stood for a moment side by side, the cold January night biting at her face while she watched Jack slip his hands into the pockets of his jeans, acting like a kid who didn't know what to do next.

"You have a nice night," she'd said and started to walk toward her ride. "You were a perfect gentleman."

"Can I take you out, sometime?" he had called to her just before she'd stepped into the car. "I really would love to see you again."

"You can come see me any time you want," she'd said coyly. "Except Mondays and Tuesdays."

"What's your name?"

She had looked at him a long time, trying to decide if this was some nut job who actually was giving the performance of a life-time, or if, as her gut told her, he was a genuinely good guy.

"Sarah," she'd said and climbed in the Uber before he could say anything more to her.

As the car pulled out of the parking lot, she'd looked from the corner of her eye and had seen him just standing there, a grown man looking like an awkward boy. At the last second, he had raised his hand and given her a small wave.

When she'd gotten home and locked the door behind her, she'd been mad at herself for breaking her own rules that night. If she was lucky, he was going to go home and forget all about her.

It was best for them both if she never saw him again.

"For the most part they're just guys out for a good time," she told Hailey. "And they tipped well."

"Why would my dad go to a place like that?"

"The guys from work took him out for his birthday. He'd become a hermit since your mom left."

"She'd been gone like ten years by then."

"One of his buddies said he never went out."

Hailey looked at her suspiciously. Maybe if Sarah was to win her stepdaughter over, she should tell her everything. It's not like their relationship could be tarnished any more than it already was. At the very least, Hailey would finally know who Sarah had been.

Which wasn't who she was now.

"When I met your dad," Sarah said, swallowing, "I was one of the strippers at the Gentlemen's Lounge."

CB ꝏ

Hailey wanted to gloat because she'd finally found out the truth about Sarah, but her moment of triumph was stifled by a sobering thought: if what Sarah had just told her was true, what sort of man did that make her dad?

More lies from that wench.

How much could Sarah have really loved her dad if she was spewing these lies about him? Her dad wasn't a pervert. He got embarrassed watching romantic movies when the couples made out. Or was that just an act?

No! Hailey knew her dad. He was one of the good guys, a great father, a hero who gave his life to save others. That's not a man who went to strip bars and married strippers.

Angry words jammed the back of her throat. She couldn't swallow. Why was Sarah so vindictive? If she loved him like she kept telling Hailey, it didn't make sense for her to hurt Hailey with these lies. Hailey's head felt too small, busting with confusion. She could feel this pain between her eyes, making it almost impossible for her to think clearly. Her dad didn't do what Sarah was saying.

"You're a pathetic hooker," Hailey said through gritted teeth. "You tricked him."

"I was a stripper," Sarah said to defend herself. "I wasn't a prostitute. I didn't sleep with men for money."

"No, you just married them and stole everything from their family. You're such a low life."

"It was nothing like that."

"There's not a single word of truth coming out of your mouth," Hailey yelled and stepped out of the closet. "You seduced my dad and stole my house."

"I loved him," Sarah said in a voice full of pain. "He saved me from that life, don't you get it? He saw who I was, really was, which wasn't a stripper."

"Stop lying!"

Peanut whined and hid under the bed. Hailey gave the little puppy a quick saddened glance.

"You're scaring Peanut," Sarah cried.

"It's all your fault for saying all those lies about my dad. He would never go to a place like that."

Sarah wiped her nose with the back of her hand. "You don't want to hear anything I have to say."

"Because only lies comes out of your mouth," Hailey said, her fists clenching at her side. "My dad would never date a whore and he definitely wouldn't marry one. You lied to him about what you did at that place. You had to."

"I danced for him—"

"Liar."

Tears were flowing down Sarah's face. "The guys paid for a lap dance and it was me—"

"Shut up!"

"I'd never seen a grown man so red-faced when I approached and started to dance."

"Shut. Up!"

"He was such a gentleman," Sarah said through her tears. She tried to wipe them but more kept coming. "He wouldn't even look at me dancing for him. He was too embarrassed."

"Stop," Hailey said in a voice full of anger. "I don't believe you. My dad wouldn't go to a strip joint. He just wouldn't. That's not *my* dad."

"Not on his own," Sarah said, regaining a bit of composure. "He didn't even know where the guys were taking him for his birthday. He even tried to walk away once he realized where they were, but the guys practically forced him."

"You're making this up."

"He told me all of this on our first date," Sarah said. "He wanted to make sure I knew he wasn't the sort of man who went to the Gentlemen's Lounge all the time. He'd actually not been to a place like that in years, not since he was young and he and his friends went as a joke."

"I told you, my dad wouldn't go to a place like that," Hailey said in a voice which was full of doubt now. "My dad—"

Her dad made snow forts in the front yard and put up Christmas lights along the eavestroughs and around the evergreens, he made cannonballs in the pool like a stupid teenage boy just to splash her. Her dad made chocolate chip pancakes on the weekend and roasted marshmallows in the backyard fire pit so Hailey could make s'mores.

Her dad didn't go to no goddamned strip clubs to marry whoring strippers.

"Why are you lying?" She was sounding like the little four-year-old who'd kept asking why Mommy had left. "Why?"

"Why would I lie about the man I loved more than life."

Hailey's facial expression became hard. "I wish you'd died instead of him."

Sarah took a step back as if she'd been shot. "That's the cruelest thing anyone has ever said to me. I would never wish that for you."

Hailey clenched her jaw so hard that all that could be heard in the silence were her teeth grinding. She didn't care. She wanted Sarah to hurt as much as she did. No, she wanted Sarah to hurt more.

She wanted to break Sarah's heart.

"Your lies are the cruelest thing I've ever heard, especially about *my* dad. And you say you loved him."

"More than you'll ever know."

☙ ❧

Sarah recalled how Jack had showed up the next night without any of the other guys. He'd sat at the bar nursing a Diet Coke, waiting for her all night long to come and say hi. But she never did. She had done her job and then snuck out the back and went home.

For a week he came and sat at that bar all night long. She had begun to worry that he might not be such a gentleman after all, but some psycho she shouldn't have been so quick to give her real name to.

Her stage name had been Sky.

But he'd looked harmless and so cute that night of his birthday. She'd let her guard down. When the guys had asked her if she'd dance for their firefighter brother, and once she'd seen who the guys were pointing to, for a moment she'd forgotten the rules—not the establishment's rules, but her own rules.

To keep it professional. Dance. That's what they were paying for. Be nice but not too friendly. Make sure everyone respected the line that shouldn't be crossed.

But she had crossed it by kissing his cheek. And she'd given him her real name.

And then for a week he'd shown up, always keeping his back to the stage but she would catch glimpses of him looking at her from the mirror behind the bar. But not in a creepy, stalking sort of way.

Just a boy waiting for his chance to talk to a girl.

A girl he liked.

By the seventh night, she was looking forward to seeing him and when she came on stage and didn't see him, her performance faltered a little. She wasn't quite into her act that night until he showed up around eleven. Selena had been quick to point out that once prince charming had entered the premises, the little want-to-be princess had gotten a smile she couldn't quite put away. Her eyes had been pretty much glued to that handsome hunk sitting by himself at the bar with his back to her.

But they were watching each other in the mirror.

Like two lovers.

She'd told herself she was imagining something that simply wasn't there, that couldn't possibly be there. No man in his right mind would want to be with a stripper. It was barely a step above being a prostitute. Why would a gorgeous firefighter like him, someone who saved lives, who could have any girl, any respectable girl, want a high school dropout who earned her living by dancing naked in a downtown bar?

He had no idea who she was. Maybe she should just go talk to him, put him out of his misery. Once he found out about her, she knew he'd never be back.

Not if he was as smart as he was good looking.

She cut her shift short about half an hour, got dressed, and made her way to the bar and sat beside him. She remembered being nervous and she'd wondered if that's the way girls typically felt when they were close to a boy they liked. She'd never experienced anything of the sort back in high school because she'd dropped out, and with all the moving they'd done she'd never gotten to know anyone.

She knew this wouldn't go anywhere. None of it made sense. But it was nice to meet a man who apparently liked her enough to come see her work every night since they'd met. It was odd, for sure, but she had to find out why he kept coming back.

"Hi Jack," she said once seated.

"Hi Sarah," he said, looking at her via the mirror behind the bar. "I didn't think you'd ever come."

"I didn't think I would either," she said. "I never do."

He sipped his coke. "What changed your mind?"

The bartender gave her a club soda. "I figured if you're a firefighter, you're probably not a psychopath. At least, I'm hoping you're not."

"I'm a single dad with a fourteen-year-old daughter."

"Then why are you here?"

He turned toward her. "Because I can't get you out of my mind."

"You look like a good guy," she said. "You're a father. This isn't the place you're going to find a new wife."

"What if you're wrong?"

She sipped her club soda. "I'm a stripper."

"No," he said. "That's what you do."

"Is there a difference?"

He gave her a tiny, soft smile that went all the way up to his stunning green eyes. "I doubt that this was your ideal career path growing up."

"You don't know me," she said. "What if it's all I ever aspired to be?"

"Was it?"

She sipped her club soda and finally looked at him.

"It wasn't my first choice." She forced a smile. "Did you always want to be a firefighter?"

"I wanted to be a surgeon," he said. "But I found out I hated biology in high school."

"Widow or divorced?" She had no idea why she'd asked. "You don't need—"

"Divorced."

They sat in silence but it wasn't uncomfortable. It actually felt natural, like they'd done this hundreds of times. Two old friends catching up.

"She never wanted to be a mother," he said. "She never wanted to be with me. We met at a party and got carried away. We were both young and stupid."

"And now you have a daughter."

"Like I said, we were young and stupid. Mostly stupid."

"Maybe I should save you from making another mistake," she said. "Because we both know that is what this is."

He finished his drink. Looked at her with kindness in his eyes. It actually scared her a little because she could fall into those eyes and never want to come back out.

"Is it?" he said.

She tucked a strand of her long strawberry blond hair behind her right ear. She always wore it in a tight ponytail when she danced but loved to have it loose otherwise.

"You saw a pretty face, that's all I am."

He grinned. "A little full of yourself."

"Better than to say you saw a gorgeous ass."

He laughed out loud and she thought he sounded delicious. The more time she spent with this guy, the more she liked him. That was a big problem.

"You are extremely attractive," he said. "But that's not why I'm here."

"Why are you here?"

"I can't stop thinking about you," he said. "I never felt that way about my ex-wife and she sure didn't feel that way about me."

"Was she blind?"

"No," he said. "I think it just took her a long time to figure out she'd rather be with a woman."

"Oh," Sarah said. "Not that there's anything wrong with that."

"If you tell me right now that you're gay, then I'll leave and never bother you again."

Sarah teased him with her eyes. She was getting herself into so much trouble but she couldn't stop. She'd wondered for a long time if she'd ever be able to have a normal relationship with a man, and sitting beside Jack having a very open conversation gave her some sort of hope.

Sadly, she'd never been in love. What had happened to her when she was twelve had spoiled that for her. And being a stripper gave her reason to stay distant. She didn't have to care about her clientele. She just turned off her mind, let herself get carried away by the music—yes, there were some substances consumed, too—and didn't worry about her feelings getting hurt.

But it could be very lonely.

And she was tired of that. Eating by herself, sleeping by herself, going to the movies by herself. Some of the other girls lived that wild lifestyle common with those who did the kind of work Sarah did, but she didn't. It was a job that paid the bills. Lately, she'd been yearning for a lot more.

She wanted someone in her life.

"I was abused when I was barely a teenager," she said and saw his face fill with sorrow. "I'm basically celibate. But I'm not gay."

"Me, too," he said, looking at her. "No one since my wife left."

"You know you're an attractive man, you could easily get any woman in bed."

"The thing is," he said and took her hand into his, "I made that mistake once, and I don't regret it because I have the most wonderful daughter any father could want, but I don't want to sleep with a bunch of women. I want to find the right one."

She snorted. "You're not finding her here."

"One man's trash is another man's treasure."

"So, now you're comparing me to trash."

His face reddened and she totally adored how easily he got embarrassed.

"God, no," he said. "Like I said earlier, this is what you do, but I'm sure it's not who you are."

"You're sure?"

He still held her hand and she made no attempt to pull it away. His hands felt nice and warm. Nothing like this had ever happened to her and she honestly didn't know what to do. Her common sense said to just get up and go home, but the lost girl in her wanted to see if this might lead to something. Was there any harm in that?

She didn't want to be alone the rest of her life. Her mom had made her want to hide from the world so she couldn't get hurt, but she was tired of hiding. Loneliness was exhausting. Loneliness made her afraid. Loneliness was sucking the life out of her.

"Go on a date with me," he said, pulling her out of her thoughts. "Just one date and if you hate it, just ask me to take you home and I will and I'll never bother you again."

She gazed into his eyes and saw honesty in them and a lot more. She could see herself gazing into those eyes for a lifetime.

"One date," she said, echoing his words. "And then you'll leave me alone?"

"If you ask me to."

"And if I don't?"

He tried not to smile. "Then I guess we try a second date."

"A second date," she said as if thinking to herself.

"I'm a nice guy."

"Said the psychopath before he locked me in his torture chamber."

"You watch too many horror movies."

"I don't even own a television," she said. "The movies I see at the theatre are always romcoms. A girl has the right to hope."

He gave her hand a gentle squeeze. "Hope is asking you out on a date."

TWENTY-FIVE

Hailey watched Sarah closely, the two standing maybe five feet apart but a world away, wondering why she'd gone so quiet and why her face looked so serene. It unsettled Hailey which didn't happen often or easily.

The woman was strange.

Made Hailey distrust her even more. She had to have manipulated her dad. That's the only thing that made sense.

"Why would he want to date you, a *stripper*?"

"Why do you say it like it's a disease?" Sarah said. "I had no choice. At seventeen I was all alone, and needed to take care of myself."

"You could have gotten any other job."

"It always looks easy from the outside," she said. "I dropped out of school in the middle of grade ten when my mom died."

"You would only have been fifteen."

She shook her head. "We'd moved so much I was back two years."

Hailey grinned. "You were seventeen and still in grade ten?"

"Like I said, we moved a lot."

"So you dropped out of school and started to strip? You were just seventeen, you couldn't have."

"Do you look seventeen when you put on a little makeup?" She didn't wait for Hailey to answer. "I needed money. All I knew was that world. It wasn't very hard to convince the club owner. He knew I was going to pack the place."

"Like that's something to be proud of," Hailey said. "Why are you telling me anyway? Am I supposed to feel sorry for you?"

"No," Sarah said. "I just want you to know who I was and why I fell in love with your dad."

"I really don't care to know you, and I really don't want to hear your lies about you loving my dad."

"They're not lies," she said so quietly Hailey wasn't sure if she'd heard. "He was my heart."

"And he was my dad." Hailey felt her anger return. "And you stole him from me."

"He was capable of loving us both."

"But I didn't want to share him with you," she said. "Why can't you get that? He was my dad . . ."

"And he was my husband, my friend, my protector. He saved me from a horrible life because he believed that I was better than I thought I was. He didn't see a stripper when he looked at me, he saw a woman he could love. He was able to see past all of my brokenness and put all the pieces back together. How could I not love a man who could do that? And when I saw him with you, how tender and loving he was, how could I not want to spend the rest of my life with him?"

"It was all about you," Hailey shouted. "Did you ever think about what I wanted? No, you didn't. Poor broken Sarah who was abused saw her lifeboat and she clung to it with all her might and she didn't care who she hurt. So now I'm the one who's broken and parentless, all because of your selfishness."

"That's not how it was."

"Stop," Hailey said.

"I loved your dad," Sarah said. "You were the family I'd always wanted."

"That makes you sound crazy and pathetic," Hailey said. "You can't hijack a family."

"You're twisting my words."

"You tricked my dad."

"No, it wasn't like that."

C8 80

Jack took her bowling for their second date. She had never bowled in her life; she didn't know how to grab the ball or how to roll it down the lane.

They had pizza and beer while they bowled. Everyone was eating and drinking while bowling. There must have been twenty lanes on the lower floor where they were, and another twenty lanes on the upper floor; the place was packed and filled with laughter and the constant crash of bowling pins being knocked down. Jack helped her the first couple of times, stood behind her and grabbed her hand with the ball in it, and showed her how to release the ball so it would roll down the lane more or less straight. And when he guttered his first ball, she laughed so hard she thought she was going to pee her pants.

She had no idea a date could be so simple yet so much fun. She had never laughed so much about the silliest things ever.

There hadn't been many reasons for laughter in her past. They played five games over three hours and by the time she threw her last ball and got a strike, she was exhausted and it was only ten o'clock.

He drove her home, wished her good night, waited until she entered her apartment building, and then she watched him drive away.

Her heart sank.

Jack hadn't asked her for a third date. But then she saw his car come back around the parking lot and she rushed outside. He lowered the passenger side window and she stuck her head in the opening and waited, forgetting to breath.

"Would you like another date?" he asked.

"Going to be pretty hard to beat the first two," she said.

"Is that a yes?"

She nodded, her entire face hurting from smiling so big. "That's a big yes."

He handed her his phone. She entered her number. He said goodnight and drove away.

She knew it had only been a couple of dates—but both had been awesome—and she knew there was no guarantee this little fairy tale was going to last, but what if it did? She couldn't take the chance of not finding out. Wasn't she allowed to find some happiness? She wasn't her mom. Her mom had been stuck in that life because she'd been a drug addict. She'd been unable to get out.

Sarah had stayed away from the hard drugs. Some nights she drank too much, to help her make it through another performance when she wasn't feeling up to it. But that was it. She hadn't planned on doing this for this long, but somehow the years had gotten away. Maybe that's the way her mom had felt too. But her mom hadn't been able to handle being alone. Sarah had made a point of it. Better to be lonely than pulled deeper into a life she hoped to get out of.

She watched Jack's car turn onto the main road and disappear. She smiled, turned, and walked back to the apartment building's front door.

Jack wasn't one of her mom's deadbeat boyfriends.

CB ℰ℺

Hailey was getting tired of Sarah. She just wanted the woman out of her home, out of her life. She was still reeling at the fact that her dad had made Sarah the beneficiary of the house. She couldn't get passed that.

"You keep saying you loved him," Hailey said. "But those words are meaningless now that he's gone."

"Not to me they aren't," Sarah said. "The way he loved me made all the difference in my life. He made me happy and I made him happy, too. I know you didn't see that, but he was lonely. He loved you and loved being a father, but he needed me as much as I needed him. Someday, you'll understand what I mean."

"I really don't care."

"He was your dad but he was also a grown man," Sarah said.

"You're barely older than me."

"I know I'm not old enough to be your mother," she said. "And I never tried to be. I just wanted us to be close, maybe like sisters."

"I don't want a sister."

"A sister could help you, care about you."

"I can take care of myself," Hailey said quietly, almost afraid to voice it just in case it wasn't true. She knew she could look after herself for some things like cooking simple meals and doing the laundry, but she really didn't know much about paying bills and stuff like insurance and getting the car fixed, or even who to pay for her hockey. But there was no way she was telling that to Sarah. She'd figure it out. She could call her grandparents.

Maybe all of this wasn't worth it. Maybe she could just get on a plane to the west coast.

"I'm sure you can," Sarah said. "But—"

Hailey had had enough. She shoved Sarah as hard as she could and watched her stepmom's face fill with disbelief as she lost her footing and fell, smacking her head against the wooden chest that sat at the end of the king-size bed.

Hailey grinned.

;;

Sarah couldn't believe what Hailey had just done. The back of her head hurt and she could feel a kink in her neck. But the biggest fear lived inside of her.

Instinctively, she put a hand on her stomach.

"You hurt me," she said.

"I don't care," Hailey said and walked away.

"I would never hurt you."

"You've hurt me plenty."

Sarah tried to sit but the pain in her neck and back made her wince. She managed to lean against the wooden chest.

"I'm pregnant," she said as Hailey was walking out the bed-room. "You could have hurt the baby."

Hailey stopped in the doorway, hesitated for a second, then walked away without saying a word.

"Hailey," Sarah said. "We need to talk about this. We need to make things better."

TWENTY-SIX

Hailey couldn't believe what Sarah had just told her. If she'd expected it to make a difference, to somehow make then become a family, there was no chance of that. Just Sarah trying to manipulate her like she'd done to her dad.

So pathetic.

As if Sarah having a baby mattered to Hailey. Why should it? She was probably lying about that, too. Everything Sarah said was a lie. Hailey was so tired of hearing Sarah lie about everything, about how much she'd loved her dad and what a savior he'd been.

She. Didn't. Care.

All she'd wanted was to get her poster of Brady Tkachuk back, and it was obvious that Sarah must have thrown it in the garbage. Hailey could buy another, but it wouldn't be the same as her dad having bought her the original one. That's why it mattered so much to Hailey.

Pregnant?

Why should she care? That baby was going to make Hailey even more invisible. That baby was going to be Sarah's, and there was no way Sarah was going to care about Hailey then, no matter how much Sarah denied it wasn't going to change anything. That baby was going to be Sarah's and only Sarah's.

Hailey was just a stepdaughter, not really Sarah's. You couldn't love a stepchild the same as your own. Hailey was old enough to get that. That's just the way we're programmed, to care more about our own.

And even that wasn't always true.

When Hailey thought of her own mother unable to love her the way she saw Andréa and her mother or Madelaine and her mother love and care about each other, it was hard not to be jealous. Her dad had been her everything, and without him she felt abandoned. She knew most of her friends always acted like they didn't like their parents, but that was easy to do when you went home to them every day. None of them understood the depth of the loss Hailey had to live with now.

She felt utterly alone. There was no one left who truly loved her. Yes, her grandparents loved her, but that hadn't stopped them from moving out west to be closer to their *younger* grand-kids. Because everyone knew that younger grandkids needed more attention, more care, more of everything. They were cuter, easier to love. Teenagers were the hardest to love.

But she wasn't. She still liked to hug her dad before going to bed and hear him say he loved her and to have sweet dreams. She couldn't just turn her own feelings off, not need him anymore. Deep down, she was still a kid who craved to be loved by her parents, but one was dead and the other didn't care.

The other had never wanted her to begin with.

That was a truth full of jagged edges. Impossible to swallow. Sarah wasn't the only one who'd had a shitty mother who didn't care. Her stepmom wasn't anyone special in that respect.

Her dad had made Sarah happy.

Hailey didn't want to hear that.

Her dad had been able to see beyond who Sarah had been and see who she could be.

Hailey didn't care.

Her dad had fallen for a goddamned stripper.

Hailey was so mad at him.

And now Sarah was carrying her dad's baby. She felt nothing for it. It was just one more thing that hurt, that made Hailey feel like she mattered even less.

Hailey walked into the spare bedroom that her father had been renovating. She guessed Sarah was going to have to get someone to turn it into a baby's room. No one had been in here in two months. Everything was exactly the way her dad had left it.

She picked up the utility knife that was lying on the window sill. She pushed the blade out. Then retracted it back in. Pushed it out, retracted it back in. The view from the window was of the side of the house where the garage was. The roof was full of snow.

Hailey turned and eyed the mess her dad had left. There was dust covered drywall pieces littering the floor and a small step ladder leaning against the wall. She saw gloves and a crushed dust mask, his hammer and reciprocating saw shoved in a corner. Still plugged in was his drill and there was a box of drywall screws lying open beside the drill.

She continued to play with the utility knife.

This was supposed to be Sarah's little workout room. She was too good to go down to the basement where the equipment was. There was that new Peloton her dad had bought for Sarah, but she knew Sarah didn't like going down there, and an old treadmill and a Bowflex machine Hailey normally used but couldn't remember the last time she'd been down there either. Since she'd lost her memory for two weeks, she probably hadn't worked out in that long. Her dad had cleared a space for her years ago where she could practise shooting pucks against the cement wall whenever she wanted to and not damage anything.

Hailey looked at her wrists. Those little white scars were a call from the past when she'd been miserable. All thanks to her mom. And Sarah.

Sarah, Sarah, Sarah.

She hated that name. She hated her mom. Seemed the women in her life had been nothing but big disappointments.

Hailey pushed the utility knife blade out.

Scrutinized it.

Touched her skin with it.

Pulled the blade back.

She remembered cutting herself when her dad had started to date Sarah. She'd read lots of stories on the internet, why kids, teenagers mostly, cut themselves. The tiny scars on her wrists were barely visible, like her.

They'd only been visible to her dad.

But he'd died.

He'd been all she'd had.

And he'd died trying to save someone else.

He should have saved her. He'd deceived her. He hadn't told her the truth about Sarah. She wondered why? Had he been embarrassed for falling for her? Had he been ashamed of having been manipulated by Sarah?

She missed her dad.

His presence was fading from her memory. It had only been two months. Would she remember him at all after two years? Ten years? Twenty?

She pushed the utility knife blade out and gave herself a little cut just like she'd done all those times before.

Why did her dad have to die?

Another small slit.

His carelessness had made her an orphan of sorts, maybe not in the technical definition of the word, but really, who did she have left? A mom who didn't want her? A stepmom who was a former stripper and was apparently pregnant with her own baby, so why would she ever care about Hailey? Oh, and grandparents who had moved across the country to be closer to their new grandchildren.

Nobody really wanted her.

A third cut.

They weren't deep enough to really bleed. The first one was already congealing and the second one looked more like a scratch. Hailey stared at her wrist for a long time.

She wanted more relief. She needed more relief.

അ ഊ

Sarah pulled herself up with the help of the king-size bed's foot-board and felt an ache in her back. Her mind reeled with worry and she put a hand on her stomach.

Her appointment Thursday with her family doctor confirmed what the pregnancy kit had already told her: she was two months pregnant.

Leaving the doctor's office, she had been walking on cloud nine. Of course, she had longed for Jack, but what a gift he'd left behind. And to think that they'd almost skipped sex that morning because he was running late and she was feeling sort of blue.

She sat in the car outside the medical building feeling both exhilarated and horribly devastated that he wasn't here with her, that he would never know this child.

Their child.

Sarah felt his absence every day but she'd told herself that she needed to go on, which was why she'd fallen in love with the idea of buying the flower shop. She still wanted to buy it but wasn't sure how she was going to handle it and a new baby. It was probably too much, but she didn't want to give either up.

She sighed.

Spotted her phone on the floor and bent to pick it up. It must have slipped out of her back pocket when she stumbled and fell after Hailey had shoved her.

That had been so unexpected.

Scary.

All because of a stupid poster Sarah had not touched. Why would she? The last time she'd gone into Hailey's room was to vacuum and she couldn't remember if it was before or after Christmas. That day seemed months away now. So much had happened. If only Hailey could remember how they'd been when she had amnesia. Sarah had loved how they could just spend time together, the way she'd always imagined.

All gone now.

Hailey seemed so much worse. Angrier. More determined to tear them apart. It didn't make sense to Sarah why her stepdaughter had so much hate for her. She just didn't understand what was going on in Hailey's head.

If only Hailey would talk to her, really tell her what was going on, maybe she could help. She couldn't believe her hateful behaviour was all because Hailey thought Sarah had stolen a poster, or because she'd been a stripper when she'd met Jack.

That just didn't make sense.

There had to be more to it than that. Had to be. Sarah had had reasons to hate her own mother—her mom hadn't protected her from Axel—but Sarah had never shown anything but a desire to be close to Hailey. She'd meant it when she'd said that they could be like sisters. That definitely made more sense since they weren't that far apart in age. Twelve years. Some siblings had more years between them.

A pain in her stomach stole her thoughts and filled her mind with worry. She couldn't lose the baby. She prayed to Jack to not let her lose the baby. That would be like losing her heart all over again. Finding out she was going to have Jack's baby had been a gift she couldn't have foreseen and definitely not one she ever wanted to give back. This baby was a miracle. It was giving her the strength to move on.

She really wanted to share the experience with Hailey. This baby was her father's child. This baby was going to be her brother or sister. How could she not be thrilled?

Sarah had to help Hailey get past her anger.

But would her stepdaughter ever let her?

She had to keep trying. That's what a parent would do. A mom would never give up. A sister would never give up. Hailey was Jack's child just like the one she was carrying inside of her, and Sarah knew she couldn't abandon either one. It didn't matter that she hadn't given birth to Hailey. All she'd ever wanted was to be someone Hailey could trust and depend on.

Sarah had to make her stepdaughter see that she'd always be there for her, no matter what. Something had to have happened on that Sunday Hailey found her mother. Maybe if she could get Hailey to talk about it, she'd be able to help.

It seemed like an impossible task the way Hailey was right now, but if Sarah kept trying, maybe, hopefully, she'd get through to her. That anger couldn't last forever.

It would destroy Hailey before long.

Sarah felt something nuzzle against her leg and when she looked down, she was surprised to see Peanut. The poor dog looked sad and confused. She bent down and picked the Maltese into her arms.

Sat on the bed.

Patted her head gently. "Do you have any advice for me?"

Peanut did that thing with her head, leaning sideways and giving Sarah a questioning stare.

"Nothing, hey?" Sarah said and continued to pat Peanut. "She's not a bad person. I know she's not. I don't know what I can do. I want to help her so much but she keeps pushing me away. Literally, today."

Peanut made a whining noise.

"I share your sadness," Sarah said. She turned Peanut so she could look into her eyes. "But we won't give up, you and I. I've survived worst abuse. This is nothing. Nothing."

Peanut kissed her.

"Maybe we can help her find her poster," Sarah said putting Peanut down. "Hopefully, she didn't throw it out when she had amnesia."

Peanut gave a tiny bark and walked ahead.

"I'm coming," Sarah said. "You lead the way."

Peanut wagged her tail as she crossed the hallway and walked toward Hailey's room. But then she stopped and dashed into the spare bedroom, barking like crazy.

Sarah entered the room and for a second stood frozen in the doorway, her mind unable to understand what her eyes were seeing.

Hailey was holding Jack's utility knife, the blade against her left wrist, blood drenching her stepdaughter's forearm.

Everything was so red.

"Hailey, stop!" Sarah screamed.

TWENTY-SEVEN

Hailey was surprised when Sarah entered the spare bedroom and screamed. She jerked her hand sideways and dropped the utility knife, but she'd already cut herself. The wound wasn't as long as she'd planned, only an inch or so, but she'd been smart. She knew a perpendicular cut wouldn't do it.

She'd cut up her wrist, along the vein.

Red warmth flowed over her wrist and was dripping onto her legs. She was sitting against the wall beneath the window, her legs crossed Indian-style.

"What are you doing?" Sarah shouted.

Hailey looked up at her stepmom and there was absolute calmness inside of her. She knew her pain was going to stop soon and she'd be with her dad. She couldn't wait to see him again. She was going to forgive him for all the stupid shit he'd put her through these last two months.

These last three years.

Sarah looked funny, kind of fuzzy, fading like a ghost. She was freaking out but Hailey couldn't understand what Sarah was saying. Hailey smiled at her stepmom. She looked so lovely.

Beautiful, really. No wonder her dad had fallen in love with her. She wished they could have gotten along, but Hailey just couldn't. She'd never wanted to share her dad with anyone. It was all her mom's fault for leaving them. She'd made Hailey afraid of losing her dad so she had owned him. Sharing him had been an impossibility. Sarah just couldn't understand that. She thought they could share him.

Beautiful but dumb.

Hailey didn't mind dying. Sarah would have her baby so she really wouldn't need Hailey anyway. Sarah wouldn't be alone. Things would be better with Hailey gone.

She was getting cold.

She couldn't focus on Sarah any longer. It's like her stepmom had disappeared. Maybe it was just a magic trick. Sarah was really there but hiding behind a black curtain.

Sarah was sneaky that way. What you saw wasn't always real. She had tricked her dad. She really was a master magician. But Hailey hadn't been fooled. She'd stopped believing in magic long ago when her mom had disappeared.

But hadn't.

Smoke screen.

Her mom, just like Sarah, had been hiding behind a life of lies. All the women in her life had been liars. Both had tricked her dad.

Both had failed to trick Hailey.

In the end, she'd found out what a fraud her mother was and today she'd found out Sarah had been no better. She had felt it all these years and now she knew.

She was tired.

She just wanted to lay her head down and sleep. Maybe in the morning things would look different, but right now she was cold and sleepy.

Exhausted.

Hailey looked up at Sarah once more, tried to say something, but she didn't have the strength to move her lips. She simply gave Sarah one last smile.

Then everything went dark.

CB EO

Sarah's fear was gutting her from the inside as she stood staring at all that blood oozing out of Hailey wrist, hypnotized by the unbelievable sight happening before her. She had never suspected Hailey capable of doing something so drastically final.

Not for a *bloody* poster of that Senators hockey player. She couldn't think of his name right now, she couldn't think of anything right now. This made no sense. Why would Hailey do this? It was just a goddamned poster.

No, no, no. This couldn't be happening. She had to stop this. She couldn't let Jack's baby girl end her life. No, no, no. She couldn't let Hailey die.

"Why?" she said over and over as she finally found her legs and moved toward her stepdaughter. She saw one of Jack's clean rags hanging on one of the ladder's steps and grabbed it, twirled it like a tourniquet while she dropped to her knees beside Hailey and tied it as tight as she could just above the cut.

"Hailey, honey," she said while running her shaking hand across her stepdaughter's forehead to brush away her hair. She was trying to see if Hailey's eyes were open. "Hailey, honey, answer me. Please."

Hailey was unconscious.

Sarah shifted to a sitting position and wrapped her arms around Hailey. "Hang on, honey. Hang on."

She pulled her phone out of her back pocket and dialed 911. She had never been so scared. So unprepared.

"911, what is the nature of your emergency?"

Nothing came out. Her tongue had filled her mouth with fear and wouldn't allow a sound to come out. She tried to swallow but couldn't.

"Are your hurt?" the lady on the line asked.

"It's my stepdaughter," Sarah finally said, relief washing over her. "She's seventeen and just slashed her wrist. I wrapped a tourniquet but she'd bleeding bad. We live at 1025 Rushmore Road."

"Help is on the way . . ."

TWENTY-EIGHT

S arah was standing in front of the living room window, feeling the warm spring sun against her face. It felt really good, the way seeing an old friend did. After the last few months, she was looking forward to long warm days, to greenery, to flowery colours.

Her back was aching.

She was only six months into her pregnancy and already she felt huge. Whoever was growing inside of her—she'd decided not to find out the sex—was very active lately. Every once in a while, a tiny twig of a foot poked at the side of her belly and she'd gently rub it and it would pull back in. She wasn't sure if the baby was ticklish which was why it was pulling the foot away, but it made Sarah smile each time. It's like they were playing a game.

She didn't care so much for when the baby pushed on her bladder though, which always seemed to be in the middle of the night. She was tired a lot.

But loving every moment of it. Her only regret was that Jack wasn't here with her. She knew he'd gone through this with Hailey's mother, but she would have loved to share this experience with him. She still had no idea how she was going to explain to the baby what had happened to her or his father, but it would be some time before she'd need to talk about it.

She'd spoken to Ruth just last week and suggested that if she wanted to sell the shop to someone else, maybe that would be best, because Sarah had no idea if she'd be able to handle a new baby and her own business any time soon. As much as she'd wanted to, she'd realized it would be too much.

Ruth had put her at ease. Until that day they'd spoken, she'd had no plans to sell anyway and was quite fine keeping the shop until Sarah was ready. Besides, being stuck home with her husband all day, as much as Ruth loved him, might get a bit much quickly. Part of the allure of the flower shop was that it was her own space and the hours just flowed by unnoticed while she worked. It had never really felt like work to her anyway.

Sarah had thanked her and reiterated that if another seller came by . . . but Ruth told her to hush and just take care of that baby and they'd talk again when the time was right.

She'd burst into tears. Ruth was the grandmother she'd never had. How could a stranger be so kind and caring?

A flock of geese flew by in that V formation they were known for. But instead of heading south, they were coming back and heading north.

The sun slipped behind a lonely white cloud, leaving Sarah with a slight chill. The winter had been long and there was still a small patch of snow on the north side of the property where the sun didn't shine, even though it was May first. The past week had been beautiful, and Sarah had seen the grass turn from winter brown to spring green. Another week of warmth and the lawn would be a deep luscious carpet she could walk barefoot on.

She'd have to hire someone to mow the lawn this year. She was sure she could do it if she weren't pregnant—Jack's John Deere snowblower morphed into a ride-on mower for the summer—but she didn't think it would be a good idea to be bouncing around like that in her condition.

And she'd have to get a pool guy, too.

Such small worries considering everything that had happened in the last six months. She'd hired a contractor to finish the baby's room, had the main bathroom gutted and redone—with a thermostatic valve to regulate the water. She'd remembered Hailey telling Jack all the time that whenever she was in the shower and someone used water somewhere in the house, she got scalded. And she'd had that dent she'd punched in the hallway wall by the front door repaired.

The house was ready for the baby.

All that was left to do was wait.

Sarah watched the car drive up the driveway and disappear from her sight as it got closer to the house. The sun cast aside the cloud it had been hiding behind and Sarah felt its warmth again. A little sunshine made such a big difference, chased away aches and pains, brought back hope.

The front door opened and Peanut went to see who it was. Moments later, Sarah could feel a presence beside her. She didn't make eye contact, just kept staring outside.

Hailey did the same.

They stood in silence for about five minutes and then Sarah turned her head. A smile lit her face.

"I like it."

"It feels so different," Hailey said while shaking her head. "I've had my hair long my whole life. It feels like I'm bald."

She had just returned from the hairdresser. Her hair barely touched her shoulders, and she'd had it layered. Hailey had been away since her suicide attempt, but when she'd come home yesterday she'd asked Sarah what she thought about having her hair cut shorter.

The part that had gotten Sarah was that Hailey had come and asked her for her opinion. She'd been floored and had had to fight off her emotions. She had to be strong. She had to be the parent. Hailey was still fragile, but her time as an inpatient at the Robertson Mental Health Crisis Centre these last few months had been crucial to getting Hailey feeling safe and healthy enough to return home. She told Sarah she'd kept telling the therapist at the beginning that she hadn't meant to cut herself like that, but then again she'd been so full of anger all the time since the death of her father, and on that day she'd just been emotionally overwhelmed.

Hailey told her that she really hadn't wanted to die. It had taken her two months to let Sarah come see her. When Sarah went to that first family session, by the time she got home, she was completely drained and anxious. She was afraid of how her mental state might affect the baby. She understood family therapy was critical for Hailey's recovery, and she definitely didn't want to make Hailey think she didn't matter as much as the baby, but those first few sessions were emotionally brutal.

Sarah bore her soul to Hailey, told her stepdaughter everything that had happened in her life before she'd met Jack, and how she knew she'd never find a love like that again.

"You look beautiful," Sarah said.

"Thank you."

"What are your plans for today?"

"The last few months were so structured that I've become used to following a strict schedule," Hailey said. "I should probably get in touch with my friends, I guess, but not today. I really just want a quiet day at home."

Sarah nodded.

"I'm sorry for everything that happened," Hailey said.

Sarah was staring outside, her face slightly angled toward the sun. It was during the third family session that Hailey finally fell apart and let Sarah hold her. It didn't come naturally to either one, but Hailey didn't push back and Sarah started to learn what it took to be a parent. She really didn't think of herself as a big sister because it's not what Hailey needed. At least, Sarah didn't think so.

Not at that moment and not right now.

"I know."

They stood side-by-side, keeping a small space between them that Sarah hoped would eventually vanish. Hailey had made a lot of progress in these last few months, accepting that she'd been in and out of depression since her mom had left, using hockey as her escape. Ramming that girl into the boards, she'd told Sarah during one of their sessions, she'd been thinking of Sarah as she did it. She had wanted to hurt Sarah so badly for stealing her dad and taking her mom's place, taking away any possibility that her mother could come back if she wanted to.

Hailey's fantasy of having her parents back together ended that Sunday she found her mom.

"I said some horrible things when you sent me to rehab," Hailey said.

Sarah turned to her stepdaughter. "You were in a bad place. I didn't take it personally."

Hailey didn't need to know the truth. Of course, it had hurt Sarah to hear Hailey say how much she hated her for saving her life, that she wished she was the one who'd died instead of her dad, that she hoped she miscarried the baby. But Sarah told herself it wasn't the real Hailey talking, it was the Hailey who was hurt and scared and completely heartbroken.

Her stepdaughter had needed someone else to feel the pain she felt. Sarah had heard the desperation, the cry for help in every word Hailey had spoken. Not that each word hadn't cut deep into Sarah, but her love for Jack had helped her let that anger bounce off of her. Leaving Hailey at that centre that day had nearly crushed her, and she'd had to keep telling herself as she drove home to her now empty house, that this was the right thing to do, that Jack would be behind her one hundred percent—Hailey had tried to kill herself and she needed professional help to get through this. Just taking Hailey back home so she could look at Sarah every day, her hate still present, would have been a mistake.

And maybe given Hailey reason to try again.

Sometimes, doing the right thing hurt like hell but not doing it could be disastrous. And Sarah had had to admit that she'd been afraid of Hailey at the time and hadn't been ready to share a home with her. Time apart had been the best remedy.

The only remedy.

"You're a bad liar," Hailey said.

Sarah hid a smile. "You didn't always think that."

"I was wrong about a lot of things," she said. "I was wrong about you. I guess I never listened to what you were telling me about your childhood."

"It was never something that I liked to talk about," Sarah said. "I wasn't looking for sympathy. I just wanted you to know me, to see I wasn't a bad person."

"I didn't want to know who you were."

"Your father is the only person I'd ever bore my soul to," Sarah said. "When we first started to date, I wanted to scare him off."

"He didn't scare easily."

"Don't I know it."

They both laughed quietly, as if afraid to invade one another's space.

"I guess you don't scare easily either," Hailey said.

Sarah turned to her stepdaughter and looked up into those beautiful green eyes that reminded her of Jack so much, and slowly raised her hand to Hailey face.

"I was horrified when I saw what you'd done," Sarah said. "I didn't want to lose you too."

 beginning-of-section-ornament

Hailey actually closed her eyes and let herself feel Sarah touching her face. There was such gentleness in that touch, it made Hailey realized that Sarah didn't need to be her biological mother to care about her, and really, was there anything horribly wrong with letting this woman her dad had loved take care of her?

She no longer thought so.

In some way, they had a lot of similarities, both had had heart-breaking upbringings. Sarah had suffered in silence at the hands of her abusers—and while Hailey's mom's neglect and abandonment may not have left the scars Sarah bore from Axel, it was an abuse all the same that had consequences, she thought—and Hailey had stifled her suffering by cutting herself and hiding it, and pretending that everything was perfect in her life when it really wasn't. In a way, she'd been somewhat neurotic with her obsessive possession of her father, driven by a fear of losing him.

Sarah became her nemesis whom she'd needed to destroy at all costs. Unfortunately, it had nearly destroyed her, as well.

Sarah pulled her hand away and Hailey felt a little sad. She wouldn't have minded the moment to last a bit longer.

She opened her eyes and saw true love in Sarah's face, and for the first time in a long time, since the day her mother had left, Hailey believed that she was going to be all right, and that was all because of Sarah. It was a bit unsettling, this serenity settling inside of her, and she hoped it wasn't going to be one of those short-lived feelings.

"I guess I never believed that a stranger could actually care about me," she said. "Just because you fell in love with my dad didn't mean you'd feel anything for me."

"When I first met you, I saw immediately that you weren't going to make it easy," Sarah said. "But I didn't think you were going to make it impossible. I admit, I wanted to give up plenty of times. You know, wait it out until you were old enough to move out."

"I was only days from turning fifteen."

"Yeah, you weren't moving out any time soon."

"Guess you really did love my dad."

"I wasn't going to give him up," Sarah said. "Not after waiting my whole life for him. I was going to put up with his spoiled brat of a daughter until hell froze over."

Hailey laughed. "I deserve that."

"No, you don't," Sarah said. "You were just as broken as I was, in your own way. Once I realized that, I knew I had to try harder."

"Which made me hate you more."

Peanut barked and Hailey looked down at the same time as Sarah did.

"I'd forgotten she was there," Hailey said and bent down to scoop the puppy into her arms. "How could we possibly forget about this cuteness?"

Peanut reached up and licked Hailey's chin who kissed her back.

"Thanks for getting me that new poster of Brady."

Sarah smiled. "I didn't. I found your poster rolled up under a mountain of clothes in your closet when I was cleaning up one day."

A tear streaked down Hailey's face. "I'm so stupid."

"Don't be so hard on yourself."

"Hard not to be."

"Let's put the past behind us and look at what's ahead," Sarah said.

Hailey was quiet for a moment. "Thank you. And speaking of looking ahead, did you decide on a name?"

Sarah stared out the front window, looking pensive. Hailey noticed how motherly Sarah had started to look. Considering all the bad that Sarah had gone through in her life, Hailey really believed that Sarah was going to be a good mother.

"If it's a boy," Sarah said. "I can only think of one name."

"Jack," Hailey said.

Sarah nodded.

"And if it's a girl?"

"I like Jackie," Sarah said. "Not Jacqueline, just Jackie."

Hailey nodded. She loved both names. She was pretty sure her dad would be okay with those, too. If he hadn't died, Hailey was sure they would have chosen completely different names, but considering he wasn't here, and knowing what he'd meant to both her and Sarah, she was happy that Sarah was going to honour him this way.

"I can't wait to be a big sister."

Sarah grabbed her hand and squeezed it. It happened so unexpectedly that Hailey almost pulled away, but then realized it was okay to enjoy this closeness between her and Sarah, that family used touch to show their love and affection.

Family.

She'd actually just thought of Sarah as family. Not something she would have done a few months ago, but Sarah was her stepmom, and was going to be the mother of her brother or sister. The three of them would be a family.

A new family.

A new beginning.

"I'm so happy to hear you say that," Sarah said. "You have no idea what that means to me."

Hailey put Peanut down because she'd become a wiggly worm in her arms. She then did something spontaneous, something she definitely wouldn't have done a few months ago. She put one arm around Sarah's shoulder and touched her belly with her other hand.

"Feel that?" Sarah said. "That was the baby kicking."

"Does it hurt?"

"When she kicks me in the bladder or appendix it does."

"She?"

"Or he," Sarah said. "I don't want to call it an *it* and saying he or she all the time is tiresome."

"Are you scared?"

"Sometimes," Sarah said. "What if I'm a lousy mother? What if I'm as horrible as my mother was."

"I don't think you will be," Hailey said. "I know firsthand how determined you can be. This baby is going to love you."

"You really think so?"

"Yeah," Hailey said. "I'll make damn sure of that."

They stood like that for a few minutes, Hailey with her hand on Sarah's belly, feeling the baby move around. After a while, Hailey pulled her hand away and stared out the window.

"I guess I should learn how to use the mower," Hailey said.

"I was going to hire someone, but if you want to give it a go, try it."

"I watched Dad doing it for years. He was going to show me this summer."

"I can help," Sarah said. "I did use it with the snowblower attachment. We just need to figure out how to remove it and put the mower attachment on. The tractor is easy to use."

"Aren't you the handywoman?"

Sarah laughed. "I surprise myself. Did you look at the spare bedroom when you came home yesterday?"

"It looks nice," Hailey said. "Did you finish it?"

"I'm not that handy," she said. "I hired someone but I did paint it."

"Like I said," Hailey said. "You're going to be a great mom."

"I hope so."

"I'll help."

"I'd love that."

Hailey and Sarah stood side by side, Hailey's arm around her stepmother's shoulder, a feeling of being home overtaking Hailey. It had been a long time since she'd felt this way, like this was her home, too. And she really was looking forward to the baby's arrival.

"Look," Sarah said, pointing out the window. "Spring is finally here."

"Buds," Hailey said, her face glowing. Spring this year had a different meaning for her. It was like she'd been given a second chance, that a new life was possible. "The trees have buds."

Did you enjoy
The Trees Have Buds?

You can make a big difference. Reviews are incredibly powerful. There is no better way to let other readers know if a story is good. And since I can't compete with authors who have the financial backing of a big publisher, your review means that much more to me.

I'd be extremely grateful.

Best places to leave your review is where you typically buy your books and ebooks, and also on BookBub and Facebook. Nothing is better than word-of-mouth.

If you're not part of my Insiders Group, you can join and receive updates about future novels, special promos or giveaways, and reviews about books I've read and want to share with you. I really value that you've welcomed my books into your life and will never spam you. You'll be able to unsubscribe from my Insiders Group anytime you want, but I hope you'll stick around because more stories are coming.

And you'll get a FREE ebook when you sign-up.

Excerpt from

THE LITTLE
LIES WE HIDE

ONE

Why are you behaving like a dumbass?"

"I'm not!"

"Of course you are."

Bradley glared at Kate from across the living room, the black leather couch between them acting like a bored arbitrator. Behind him, a wall of windows looked out at the Vancouver skyline from the seventeenth floor.

This was Kate's three-million-dollar condo. He had a tiny apartment about a tenth of the size in the old part of downtown. It was within walking distance of the radio station he worked at as the Program Director, so the location suited him fine.

Besides, Bradley didn't own a car.

Kate, on the other hand, had a brand-new BMW 4 Series Convertible in a gorgeous Melbourne Red Metallic. It complemented her high-powered position as Executive Vice-President of the conglomerate that owned, amongst many things, the radio station Bradley worked at.

"We're going to be late for work," he said. "Can we talk about this later?"

"Well, *you're* going to be late for work as I can pretty much come in as I please, and no, we're going to talk about this right now."

"Oh, pulling the old boss trick on me."

Kate crossed her arms and focused her emerald green eyes on him. He could feel the sharp intensity radiating from them cut him to pieces. He hated it when she pulled rank. Didn't make for fair play.

But damn it if she didn't look beautiful. At forty, she put to shame girls half her age, and in the boardroom, she ate grown men whole with her sharp tongue and sharper intelligence. Why she was with him, he still couldn't quite figure out. And this argument they were having left him even more confused. Had she really just asked him—?

"Whatever it takes," she said.

"Whatever it takes? You make it sound like I'm some deal you need to close before breakfast. And I haven't even had a cup of coffee. Why can't we get a damn coffee machine in here?"

"If that's what you need to say yes, then I'll have one installed this afternoon."

Bradley ran a hand through his longish auburn but slightly greying hair. A few weeks back, he'd told Kate he was thinking of getting his hair cut short, but she hadn't liked the idea. She'd told him the long hair, the goatee, and the earrings fit his radio persona to a T. And then she'd added *makes me weak in the knees*.

Nothing made her weak in the knees, as far as he knew. They had met about three years ago when her company had bought the radio station he'd been working at. The station had gone through different ownerships over the years, changed format a few times to try to cater to new markets, and there had even been rumours of being shut down. But then Kate had showed up one Monday afternoon and gathered the staff and told them they'd been bought. No surprise there for anyone, and of course all the mumbo-jumbo coming out of Kate's mouth about them turning a corner and becoming *the* radio station of Vancouver had fallen on deaf ears. They'd heard it before, including Bradley.

Except that he hadn't been able to keep his eyes off this tall brunette wearing a power suit that probably cost more than his monthly wage, and the faint aroma of her perfume had been just strong enough to make him imagine that her smile was filled with hidden messages and possibilities.

Not the first time he'd been fooled so easily.

And as quickly as she had materialized on that day, he'd barely seen her the next three months. The station still sucked, the format was still awful and dated, and just like before, rumours of being shut down floated through the stale office air like a bad cold.

Then things started to change, and fast. The previous Program Director was shown the door, Bradley was told he was the new PD (he'd sensed he couldn't refuse, unless he viewed being unemployed as a better career move), and Kate became a permanent resident of the station. Three months later, the station had been well on its way to becoming *the* radio station of Vancouver and Bradley had found himself falling hard for Kate.

So why was he freaking out at her marriage proposal?

CB ꙮ

He should have known something was up this morning when he found Kate still in bed at five. She never skipped a day to run her 5k before work. He'd thought maybe she was sick, but he'd never known her to be sick. The woman was all about healthy lifestyle. She popped vitamins like they were M&Ms. Probably when they then made love, that should have told him that something was definitely up, but when Kate O'Grady made love to him, she was like a drug that left him completely and utterly in her possession.

He wasn't complaining.

He really did love her.

But why did they need to get married? Hadn't she been the one who had said two years ago that although she wasn't looking for a fly-by-night fling, marriage wasn't on her horizon either? That had suited him just fine. This was 2018 and no one needed a marriage certificate to *seal the deal*. He hadn't needed a piece of paper to confirm his feelings for her, and neither had she.

Until this morning.

"Marriage? Why now? What's changed?"

"Not exactly the response I'd expected," she said and softened her stance. A little. "What's changed? I guess *I* have. I'm not twenty anymore."

"So?"

Kate looked at him as if he were a bad puppy who had just peed on the floor, and she was about to reprimand him. He hated feeling so inferior to her. Maybe that's why he didn't get the marriage thing all of a sudden. She really didn't need him, but he hoped that she still wanted him. Of *course* she did. Why else would she want to marry him?

Well, he knew one person who would be thrilled at the news: his mom. It had been a long time since he'd spoken to her—last Mother's Day, he thought. It was September. Crap, he'd let time fly.

"You here?" Kate said with a flash of annoyance. "Bradley Knighton?"

He was in trouble now. She only used his full name when she was getting pretty pissed with him. "Just thinking about my mother."

"Seriously?" she said, now totally irritated. "I ask you to marry me and your mom is what pops into your head."

"Yeah," he said, getting defensive. "I was thinking that if anyone was going to be thrilled at the news, it will be her."

"Well, that's exactly why I've asked you to marry me," Kate said with a hint of irony. "So I can meet her and the rest of your family."

Bradley became distantly quiet.

"What is it with you and your family?" she said, softening her tone. "You never talk about them. When's the last time you actually went home?"

"A while," he whispered.

"You might need to right whatever is wrong there," she said. "I won't put up with any family ill will at my wedding."

"So, it's a done deal?" he said, sounding like a six-year-old. "I don't even get to say what I want?"

"Jesus, Brad!" She closed the distance between them and stood a foot away. "Do you love me?"

"Of course."

"Then what's the holdup?"

He tried to step away but she grabbed his arm. He looked down at her grasp, a sudden burn churning deep inside of him in a place he couldn't reach. "I don't know. I guess it's not something I ever thought we'd be discussing. I didn't think we needed it to be together."

She let go of his arm. "I didn't think I needed it either before . . . before I met you. You're special to me. No other man has ever made me feel this complete before. I guess . . . I guess I don't want to lose you."

He looked into her eyes, the depth of her love pulling him in and driving it home that he was a fool not to put a ring on her finger. Still, he couldn't silence the nagging burn. "Marriage is no guarantee. We both know that."

She stepped into him and rested her head in the hollow of his shoulder. She was the strongest woman he'd ever known and it always caught him by surprise when she showed that she had fears and insecurities; that, like everyone else, she had vulnerabilities.

He wrapped his arms around her and took in the scent of her perfume. Why couldn't he say yes?

The answer was nineteen years in the past and thousands of miles east.

03 80

Bradley was standing at the massive kitchen island, a glass of orange juice in hand. He set it down on the granite countertop, his hand running against its smooth surface, not finding any of the chipped edges that were so prominent along the worn laminate countertop at his apartment. The more time he spent in Kate's condo, the more he realized the huge gap between their lifestyles.

When is the last time she's been in my apartment?

"Don't worry about it," Kate said, back from the washroom. She looked ready to take on the world for another day. "You obviously don't feel the same as I do."

"It's not that," he said in a voice full of regret. "I'm crazy about you."

"But?"

"There's no but," he said, his hand still running across the granite. "Look at this countertop."

Standing on the other side of the island, she crossed her arms. "What about it?"

"It's gorgeous."

She sighed. "Brad, really? And your point?"

"I make about sixty thousand a year. I live in a shabby apartment in a downtown area that's not the safest. You live along the waterfront in this luxurious condo. I know what these condos sell for."

"Again, what is your point?"

He rubbed his goatee. The grey in it was starting to bother him. Why was he getting so much grey lately? He was only thirty-eight. Then again, Dad had been mostly bald by forty, so maybe grey wasn't so bad.

"I'm not with you because of your money. That's not who I am."

"I know," she said. "But it's never bothered you before that I have a slightly higher standard of living."

He raised an eyebrow. "Slightly?"

322 | François Houle

Her embarrassed yet slightly coy smile was framed by uncharacteristically blushing cheeks. "Touché."

They stared at each other, two people madly in love but being held back by baggage that should have been tossed long ago. Was he afraid that if he finally said yes, he'd be closing that door from his past forever?

"Talk to me," Kate said. "You need time to think about it? Then take it. I know I blindsided you a little . . . okay, a lot."

"I just don't quite get it. Why now?"

"I turned forty back in May."

"It was a great party."

She smiled. "It was."

"So?"

She reached for his hands and took a moment before she looked at him. "I'm forty and I want to have a baby with you."

The look on his face was that of a man who'd been shot and hadn't realized just yet that he was bleeding out.

 os 8o

Bradley pulled his hand away like he'd just touched something hot, and backed away. He looked at Kate as if she were a stranger. "A baby?" he said, sounding as horrified as he felt. "You want to have a *baby*? You? Do you know what that will do to your career? Are you going to become a stay-at-home mom? I can't afford to keep us in this condo, and my tiny apartment is going to get real cramped real fast with three of us living in it. A baby! Really?"

He started to pace the length of the island like a dog needing to go out for a pee. Or in his case, flee.

"Brad, stop!" She waited until he stood still and looked at her. "No, I'm not going to become a stay-at-home mom. I don't know the first thing about babies, I admit. But there are lots of great nannies out there. I'm not giving up my career, but I'm willing to make concessions. Having a baby with you is the purest sign that I know of to show how much we love each other. And I want our child to have married parents. That's important to me. My parents are still together after fifty-one years."

"And they already have ten grandkids thanks to your brother and sisters."

"But not from me and you," she said. "You know they're very fond of you."

They were great people who'd been good to him. Her entire family was what he thought families should be like: lots of laughter, innocent ribbing, and a ton of love and support. And they had accepted and welcomed him into their stronghold instantly, easing the estrangement from his own family.

But a baby?

At this point in their lives?

Boy, she was full of surprises today. First, she proposed to him, and now she wanted a baby. None of these things had ever crossed his mind before, and he was pretty sure they had never crossed her mind before either. The last thing he'd ever seen himself as was a married man and a father.

And then it hit him, the irony of his predicament. If—and that's a big if—things had worked out all those years ago, he'd probably be married now and odds were that he'd have at least one kid, probably more. Maybe what had happened was a blessing, because he wasn't convinced that he was cut out for either of those.

So, what exactly was he cut out for? What did he want?

What he was cut out for and what he wanted was what his life already was: Program Director of the most popular radio station in Vancouver, and sharing his life with the most wonderful woman he'd been lucky enough to find. That was enough for him.

Apparently, it was no longer enough for her.

"We can't have a baby for your parents' sake."

"That's not why I want one."

"This is coming out of nowhere. You can't return it after it's born, there is no thirty-day money back guarantee. A baby comes out screaming and turns everything upside down. Not unlike the Tasmanian Devil."

"You're comparing our child to the Tasmanian Devil?"

"Our child?" A worried frown wrinkled his forehead. "Are you already pregnant? Because if you—"

"Relax," she said with that tone she used at the office to take control of a situation just before it got out of hand. "Take a breath. I'm not pregnant. Give me some credit here. I'm not trying to trap you into a situation that would be based on a lie. I want you to be as committed to us as I am."

Bradley clenched his jaw and gritted his teeth, a habit he'd developed long ago to control his anger when all he'd wanted to do was take a baseball bat to David after another humiliating prank by his brother. Like then, he now felt trapped and helpless; he loses and someone else wins. He'd really believed that twenty-year-old loser Bradley had been left behind in Ottawa, that finding Kate had been meant to happen all along, that finding her had been the biggest win of his life, a win that big brother David couldn't ever take from him.

But now he feared that if he didn't go along with Kate's plan, he'd lose her. No David to blame. Just himself.

He was so damned tired of being on the losing end.

"I am—"

His cell phone began to play *Time Bomb*, a song that had resonated with him as a teenager and had seemed fitting as his ring tone—the perfect anthem to his chaotic and messy life. Definitely fitting for today.

"Who is it?"

Bradley looked at the number on the screen and his face folded into a questioning frown. "My sister."

Connect with François Houle

www.francoisghoule.com

www.facebook.com/francoishouleauthor

www.bookbub.com/authors/francois-houle

Acknowledgments

The first draft of this novel was written before COVID-19 became a way of life in March 2020. It certainly has been a strange year but being a writer, the isolation wasn't a big adjustment. I do empathise with those of you who have struggled and hopefully this book has provided a welcomed distraction for a short while.

I'd like to thank my new editor Geffen Semach who wowed me with her fabulous developmental edit. The story is stronger because of her.

I also want to say a special thank you to Gillian Nidd and Lucie Arsenault for their wonderful review of the medical scenes and their suggestions made those scenes that much better.

Once again, a big thanks to my real estate agent Nim Moussa for his invaluable insights on owning and selling a shop in a small town.

And of course, a big thank you to you for reading another one of my books. I do hope you enjoyed it.

Hopefully, you won't have to wait as long for the next one.

Happy reading!

Also by François Houle

We Became Us
Broken Hearts
It Happened to Us
Beautiful Midnight
The Little Lies We Hide

About François Houle

François Houle's first novel *It Happened to Us* spent multiple weeks in 2019 as an Amazon top 100 best seller in two categories. His fiction explores themes that are universal such as family and friendships, love and grief, and anything else that makes us all human. Reviews often refer to his books as "beautifully written," "heartbreaking and heartwarming," and "intense and emotional."

François is one of five boys so it's no surprise that family is a strong theme in his books. A lot of the inspiration for his first two novels *It Happened to Us* and *Beautiful Midnight* came from the passing of his father in 2005.

François grew up in a small town outside of Montréal, moved to Toronto when he was ten, and currently lives in Ottawa. An avid reader from a young age, he tried to create a comic book when he was twelve, penned hundreds of song lyrics as a teen-ager, and wrote his first novel in 1985, a sci-fi influenced by the novel *Dune*. Several horror novels followed, and although none of these books will ever be published, they were important in his development as an author.

In 1985, at the age of 22, he graduated from college with a Programmer/Analyst diploma and then went into the ice cream business with his family, owning three Baskin-Robbins franchises for about 6 years. In 1991, he started his IT career, and from 2003 – 2017, he was a Certified Professional Résumé Writer and oper-ated a part-time business writing résumés, which helped while his wife took a sabbatical from work to stay home and care for their two kids.

If you'd like to stay current with what he's working on, please like his Facebook page and join his Insiders Group at *www.francoisghoule.com*.

Fun Facts About Me

1. I'm a big hockey and football fan.
2. I love alternative music (*The Twilight Sad* is one of my all-time favourite bands).
3. I enjoy woodworking.